THE PROMISE

Dreams Not Deferred But Denied

A Historical Novel

BY MAHAILIA ADAMS

Copyright

ISBN 979-8-234-06897-2.

Contents

Prologue

The gospel song is moving, almost seeming to shake the walls of the cabin to the cadence of the lively music, making one want to look for a tambourine to add to the syncopated rhythm. The poise and confidence of the tall figure bouncing and swaying on the piano bench gives Julia the air of someone much older than her fourteen years. She is playing the song from memory, having practiced it many times while her father was away on the circuit. Julia is determined to hold up her end of the promise.

As she plays, Julia thinks, "My piano playin' is getting better and I've kept up with my schoolin' so next year I can move to Houston! I've worked hard since I was 5 years old, ever since Aunt Lily and Aunt Mabel made me the promise. Mama has told us stories many times about how different Houston's Colored ward is from Texarkana. They have fine schools and churches – and even a hospital. The streets are made of bricks and the businesses and homes are owned by Coloreds! Aunt Lily is even better at playin' piano than mama, so when I start my trainin' with her and add on some singin' lessons, I will be on my way. Maybe I'll take over for Aunt Lily in their big church or continue my schoolin' and become a teacher myself. But my real dream is to become a star – entertainin' the well-dressed Coloreds in South Texas! But one thang for sure; I ain't never coming back to this ole farm!"

As she finishes the song, Julia turns and looks over at her mother for her approval but instead sees that Emma has collapsed back into the chair, appearing exhausted. She was so into playing and daydreaming about her bright future, that she didn't realize her mother had stopped clapping to the beat. Julia helps her mother back to bed, but her mind stays on the promise as she plans how she can continue to help more around the house while her mama rests and sneak time to keep up her piano practice and school lessons. She doesn't realize just how much her life is about to change. Will the promise be snatched away from her?

Teresa Holliday

Part I

1

The Funeral, October 1900

A group of somber faces stands behind a family circling the open grave. Dressed in simple cloth robes, their voices rise singing "Nearer My God to Thee…" The minister fills the shovel with dirt. He hesitates, then heaves it onto the wooden box. Six men hold ropes hooked to the pine casket, three on each side of the grave, are struggling to lower the casket in unison. The minister, also dressed in white sackcloth, lifts his head to the dark sky. Tears are rolling down his cheeks. He chokes a little. He utters, "from ashes to ashes, dust to dust we return O Lord…"

Julia stands staring at the action of her father, the minister, with her jaw set so tight that the strain pulsates the veins in her temples. A blast of wind whips around the small group. An updraft soars, carrying twigs, branches, and small trees as they tumble through the air, ravaging the cemetery. An unexpected chill fills the air. Dark clouds roll in rapidly. Her little sister, Laura, stands next to her, her hands wiping her eyes as tears fall down her cheeks onto her thin, handmade coat. She pulls at Julia's dress, shivers and shrieks as a gust of wind pushes at the backside of the mourners, threatening to shove them all into the open grave. They clutch at their shawls and wrap them around their bodies to draw closer together for warmth. Julia bends down and whispers, "Shush" as she lifts the child, shakes her, and pats her on the back. Laura cries out again as Julia covers her face with her shawl to smother the cries into whimpers. She continues to hold her, sheltering her from the wind that whips around them. Julia digs her heels into the ground as if she might still the wind and the cries.

The dirt hit the wooden box in a growing heap. The mourners come alive with cries of "Have mercy, O Lord."

Six pairs of arms with shovels throw dirt that soon fill the grave. Julia shudders and becomes rigid; a single tear rolls down her cheek as she clinches her fists, gripping the child. Little Laura quiets as Julia cuddles her to her breast. No longer watching the rhythm of the arms as they move in synchronization piling the earth that swallows her mother's casket, Julia looks up at the clouds, wondering how everything had gotten so out of hand.

This is not happening. This can't be real. My Mama's gone!

"Mama took to her bed just last fall with a cough and fever and stayed there off and on until spring. When it was warmer, she stepped out to lounge on the porch in the sunshine for a period each day. She seemed to get stronger, and she didn't cough nearly as much during those summer months as she did when the cold air set in again this fall. How did this happen?

Mama's consumption was diagnosed after she gave birth to her fifth child, according to Papa. She lost most of the weight on her slight frame after the birth and death of her sixth child. Later, following the seventh unsuccessful pregnancy, she was in bed with my small, whining sister, Laura. My mother and sister would spend afternoons resting, and I was called upon to accept more responsibility. As time passed, Mama grew weaker. Soon the hours she lay in bed ran into one day and another. For a long time, she managed to get up and sit in the front row of the church on Sunday morning, though she no longer played the piano or attended the revivals. By the end of the summer, she was too tired after dressing to go out, as the coughing racked her thin body. She would sometimes sit in her favorite chair, watching the little ones play as I practiced on the piano. There were inquiries made by neighbors and church folk as to her progress, but friendly smiles never revealed to me the concerns they had for her health. The church community rallied to the aid of our family when she became so weak she could not manage the household. I accepted this situation as a temporary inconvenience to be dealt with only until my mama got better.

The times when I could be alone with my mother were precious, even though I had to share them with baby Laura. I would lie with Mama and read poetry and the Bible. Mama listened to me as I talked about my future and the career I looked forward to, relating every detail. I will miss our times together. I never thought I would have to live without my mama. Did she know how much I loved her. I wonder if Mama knew she was not getting better and felt her life slipping away. Why didn't she tell me she might not live, and she would not be here to see the bright future we had spent so much time planning, sharing what may not happen now. Instead, she just let me believe everything was going to be all right. I no longer have her share my future. How could she do this to me?

All this time, the hardest part has been dealing with my papa. He has grown meaner and meaner. I just knew that some days when Mama was not doing so good he wanted to hit me. He hollered at me more each day because he said I wasn't doing my chores around the house.

Papa said, "You don't need to study while Mama is sick. You need to take care of your brother and sisters."

I said, "I don't have time to do so many household chores. I have to prepare for my school studies in order to keep my part of the promise."

"Forget the promise. Taking care of home comes first."

That's when we hollered back and forth and Mama came in to keep him from hitting me.

When he was around, I had to be doing something all the time, with no time to practice the piano or my studies. He doesn't seem to understand how important my studies are to me. When I was just five years old, Aunt Lily said I had such beautiful long fingers, perfect for playing the piano. She promised that if I got good grades and practiced my piano lessons well, I could study music and singing lessons from her on the grand organ she played on Sundays in that large stone church. From that time on, I have thought of nothing else but my new life away from Bowie County. There are greater blessings in store for me in Houston, an exciting life full of music and good times. One more year and I would have graduated and moved to Houston to attend Normal Teaching College for music and teacher's training.

I know I am better than the average country girl, not just because I am Reverend Todd's daughter; most country girls just want to get a man, marry and have lots of children. I have a plan for my life. Marrying one of these country boys and having a lot of children is not something I plan to do. I will not be like my poor mother.

Julia's two aunts stand next to her, dabbing their eyes and cheeks in grief at the loss of their beloved sister. Their sniffles bring Julia back to the funeral. She turns to look at them, wondering if they will remember to keep the promise.

I remember members of the congregation had been dropping by often with food and performing some housekeeping. There was always sister so-and-so sharing her recipe, making it possible for the family to have plenty to eat. The prayer meetings continued each Wednesday evening as the deacons and stewards took over when my papa left on the circuit. Members came on each occasion before the Bible studies to clean and prepare the house to relieve Mama of her chores. All looking forward to their beautiful first lady being back on her feet.

I met her father's demands on my free time with arguments and bargains for her efforts. I slipped away as often as possible to neighbors or to any social event where I could be the center of attention. I needed a break from the expectations around the house.

These escapes took my mind off the deteriorating situation at home. The arguments with papa about the chores escalated. I sought protection from mama when he threatened to thrash me. Although he contained his anger and stalled the thrashing solely to appease Mama and not hinder her recovery.

Somehow, the fact that Mama would not get better escaped me until the day she died. I ignored the warnings from neighbors that I should stay close to home. They saw what I failed to see. The veiled compliments on my bravery were accepted as the tribulations I had to bear until the situation got back to normal.

Mama didn't tell me she was going to die. What is going to happen to the promise? Mama is gone. She is gone forever. What am I going to do?

Emma's sisters arrived the day before the funeral. The sisters alighted from the train and greeted the motley ensemble from the church there to welcome them. It was rare that ladies of their station came to this small community. Lawrence Jr. picked them up in the wagon. He recognized his aunts by the way they were dressed. Although he knew nothing of popular styling or fashion, there was no mistaking them. His Aunt Lily wore an Anne Boleyn bonnet in black velvet, turned up in front and lined and trimmed in scarlet; a scarlet feather in front stood out. Aunt Mabel wore a bonnet of pink silk, trimmed with black ribbon and a black feather, with black lace around the front. They wore bustles, rarely seen here in the country. The Benolton chains which were long beads of filigreed gold and silver, hung from each side of their hats and draped across the bosom. For warmth, they wore petticoats of wool and boas of beaver skin around their shoulders. Their arrival, dressed in such finery, caused quite a stir among the church crowd. On this funeral day, their black clothing quieted murmurs.

The death of their sister is a surprise to them as well. They had received letters written by Emma, telling of her illness. When the letters stopped, Julia continued to write using positive news of her mama's progress. She did not say how serious her mama's condition had become. Instead, the word was "hope" that she would get better soon.

Her death was sudden. That morning, Reverend Todd woke to find her cold. She passed away in her sleep. Emma had been up with friends the day before and appeared a little stronger. She had even helped prepare the evening supper. Later she listened to Julia play the piano and seemed quite content. She retired to bed at the usual time, which was early. She appeared to be resting well when Reverend Todd lay beside her that night. The children, along with Julia, were inconsolable when Reverend Todd told them the news in the morning.

"Receive the soul of your servant, Emma, in glory, oh Savior."

These words bring Julia back to the present; tears flood her eyes as she looks at the heavy layers of soil hitting the coffin. She bends over and drops a prized patchwork quilt over the coffin as it disappears under the dirt. Emma and the girls had spent long hours stitching the pattern. It won't be used by anyone now, so it should rest with mama.

The wind has died down, and the once great force has now become drenching rain. The crowd turns to leave the gravesite, seeking shelter. Aunt Mabel put her arms around Julia's waist to comfort her. Julia ignores her.

"You are a strong girl, Julia. You have to be even stronger now that your mother is gone."

"Come on back to the house, child, we need to talk," said Aunt Lily. "Come on now, it's time to go. "You'll catch your death."

Mabel attempts to turn Julia while holding her waist but finds Julia is not moving. She tugs at her, but Julia is indeed strong and does not budge. Both females glance at one another, shrug their shoulders, and cinching their boas nearer to their frames, pivot and hasten toward the residence.

"Don't linger too long, the rain is soaking us," said Lily.

Julia stands motionless, the rain soaking her and the wind threatening to blow her over. She stares at the mound as though the living part of her is buried in it. The ground can no longer hold the water, and puddles begin to rise. Julia, saturated to her skin, shivers now from the cold. Her father, missing her at the house, picks up a blanket and starts across the field to look for her.

Meanwhile, a few neighbors who didn't attend the graveside service are busy in the house preparing food for everyone. The entourage from the gravesite enters the frame house by way of stone steps that lead to the porch, which stretches the full length at the front of the house. When they enter the door, the first sight of the glowing fireplace sends warmth throughout the room and a respite from the chill of the wind. The big room is the company room as well as the kitchen. The fireplace has a reservoir where a kettle of hot water is steaming, hanging from a crane over the fire. A church member is standing nearby at the wood stove, stirring a pot of stew.

The family uses the screened-in back porch to hang the killed meat to dry. An icebox against the wall holds from 50 to 100-pound blocks of ice when available.

Julia arrives draped in the blanket her father provided. She does not respond to words intended to comfort. Her grief is not visible on her face. She wears no special expression. Julia just seems to stare into space as if she were in a stupor.

Upon entering the house, she takes in the scene before her. The members of the church are milling around looking busy. A horsehair couch in the center of the room with a handmade quilt her mama made is thrown gracefully on it to protect the seat from wear. There are two horsehair-upholstered chairs in front of the fireplace, one where papa had sat reading the Bible out loud for them as they gathered on the floor. The pine floors put together tongue and groove and sealed so neither air nor water would seep through protected them from the cold. She remembers the effort her papa put into hand-waxing the floor to make it shine like glass. On the wall, the lamps have colored oil in them. Reflecting a hue of yellow as if sunlight were peeking through the heavy sackcloth curtains over the windows. There is a rocking chair made from cane, softened with pillows, where Mama used to sit and mend the children's clothes and listen to me play and sing. The piano is the focal point of the room. It is covered now with a quilt sewn by Mama and friends who came to sit and converse during the winter months. On the wall near the fireplace, there is a portrait of three well-dressed, fair-skinned women. One of them is Mama, surrounded by her sisters.

Sister Sarah, upon seeing me enter dripping wet, rushes over to take me to the bedroom to shed my wet clothes. Aunt Mabel follows. As the two women peel the garments off me, Sister Sarah says, “This poor child sho gonna miss her mama. She’s not gonna be by herself, is she? You all be here for a while?”

“Well, we may be here for a short time,” said Mabel. “There are many responsibilities waiting for us at home. From time to time we can plan to come, but we don’t get this way very often. We will do what we can.”

“So, Julia’s gonna be by herself then wit the children,” Said Sister Sarah, her expression clearly troubled.

“Julia is good stock; she will be alright, I am sure,” said Mabel. “These children have been well raised, yes indeed, very well raised.”

“Don’t nobody have time around here to help her, you know,” Sister Sarah explains. “We have been strained for the past year tryin’ to help Sister Emma.”

“The children will pull together and help themselves, I am sure,” said Lily as she walks into the room. “We will stay for another week to organize things, and Julia and the girls will take over afterward.”

Julia, not speaking and letting them dress her, grows alarmed by this conversation. They talk as if she weren’t there.

“We are ever so grateful to all of you for the love and care you have given our family. It’s going to be hard for Julia until she gets accustomed to taking care of the children” Lily says.

“What am I going to do? They’re not staying to help me?

Sister Sarah and Aunt Lily each take an arm and lead Julia back into the living room, where she is seated on the couch. The conversation with her aunts and Sister Sarah shocked her into reality. She is still not speaking but uses her silence as cover to listen further.

Soon the crowd of mourners begin to leave. The men, their hats in their hands, are nodding and shaking hands with Reverend Todd, pledging their help. After cleaning up, the church sisters put away the leftover food. Emma's sisters are busy putting the children to bed. Julia watches as if she were only a bystander in this drama. She doesn't offer any help. It's as if she imagined her aunts and the sisters of the church will now take over the care of the parsonage duties, and children, liberating her.

She looks over at her aunts, no longer assured they will be here to support her.

Soon the church members are gone, the aunts are alone. The sisters sit by the fire to chat and drink their tea. Julia watches them, wondering what they are talking about. Could they be discussing the promise? Could it be in jeopardy?

Mabel shakes her head, dabbing the tears she continues to shed.

Julia can hear a bit of the conversation. Even though they speak in whispers, if she looks at them, she can pick up bits and pieces of what they say.

"I just can't get over it. Our sister is gone, leaving these children."

Mabel sighs. "Gone are the days when we gathered around the piano while Emma sang and played for us."

Julia closes her eyes, also remembering the days of their visit when they gathered around the living room when she gave a recital for them. How proud the family has been of her and the piano. A gift to her grandfather, the original Reverend Todd, by his slave master when he emancipated him. Because of the land his slave master granted him and a piano for saving his soul, they lived well in Black folks' terms. As she played for them, they seemed so pleased with her performance. The situation has changed. A tear wells in her eyes; her shoulders drop in defeat. She looks at them in their finery and thinks how her life will change. Will I be able to keep playing the piano and dress up like them and take care of this household too?

Julia doesn't want to hear any more talk about her future. The words sent butterflies to her stomach. Her heart is beating fast and she can hardly breathe. Are they backing out now that Mama is gone? The conversation between the aunts sends Julia out of the seat, running to her room she shared with her sisters, slamming the door behind her.

What was Mama thinking, having all these children, then dying and leaving them for me to take care of? She knew she was sickly. Why would she continue to have babies? I had dreams. I had plans for myself. Now she done died and left me with this mess. I hate both Mama and Papa for this.

How could they do this to me?

Reverend Todd dealt with his grief by setting out on his circuit within a week of Emma's sisters' departure. Before leaving, he stood at the door of Julia's room as she lay on the bed.

"Theys gone now, Julia. I spec you best git use to it and start tending' da house and the youngins like you supposed to. Ya didn't much help your mama when she was living, and now da job is yours. Ya aunties are willing ta help you a bit for a while, but you the kids Mama now."

Julia didn't respond to him. He stood there waiting for a protest to let him know she heard him. She said nothing.

"It's up to you. Ya hear me now?"

Julia turned her head slowly as her father spoke. Their eyes collided for a moment.

After a long silence, "I'm headed up to Nash in the morning, got a revival going there. Tidy up the house a bit and be sure the chillren git to school come Monday morning. I'm gonna get a few things you may need. Can you think of anythin? Do you need anythin?"

Reverend Todd stood there as Julia looked at him. There was no softening in his eyes, no hint of sadness, nor warmth. He stood tall with his shoulders pulled back, his head high and chin up, his jaw tight.

She stifled her lip from quivering and looked right through him.

He stared back as a hint of pity showed in the creases around his eyes. He relaxed his shoulders a bit. His hands rolled the brim of his hat.

Julia turned her head away from him to hide her tears. When she looked back, the flow of empathy forming on his face twisted into a frown. That moment of empathy was all she saw; then it was gone. He placed his black hat on his head and walked out the door.

He shouted, "Giddy up" and the wagon rattled away. He did not come by her room to say goodbye when he left just before dawn.

The death of her mother was, to Julia, like galloping full speed on her horse across the plain and having him stop suddenly at a cliff, throwing her headfirst into the depths of abyss. Many nights she lay awake until dawn. She stayed in bed with her heart racing with anger at what was to become of her.

The grief and tears at the loss of her beloved mama overwhelmed her for years. The anger stayed forever. The choices she made for herself directed the course of her life, affecting three generations.

2

Life with the Family

From the day my Papa returned to his circuit, leaving me to fend for the family, I spiraled downward from the many changes in this household. My personal appearance, for which I have always had much pride, reflects my anger. From being neatly braided or tied, my hair has become disheveled and is shooting in all directions all over my head. I've exchanged my lovely, beautifully custom-tailored gingham dresses for sackcloth that hang over one shoulder.

My father has a lot to say about how inappropriate it is for me to be dressed like I do now and threatens to beat me for not having proper clothes on. I am stubborn and wear sackcloth to bed and around the house during the day while he is away.

Being quite tall at five foot eight, at fourteen, I look older than my age. I used to carry myself well. My aunts taught me to hold my head high, pull my shoulders back, and walk like I am holding a bowl on top of my head. Word is that I am pretty. I am happy with what I see in the mirror. Before Mama died, keeping my hair nice was important. A bun or braids in my hair with ribbons that matched my dress worked well for me. Mama made all of my dresses, sewing lace and eyelet with soft gauze, and decorating with satin ribbon. I would get dressed up for church on Sundays. My Mama told me that dressing well would denote our family's status in the community. I was almost ready to be seen in Houston society. That's out of the question now that I am stuck raising these kids.

We got dressed up for revivals. There would be this large tent needed to hold all the folks who wanted to get saved. Papa's preaching sent his booming voice from his great height across the congregation, sing-songing the sermon. He knew the keywords for the old sisters shouting "Amen" and "Praise the Lord." My Mama was sitting with all of us around her in the front seat, quiet and elegant. She fanned herself with her palmetto plant, just missing her big, beautiful hat as she nodded her approval of his sermon. I shall always cherish those memories. Well, those days are over.

Most nights I cannot sleep. Instead, I toss and turn in anger, going over the mistakes, I made in not expecting my mother's death. Other nights, when I finally fall asleep, I sleep way past daybreak and send the girls off to school with just hardtack for breakfast or what is left over from the night before. Lawrence Jr. leaves early each day to help the sharecroppers care for our land. Food is provided for their families, and the profit is divided from food that is sold. There is plenty of food for us to eat; I just need time to prepare it. We girls have never worked in fields like some of our other friends. Lawrence is the only one of us out there getting blacker by the day. There is no help for our personal garden, which is just for our family. The eggs, which I must gather daily for a hearty meal to start the day for the family, lie cracked in the nest and are unfit to eat. This was a special chore I had always taken care of for my Mama, but I failed to do it now for us. The children receive duties, but their tendency to run around playing tag requires them to be reminded.

The garden has to be weeded; the vegetables need picking and preparing. Because I sleep late, I don't gather the vegetables that should have been picked soon after dawn. No one, including me, wants to do this chore in the hot sun. The girls, who loved doing it early with my mama and receiving high praise for their efforts, do not volunteer to do so for me. Birds eat the best vegetables left on the ground during the day, and wild animals eat them at night. Fruits and vegetables must be prepared and stored to be eaten in the winter. I don't know how Mama had the time and energy it took to care for a household of seven people. When she was alive and well, she gave each child a task according to their age and ability. The brunt of the work fell on her, while I did my chores as quickly as possible and took freedom away from the house often, not being concerned about if Mama needed an extra hand.

Aunt Lily and Aunt Mabel sat with me a few days before they left to give me instructions on how to prepare and cook vegetables and how to organize and manage the household. I can't remember most of what they said. I remember nodding my head and going through the motions, but I was in a fog. None of what they told me sank in. After two weeks, both aunts packed up to return to their lives back in Houston, believing I would perk up and take over raising the family.

Luckily for me, I spent enough time in the kitchen to find out how most meals are made, although at times something in the mix seems left out or half-cooked. The preparation alone takes up a lot of the day. No sooner than one meal is finished and cleaned up afterward, it is time to prepare another. There are days the family is lucky to get sweet potatoes and fatback for supper. This is a meal the children could prepare since I can barely function. After the effort of cooking the meal, my energy level is low, sometimes depleted. I can't explain this feeling. All I know is that all of it is just too hard.

My father shops for staples before leaving to go on his circuit. Chickens and rabbits are our main course; they run around the yard. Sometimes we eat opossums. When he is home, he kills the animals and guts them. I could not be the one to wring the necks of the chickens, soak them in hot water to pick off the feathers or fur on the rabbits, and then gut them. My mama always did that part. So far, I've convinced Lawrence Jr., when my father isn't home, to do the awful task after the family went without meat for a few weeks. It was all a game for him once he realized he could terrorize us with the blood, as the headless chicken scattered spurting red sticky blood in all directions over the yard.

I find there is no end to the hard work; I am bent over the huge tub of water, scrubbing dirty clothes on the washboard. I must empty the tub, and I am the only one strong enough to bring fresh water from the well to refill it and rinse the clothes. Washing them on the washboard hurts my hands, and I'm drenched from my head to my toes when done. When Mama was alive, she had neighbors who came by and helped with the heavy chores. She paid them with food. Since I haven't harvested enough food to share, I can't pay them.

At one time, one or two neighbors would drop by to see how we were doing, but now they are busy looking after their own families. Those who volunteered in the past now request pay or refuse to tolerate my attitude, as I am told.

Since the anger has made my temperament harsh, they are not trying to help me anymore. They say that I am ungrateful for their efforts. I don't drum up enough sympathy or pity for them to keep trying to help us.

For over a year, dragging myself through the days and struggling to organize the chores properly has made me exhausted. So often at the end of the day, remembering what more had to be done or how I was going to do it was difficult. My sisters, Lizabeth, ten years old, and Deborah, eight, are assigned chores, but they often protest and neglect their duties to run and play. Checking on them to see if they have finished takes time. I complete all my chores in a daze, unaware of my actions and consumed by sadness.

Daily, I try to wrap my mind around the realization that Mama is gone and that the lives of all the members of my family are now changed forever. There is no time anymore for me to study, and no time to read the Bible. Dust covers the quilt on the piano; since there is so much to do, there is no time to play the piano, dress up, visit with friends, or go to church.

The most time-consuming part of some days is just combing the girl's hair, which is now done once a week. Mama was a mulatto with features similar to a white woman. Her hair was black with long waves, kept in a bun. The four girls' grades of hair range from tight nappy on Lizabeth to thick, heavy waves on baby Laura. Lizabeth's hair is kinky, stiff, and hard to manage. There is no point in trying to plait it since I could not even pull a comb through it. Mama could tame the tight curls with a heavy pomade, a task I am not inclined to do. Lizabeth is fond of playing in dirt, and the dust and the oil combined in her hair gives it a red hue which brings out the meanness in my father. When he sees his little girl running around the yard with red-orange peaks standing all over her head, looking wild, he begins his tirade at me about how unkempt the children seem. Jolene's hair is soft easily managed. Deborah's hair is straight and soft, but it will not stay plaited no matter how many times it has been tied together with string. Laura, the child who most resembled Mama, has very thick hair. It is black and wavy, easily managed, and I envy it.

Skin color has always played an important role in determining one's popularity, prestige, and mobility within this community. Our society thinks highly of members according to the hue of their complexions. If one is almost white and called "high yellow," then society considers them the top. I was told by Mama the origin of this notion started back in slavery. The near-white Negro, who was often the offspring of the masters, was allowed to be the house servant and did not work in the fields. The complexions of Lizabeth, Deborah, and Laura ranged from butter to brown sugar. If one's shade is olive or honey brown, people may view this person as acceptable. The walnut to pecan shades, up to black, are part of the lower realm of society who worked in the fields. None of the girls are as dark as I am. Laura's complexion is bright yellow, a total contrast to Lawrence Jr., whose coloring is a smooth raven black like Papa. Since coloring is very important, how would I have a chance in life?

My job is to care for Mama's children so they will someday shine. Here I am tending to them who will encounter less difficulty establishing themselves in this world and looking to me, the darkest girl in the family, as their guide. Their skin color will not hold them back. My skin tone will not pass the brown bag test, so opportunities to be respected and looked upon as talented beauty are slim.

The high regard of my mama and her sisters is meaningful to me. They made me feel I was the exception to the rule. Acceptance by these fair-skinned relatives was going to be my salvation. Now, I am a servant to my mama's children.

I hate myself for the fits of temper I express toward my sisters, especially baby Laura, who has always cried to get what she wants. She was only two years old when Mama died. Mama spoiled and pampered her since she was the last baby to survive birth. I carry deep resentment for this baby girl, as she was always in bed with Mama nursing whenever I spent time with her. She nursed until Mama's milk dried up. Laura, missing the nourishment coming from Mama and the comfort of being in her Mama's arms, began to cry and claw at her breast to no avail. Mama would hold her in her arms and try to feed her from a cup. The liquid often spilled over the child and onto the bed. No one else could get Laura to drink from the cup. Even though she was walking and able to feed herself, she depended on Mama to feed her. It was as if baby Laura knew that in the near future, Mama would not be around to comfort her. She was taking the time then to be close to her. Now she is missing the attention given to her. She cries and whines, and after a while she finally stops. My plate is full, no time to cater to her.

Now that I am in charge, I slap Laura and demand that she stops her whining. The other girls are afraid of me, and they keep peace by responding to my commands without restraint. Even though there are four of us girls, they are too young to be much help. No one expects

Lawrence Jr. to do women's work. At any rate, the chores never seem to get done well enough to suit my father.

Those days when I am harsh and just mean to my sisters, I chastise myself, believing that God someday will punish me for my actions. These angry feelings toward the family, as well as resentment of my duties and care of the children, I know it's going to come back to bite me someday.

Papa kept to his routine of leaving on the circuit and returning weeks later. One Sunday a month he preaches at the church in town. When he came home after the aunts had left and after the members had returned to their homes and duties, he found most of the chores had not been done. I was the subject of his anger about his loss and the resulting situation. It was important to him I knew my duties to keep the house in order, the children fed, and the chores done. My duty was to replace Mama.

When he is home, he feels his criticism of me is justified because the house is no longer kept as neat as before my Mama's death. The food is not as tasty. It is rice and beans too often, as this is, he was told, the only recipe I know how to prepare. The grits are too runny. It is hard for him to understand why the children's clothes are dirty, the girl's hair uncombed, and the beds not made. Sometimes he would come to the house, and the children are left alone playing in the dirt. I, of course, am nowhere to be seen. He would put the children to bed in their day clothes. Later that evening, I showed up after he had fallen asleep in a chair near the door. He placed himself there so as not to miss me when I arrived. Slipping by him as he snored loudly, hunched over in the big chair, his mouth wide open and spittle dripping down the side of his cheek, was easy. His belt lay in his lap, and a container of corn liquor would be half empty on the table. He remained oblivious to my arrival and would not discuss the event the following day, embarrassed by his excessive drinking. He preached against such behavior many, many times, waving the Bible at his congregation.

If he stays around the house for a few days, we clash over the conditions. His temper will flare when I talk back to him. He would take his belt and get in a few licks before I could escape out the door and down the road. He avoided chasing me and never let passersby or neighbors see him beat me. The beatings were to control my departures, but they didn't stop my doing as I pleased when he was gone.

He arrived unexpectedly one day at noon to see the girls running around in the yard half-dressed and their hair uncombed; they normally scatter in all directions when they see his expression. There was no fire in the fireplace; I was not up yet this day, and it was chilly in the room. He said he had checked the kettle, and no water was in it. I had left dishes on the table with morsels of food hardened on them. I was going to do a wash, and left clothing scattered on the floor where the children dressed and left their dirty clothes about. The entire room was out of order and showed signs I had not cleaned the house for days.

My door swung open; he found me asleep. The strap hit me while I was under the covers. Taken by surprise, I rose, wondering what was happening. The second strike caught me across the shoulders, where the covers left them bare. He is yelling about all that had not been done around the house. As I attempted to get out of bed, the sting of the strap hit various parts of my body swiftly and cuttingly.

As I screamed, raising my arms to ward off the blows, he hit me again and again. Stronger than he expected, I leaped from the bed, bumping into him. He staggered back to regain his balance, which was long enough for me to escape out of the room, running through the kitchen and out the front door. I got away by heading outside the gate. He didn't try to chase me.

As the stress and beatings escalated in the new role for me, I sought an escape. The nearest neighbor was just a few minutes away. It was great to spend some time with my friend Opal. Although I could expect a beating when Papa came home from his circuit, it did not matter, as he had any excuse to beat me anyway. The act of beating is acting out his anger for Mama being gone, as though I am somehow responsible for her death.

There was talk around the community that I was seen smoking a pipe, drinking, and carrying on with young men. It was said that I went to the juke joint and danced and was sitting on the lap of one of the young men. This type of behavior would certainly not be acceptable to my father, nor to the church members. These, of course, were whispers because all the folks in the community knew of Reverend Todd's temper. No one would be the object of such a message to his ears.

Word about my transgressions got as far as Houston and my aunts. They said they were stunned by the information about me, and the rumors concerning their niece cast them in a poor light with their friends. My disgraceful behavior needed to be checked.

As a small child, I was smart and eager to please. After receiving very little instruction on the piano, I picked it up right away. It was easy for them to look forward to my going someday to live with them in Houston. But my behavior, being talked about by visitors to their church congregation, was casting a shadow on their reputation. Aunt Lily wrote a letter to shame me regarding what they had heard.

Not knowing about the rumors traveling as far as Houston, upon receiving the letter, I opened it with anticipation. It had been a long time since I heard from them. I rushed out the door to share the letter with Opal. It was not what I expected.

"I got a letter from my aunties. They say I am neglecting the children. No talk about helping me or going to Houston to live with them."

"Did you expect them to send for you? Said Opal. They are too busy living their high falutin' lives."

"How can they criticize me? I've had to do all this work with no help. The worst part is they now say that God is going to punish me for my behavior. How do they know what I do? They say I can cover my tracks around here, but I can't cover them from God. It worries me that God don't like the ugly I do. I know in my heart they are right with what they say, but this is my life, and I know I can do better for myself. I can't let their judgement and the fear of God stop me from making my life better than it is."

Despite the church members ceasing their visits to offer help upon learning of my so-called carelessness with the children and trips to town, a few individuals attempted to reason with me. Now scolding from aunts. My heart has hardened from the endless work and beatings by now. I am neither polite nor receptive to their criticism. Instead, being glib and sassy to them is covering the fear I have in my heart that, in fact, God will punish me someday. My arrogance, which keeps me strong, hinders their pleas to repent.

3

Julia Meets Treeva

Locals sustain their diet with fresh catfish and bass from the creek near the shack, which is tucked five miles away from town, behind the woods, and where the Friday night crowd gathers to celebrate the weekend escape. They do not farm the fields surrounding the shack, which are thick with tall grass, because they think the ground's power to provide a sustainable yield has been exhausted. No one knows who owns the land because it appears deserted and without a fence for miles around. If the owners appear to claim their plot, they could tear down the shack hidden deep within the trees. A thick section of forest hides the field behind it, stretching for miles. There is a rugged dirt road leading to the shack.

The inside is lit by two oil lamps placed on a makeshift bar and three lamps hang on two by four beams at the ceiling. There is a thin sheet of tin over the two by fours which is the only roof. The three walls that provide shelter are plywood, about seven feet in height, leaving a gap between them and the ceiling. To the west, which should have been the fourth wall, is open, providing a view of the changing colors in the sky from blue to purple and orange surrounding a yellow blaze as it hides on the horizon. The floor is a permanent stage, carefully laid to provide a smooth surface. Sometimes when storms come, the shack is washed out and has to be put back together again. When it rains, the noise from the tin roof drowns out the music. There are no windows. Gaps in the ceiling and a large opening allow one to view the large field surrounding the shack from all angles.

Several yards from the shack, smoke rises from a still, unseen by the heavy growth around it. Stocky men are filling jugs and trudging unseen toward the shack through the tall grass that only bends as they travel. One man is the lookout as he follows behind carrying a shotgun. Large metal cans, which previously held motor oil, are on the side of the shack. They sit on top of a grill. The flames of a fire are high, surrounding the can. One can contains collard greens and the other chitterlings. There is a woman standing nearby over another grill turning the smoking fish and chicken, the specialty of the night. The aroma of the food surrounds the area. Smoke from the barbecue grill crosses the creek and lingers in the trees throughout the week, long after the crowd has left to go back to their various labors. The lanterns illuminated caricatures of dancers painted on the plywood walls, creating shadows. The subjects are kicking up their heels in exaggerated gyrations as they prance around. Large, wide-eyed grins are on the animated men. Their enormous lips are wrapped around their glass jars filled with brew, drinking as the fiery liquid spills down the corners of their mouths and spatters through the air.

The women are engaged in looks of rapture with their huge breasts swinging and their humped behinds swaying. They are kicking up their brightly colored skirts and showing their brown legs that are never seen on an ordinary day. At the bottom right-hand corner of the wall is a "T" resembling two sabers crossed, the signature of the artist. The "T" stands for Treeva, the local artist, handyman, and musician.

As the sun sets at the juke joint, the crowd gathers with the same expectations as the characters on the wall. The jam will start at dusk on Friday night and continue until dawn on Sunday. The musicians will come with their handmade drums, their banjos, and harmonicas. All the good folk will be here except the saintly sisters and the devoted deacons, who sometimes come under the guise of seeking to save souls. Here one also finds the gamblers, the farmers, the field hands, the players, and the wandering husbands gathered here with the available women and the errant wives. This is the time to throw off the burdens of the week, the time to forget the children, the unhappy alliances, and the sorrows of being tired and poor. This is an unlikely place for a preacher's daughter to be seen. Julia shows up here frequently when Reverend Todd is out of town. This is where her father forbids her to go.

The juke joint is freedom from responsibilities and no children allowed. During her most rebellious times, when her anger gives rise to escaping from her circumstantial bondage, Julia shows up here for release. The joint is where she can do the things her father claimed would condemn her to Hell if she did them. She dances and sings, smokes tobacco and is the object of many advances. Her actions appear to push all the limits that her circuit-riding, fire and brimstone, wrath of God predicting father could conjure. Deep within her, she believes all that he says to be true. She is offending a God who forbids drinking, dancing, playing cards, smoking, and singing the slow drag blues. This same God is going to punish her someday unless she repents. But now the devil has taken over her, and she will do his bidding and pay homage to her God on Sunday when she is under the watchful eye of her father.

Today Julia is rushing through her daily chores to be free to go out tonight. She rose early this morning to prepare meals for the day. This is the night she knew the musician, Treeva, would be at the joint. She intended to have as many chores done as possible, and the children sent to bed. She needs her sister to help her in order to be ready when her friend Opal comes to pick her up in the family's wagon.

"Lizzie, you need to bring water from the creek today," Julia shouted out the door.

"You always bring the water." Lizzie raises her voice. "Why do I have to carry it?"

"Because I said so." Julia shouted. "I'm busy right now." Julia is picking up clothing and stuffing them in bags to hide until she can wash them another day. Lizzie does not move to get the bucket.

"You going out tonight, I can tell. You always in a hurry when you are planning to sneak out."

"Mind your business and do as I say." Julia starts after her. Lizzie backs up getting ready to run. "You know you ain't spose to go out at night. Ima tell on you."

"You better not. If Papa gets me, I'm gonna get on you."

"You supposa to be here wit us. Where do you go at night time? You must be doin' somethin' bad. I know where you go, you goin' to dat joint."

"What you talking about, what joint?

"I heard said that you be at the joint. I heard you be dancing and carryin' on." Lizzie steps back toward the door as she says this knowing that Julia is liable to slap her for her sassiness.

"You don't know nothing bout what I do," shouts Julia. She moves toward Lizzie, her arm set to backhand her, but before she can hit, Lizzie is out the door.

Julia has set her mind on the mulatto known as Treeva. Her attraction to Treeva is part of her dream now that her chances for life in Houston are gone.

Julia finds his skin color attractive, with its smooth, creamy, almost white tone. Treeva, the music man, could pass for white as his dark brown hair is straight and stringy. He could have gone to the big city where he probably would have gotten away with it, but he stayed in Dodge around the countryside to make a living with his skills. He also enjoyed a bit of popularity here; he would not have in the big city. His artistry and music were the least of his talents. He is also a master craftsman, sometimes making a living by helping to build houses and furniture. People say he is a straw boss for the railroad maintenance crew that lays and straightens rail lines when they do not see him around at the joint. He is quick of tongue, artfully so, as is necessary for the call master in the work chants needed to lay the track. They are Gandy Dancers, a select gang of them. Gandy is the name for the "dancing" motion of track workers as they lunge against their tools in unison, timed by the chant. Treeva makes good money, according to gossip. Julia could see herself fitting into his world.

Julia could live well married to him. Focused on her new future, her desire is to charm this man, marry him, and have light-skinned children. The white man rules the land, and the lighter the skin of the Colored, the better his chances to succeed in life. Julia is determined that her future children will have more opportunities and receive the respect given to the fair skinned. Because her mother died, she missed the chance to become a famous socialite like her aunts. Her dreams have changed; a new plan is in place. Her family promised her a good education, but her prosperous family will take its place. The only contact her buttery-skinned aunts had with her was to chastise her. Since she is stuck here, she will make the best of her situation and get away from her father and the kids. The promise is forgotten.

Treeva had a reputation as a ladies' man and no woman had succeeded in keeping him tied down too long. Julia did not see this as a deterrent, as she was confident in her looks and attractiveness. He may be the desire of many young ladies in the community, but she was sure she could get him and keep him satisfied. She will love him enough that he would not want to leave her.

The melody a familiar staccato ricocheting between the highs and lows of a one-note blues jam. Under its spell, the room hushes; the crowd leans in as if the music has reached out and hooked them by the ribs. The sound slipping in and out as his mouth seals around the hand harp, each breath a gritty, soulful drag of air.

He slicks back his greasy hair with a quick sweep of his fingers. His clabber-pale skin bare to the waist, sun-toughened and shining with sweat and oil, gleams under the dim lights. The heat is swamp-thick, the kind that makes the body sweat just to stay alive. His arms cradle the harp like something sacred, swaying side to side in time with the pulse he's coaxing from it.

His eyes stay closed. Every note seems to move through him, filling him, hollowing him, pulling breath from deep in his lungs. He doesn't just play the music—he becomes it. Harp and man fuse into one sinuous shape, sliding and winding like a snake.

The crowd can't look away. Most Fridays, he is here—the mulatto with the battered jug at his side.

Julia makes her way through the crowd unnoticed, as all eyes are on the music man. She sits near the front on a barrel that once held sour mash, just close enough to be sure he will see her. The barrel is low to the ground, and Julia crosses her long legs, hiking her dress slightly above her ankles and showing a shadow of her calf's curve. As the crowd sways to the music, she smiles and moves her body along with the music. When Treeva finishes his solo, he rises and heads outside. As he leaves, he spots Julia, knowing she had eyes on him as soon as she sat down. This has been going on for weeks, and since he has no problem getting the attention of any attractive woman here, he had not pursued this tall, dark, mysterious one.

A group gathers around Julia, her attention is no longer on Treeva. In fact, she seems to have forgotten him. She is totally engaged in their conversation as Treeva walks toward them. Her voice can be heard above the rest as she laughs and throws her head back. She appears to be holding court. Her subjects are attentive to every word and the movement of her hands as she waves them. No one turns around, and he hesitates and decides not to approach. The fear of being rejected is great; better to wait for less competition.

Treeva stands at a distance where he has a view of Julia and her friends. When the band starts its music, a member of the group takes Julia's hand, and they dance. She doesn't miss a beat as she quick-steps; her partner nods a surprise, and they laugh. He pulls her to him and then pushes her away as she moves to the beat. It is all so smooth as Treeva watches.

"Now that is a fine piece of ass," he says out loud to himself. There is a woman standing near him.

"You talkin about me?" she asks.

Treeva spits out of the side of his mouth away from her direction and then smiles, looking her up and down. "Yeah, you fine too."

"Too, you say, who else?" she says moving closer to him.

"That tall one in the white dress wit the ribbon in her hair, the one dancing like she pretty."

"Oh! She Reverend Todd's daughter," she says. "He don't know what she up to being here. Somebody needs to tell him. She's not all that."

"Preacher's daughter, you say?" Treeva has turned his attention back to the couple dancing. "I should have a piece of that." He smiles. The woman, seeing that she does not have his attention, walks away.

Julia and her partner danced around the floor. She turns toward Treeva to see if he is looking at her, thinking; he sees me now; I know it. I have his attention, but I'll not let on that I am interested in him just yet. A little tease is all for tonight. Just enough to make him want to know me.

Her dance movements become sharper; she flings her dress and smiles in his direction. She appears to nod at him. He waits for an opening, but when the dancers turn again in his direction, she is no longer looking at him. When the music stops, Julia remains tightly closed within her circle. Treeva hesitates to see if he gets her attention again as he moves closer. She doesn’t turn to look at him but keeps talking to her friends. He stops short. Thinking better of this movement.

“I’ll save my meeting with her for when I’ll have the advantage of privacy. Now I know she a church lady. I’ll get to know her away from the joint where I won't suffer any competition.”

When he steps back, Julia and her friends go to the other side of the room and disappear for the rest of the evening.

4

Treeva Courts Julia

Treeva arrives on horseback at the church grounds early to appear relaxed before Julia and her family appear. He dismounts, then ties the reins to a tree a few yards from the entrance of the church. He wears his best pair of ankle boots, new pants, a new shirt, and a suit jacket to match his pants. His new cowboy hat covers the hair that is usually oily and stringy but now wispy and clean, pulled back in a small ponytail. He stands, shoulders pulled back in all of his five-foot - six-inch stature.

During the past weeks, he has inquired at the community store about the tall, beautiful young lady who attends the AME church pastored by her father. She is well known around town. He has been told it is best to keep his distance from her as she is considered special. Friends say he shouldn't mess around with her like he does the other young women around town. She is expected to be at church early on the first Sunday of the month. He is waiting for her today.

He falls in with a group of worshipers as they head towards the steps of the church. Treeva stops about a yard before the stairs. The church is a place he has never been, and he has no intention of entering. He had heard about being saved and having to accept the Lord or something like that. He wanted nothing whatsoever to do with it. These sheep, as he often called them, were led by a shepherd who profited from labeling them sinners. He found it logical that a person ought to be paid for causing the listeners to experience joy, not pain. Why would they go back again and again to be told they were bad? It didn't serve him well to speak very often of his beliefs, as the community was full of these Christians.

He stood waiting with his arms folded, trying not to look uncomfortable, as this was the second Sunday he had come by only to find out she was not attending that day. He looked in several directions until he spotted a wagon with a family approaching.

Lawrence Jr., Julia, and her sisters rode up in the wagon to the front of the church. Julia sees Treeva as they arrive, her heart races, but she does not look in his direction.

“Lord have mercy, there he is. What’s he doing here? I'll just ignore him.”

Julia is the first to step down from the wagon as she is giving orders to Lawrence and the girls. She continues to give her attention to her family, telling them to go into the church and sit in the front row. She is keeping her back to Treeva as the children walk past him and up the stairs.

"Good morning, God bless you," said Julia to one of the parishioners as he approached the stairs.

"Mornin’ Miss Julia. It’s so good to see ya."

"Blessed to be here," said Julia.

After the past week, she felt blessed to be there. It was time to harvest the vegetables and prepare for winter. Sister Sarah came by to give her advice on how to preserve them and fruit, but she did not stay to help. Julia and the girls had worked for days carrying buckets of water from the creek to boil the jars, then cooking the vegetables and preparing the fruit. It was sweltering hot, and the process continued until late at night. Julia was tired all the time. Household chores remained undone. There was no time for cooking meals. They ate from the jars they were preparing.

Friday night, Reverend Todd came home. He could see the chaos in the room: jars of fruit and vegetables on the table and on the floor. There were not enough surfaces to hold all of them. He picked up a jar to inspect the seal, which was very important to preserve the food.

“Sister Sarah told you how to tighten the jars?”

“Yes, Papa, she showed me. I did my best.”

He tested a group of jars on the table that Julia herself had done, and they seemed okay. He then inspected the jars on the shelf finished by the younger Deborah and Jolene. The jars were already leaking at the top. They would surely spoil and not be fit to eat. Julia and Lizzy were the only two old enough to have helped their Mama preserve food for the winter before she died. Emma always checked the seal before storing the jars.

"You didn't set the seal on the jars the younger one's filled?"

"I, I believe I did."

Reverend Todd smashed the offensive jars to the ground. Julia and her sisters came together fearing he would hit them.

"You've ruined the stock for the winter."

"Papa we did our best. I didn't have much help."

"You didn't inspect the jars the youngin's did before you put them away."

"Well I thought I did, there were so many."

"There's a special way to seal the jars. Weren't ya payin attention to what Sister Sarah told ya?"

"We were hurryin to finish. I may have missed some."

"We gonna have less food for the winter. Seems like you can't do anything like yur Mama. Jus clean up the mess."

Reverend Todd threw his arms in the air, waved in a jester to dismiss what could not be helped, and walked out the door. Julia wanted to cry and go to bed, but there was no time. She had to clean up the broken glass and the runny fruit and vegetables staining the floor. For once, all four girls came together to do their part. Laura, trying to help, cuts her hand. When seeing the blood dripping from Laura's hand, Julia became alarmed by how much was flowing. She grabs a towel to stop the bleeding. Julia is terrified and cannot bear the thought of anything happening to baby Laura. After the bleeding stopped and she wrapped her hand in a cloth, she put her arms around Laura and pressed her close. Julia lovingly takes Laura into the bedroom to calm her. She lay next to her for the night, comforting as her Mama would have, as both cried falling to sleep.

Saturday, the girls' clothes had to be washed and ironed, which took all day. Then they had to be bathed, hair braided and tied down. Early Sunday morning dressed in time for church.

Since Reverend Todd was back in town and preaching this Sunday, his family had to be sitting up front to hear him.

Julia is here in front of the church, putting on her game face. She would not let on how hard her week had been, nor how much she hated all the responsibilities she had. She could not deal with Treeva today or any day in the near future. Especially not in front of the church or where her father would see them.

She ushers the girls up the stairs, pushing them by Treeva. Once the family group enters the doorway, Treeva walks to the front of the stairs so that it is not possible for Julia to continue to ignore him. Treeva lifts his hat to address her.

"Excuse me, ma lady. May I introduce myself? I'm Treeva, Treeva Roarke."

Julia turns to look at Treeva, and although he has a handsome smile and her heart skips a beat, she doesn't smile back at him. She looks around to see if anyone sees their encounter.

"Treeva who? She sighs. "What can I do for you, Mr. Treeva?"

"I just wanted to say you're lookin' mighty good this morning."

"Thank you. Do I know you? Are you a member of this church?"

"No, ma'am, but I think you know me. Didn't I see you at the? "

"I believe you are making a mistake. We haven't formally met."

There are members arriving and walking toward them. Julia needs to stop this encounter. She heads up the stairs, not staying around for more conversation. Treeva, mystified, moves aside so the members can take the stairs. He thought she would be glad of the opportunity to meet him. Surely, since they had flirted with each other often at the juke joint, why was she acting so strange? It did not make sense that she would act as though he were a stranger today.

Julia continues to walk through the door and into the church as she greets members with a big smile. She sighs with relief to see her father sitting near the pulpit and not at the door greeting the congregation as usual. She did not want to be seen talking to Treeva and being familiar with him. Leaving him watching her walk up the stairs and into the church door, which took her out of his sight.

"So, she is going to play hard to get," Treeva remarks to no one in particular as he walks toward his horse. He rode away laughing to himself. She don't know me. I get what I want. Just you wait and see, Miss Julia Todd, preacher's daughter.

It was a month later when Treeva visited the African Methodist Episcopal Church again to see Julia. He saw her walking by herself toward the church. Dressed in white cotton and lace, she wore a bright pink sash around her waist and a ribbon of the same color tied in her hair. He rides beside her, sending dust into the air and all around her. He tipped his hat with a gleam in his eye and a big smile on his face. Julia fans the dirt from around her, annoyed at his approach.

“You lookin’ good lady. Want a ride?”

“How you going to come at me like that?” says Julia.

“Looks like I hav ta ketch you on the fly.”

“You’re not “ketchin” me at all! You making a mess.”

“Don’t play me. I know you know me. I seen you watchin’ me at the joint,” he says as he dismounts, walking with Julia. She does not pause but keeps a confident pace toward the church.

"How are we goin to get to know each other wit you acting like this," he says.

“What leads you to believe we should become acquainted?”

"Cause you want to be wit me, and you know it." Treeva keeps step with her as he looks at her with a grin, his eyes are wandering over her body.

"Don't lay those eyes on me, brother Roarke. I'm not one of your harlot women."

“I’m just complimentin’ you mis lady, not askin’ you to lie with me, yet."

"We near the steps of the church, and your standing there looking at me with lust in your heart? I see it. I know you won't have the nerve to come at me like I'm common. You disrespect me, I'm a lady and more than you can handle."

"I'm sure I can handle you if you give me a chance."

They are at the stairs now, leading up to the church door. Treeva takes three steps up the stairs to be taller than her. He is blocking her way. Julia stops at the foot of the stairs and puts her face right up to him. They are so close he could feel the heat between them. He thought they would embrace right there on the church steps. Julia has no intention of embracing Treeva. She sidesteps him, lifts her skirt, and walks up the steps and through the church door, leaving him standing there just as she did before.

Julia gives her usual smile as she walks down the aisle and nods greetings to the ladies sitting on the end seats. She meets the glances of the men who look at her, and flirts ever so casually with her eyes as a silent acknowledgment of their admiration. She takes her place in the front row, as accustomed to Sunday mornings along with her sisters and brother. Her father nods, accepting her arrival, properly dressed, a witness to the upbringing of his family.

These encounters with Julia bewilder Treeva as he is determined to get close to her. She still attends the dances on Friday, but there is no particular time to expect her to arrive or when she will leave. She stays close to her friends and seems to ignore him. Having flirted and pretended not to know him, she is now avoiding him.

Maybe I should change my approach, he thinks to himself.

Back at home. "Junior, I'll be taking the wagon from now on to town for supplies."

"Why you goin after supplies, you never did it before," Lawrence Jr. replies.

"I have things I need. Don't question me, I'll be the one pickin' up the supplies while you work in the fields."

"Goin to town is my way of gettin' a break and you are takin that away from me."

"You can take a break another day, there are special things I want that you can't get for me."

"You ain't never needed anythin' special before now. Why you need to go to town? Pa don't like you goin to town by yoself."

"How does Pa know what I do? You tellin on me?"

"No, when he beat you last week, I heard him say he knew you were goin to town. He beat you about it."

"He don't know what he saying, any excuse to beat on me. He thinks all I need to do is stay here and take care of you youngins, the house and everything without no help. I'm the one who needs the break."

"Where you go at night when he's out of town?"

"I just visit some friends. Nothing special. You not telling him are you?"

"No, I ain't tellin. You don't come back til late some nights. He's gonna find out and when he does, I feel sorry for you."

"He can't beat me forever. I have plans. Anyway, you wasting time talking to me. You have work to do. Go on get out of here."

Treeva hangs out at the country store in town every Monday with a group of men playing cards, sitting at a table in front of the store. There is no coincidence that Julia shows up at the store on the days he is playing checkers with some of the men from the local farms. It is his turn to ignore her as she speaks to everyone with grace.

She enters the store very much aware that Treeva is not looking up to speak to her. After a couple of visits during the month, he continues to ignore her. With a bright disposition, Julia enters the store, collects her supplies, and engages in cheerful conversation with other shoppers, dismissing his actions as unimportant.

While Julia is busy shopping, she looks up to see Trudy Whitman arrive in her family's wagon. She is a few years older than Julia, single and by most standards considered a beauty. Her fair skin turns heads among the young men, but she has not set her sights on any of them in particular. By Julia's criteria on beauty, she would be a competitor for Treeva's attention. The moment Trudy alights from the wagon; all four men turn their attention and stand up to greet her. One of them rushes to open the door for her. Julia is accustomed to getting attention from men, but they never rushed to open the door for her as these men did today to greet Trudy. Treeva stands with them as Trudy acknowledges him with a smile. Treeva has ignored her and now he is grinning at Trudy. They know each which is obvious.

Julia always dresses at her best and speaks out loud, trying to get as much attention as possible from whomever is around the store. She is always treated with respect and admiration. It always made her feel special. Today brings all of her fears about skin color preference right to her face. It is humiliating to see men, especially Treeva, falling all over a woman like Trudy. She finishes shopping as quickly as possible. There is never a problem of a man offering to pick up her bags and load them onto her wagon. When a tall young man offers help, Julia smiles at him and thanks him while looking at Treeva, whose attention is back with the game. Just as she attempts to climb into the wagon, Treeva looks up and speaks.

"How you doin? Miss Julia"

His voice startles her, but she responds: "Don't you have a better place to spend yur time Treeva?"

"Jest passin' the time a day is all. You lookin' good as usual." He smiles that knowing smile of his, looking at her intently.

"You always lookin at me like yur lookin through me. Your eyes all over me like they is touching me."

"If I would touch you, you'd know it. My touch would be like fire," he says, laughing. The men playing cards with him joined in the laughter. Treeva winks at one of them.

"Fire, you say. You'll feel the fire of Hell before you get a chance to light one on me."

"I'd gladly make the trip for a chance to try." Treeva is still laughing.

Chastened by his teasing and attention to Trudy, Julia says, "I don't have the time for your foolishness. It's just talk anyway."

For once, Treeva is one up on Julia. Feeling the sting, she took the reins on the wagon and headed back home.

Treeva comments: "Hm, I may have over played my hand."

His partners pause the game to look at each other. There are no comments. At least one of them has had an interest in courtin Julia, but if Treeva is interested in her, that changes his mind. Treeva's pursuit of Julia will start a lot of gossip, as he has a reputation among the menfolk. Their eyebrows are raised on this one.

Sunday evening, near the end of the day, the sun is gone, and the sky has shades of orange flowing into blue and grey. Reverend Todd left after church to go to his revival for the next evening. Julia is in the yard picking beans and dropping them into her apron. It has been a week since her encounter with Treeva in town. A look back at the last month and her conduct towards him, along with his conduct towards Trudy, made her think again about ignoring him. Acting aloof was one thing, but perhaps she had overdone it. What was going to be her next step?

She sees dust rising from the road as a rider is galloping in her direction. As the rider gets closer, Julia realizes with surprise that it is Treeva, but amused as well. Maybe her plan was working. He has been paying attention after all; here he is. Glad her father is not around. She could never explain Treeva's presence. He stops the horse at the gate, alights, and ties his horse to their fence. He removes his hat and bows like a gentleman.

"Evenin, Miss Julia."

"Evenin, Treeva."

"May I come up and visit wit ya?"

Julia is smiling this time as she unlatches the gate for him to enter. "I don't see any harm in visitin."

"We been goin back and forth for awhile here and I figure we ought to stop and see what we got goin." He is holding his hat and looking serious for a change.

"What we got here is you tryin to get over on me."

"Naw, you are playin wit me. You a fine woman, fine looking and you know dat and you bettin I'm gonna want you enough to come beggin. Well, here I am. What are you gonna do about me here now?"

"Treeva Roarke, you understand I am Reverend Todd's daughter."

"You a preacher's daughter sure I knowd that. You ain't no saint, you probably been had."

"How dare you speak to me like that!" Julia looks as if she were to strike him but thinks better of it.

"Now, now, just kiddin."

"All you do is talk. Mens like your kind talk about what they wish they had. You and nobody else know Julia."

"You see that's what I'm tryin to do. I want to git to know you," he says jokingly.

"What you got to offer Mr. Roarke? I don't cotton to foolishness."

"We getting formal now, you give me a come on, you ignore me and then you start actin like you some fancy lady."

"When you come ta court a lady, you gotta have something to offer. I am a lady, Treeva Roarke, and you best be treatin me like one if you want to get anywhere with me."

Treeva sighs. "Yeah yeah I hear you. You sure got a way bout yourself. Well, I reckon I'm goin to stay awhile unless you say I can't. I'll be handy too for ya. I will fix everything around here that needs fixin, just to be around you. You be finding out I have a lot to offer."

He walks up the porch steps and sits on the swing, dropping his hat next to him.

Glad he is here, she looks at him and says, "We appreciate anything you do for us, but being near me is not part of the deal."

Julia follows him onto the porch. She opens the door of the house. "Can I offer you some lemonade? Made it for supper."

"Thank you and spice it up a bit."

"We don't imbibe in this house," she says with surprise.

"I almost forgot, this is a house of the Lord."

"We serve the Lord here. Just make yourself at home with the lemonade."

Julia goes in and comes back with a pitcher of lemonade and two glasses. Setting them down on a small table near the swing, she sits in a chair across from him and hands him a full glass. She is prim and proper, displaying a very ladylike demure. Her legs are uncrossed. Her dress draped around her ankles. For a long while, they were both silent. Lucky for her, Lawrence Jr. is not around, and the girls have been told not to leave their room. As soon as Julia sits down, they creep out of the room and hide behind the couch to hear what is going on.

Julia breaks the silence. "I hear you been workin the Huntsville house. How is it going?"

"No problems, it's coming together jus fine. This is what I do sides playin music at the joint. I work the rails too."

"Word gets around about all you do, Treeva."

"Guess so, small community."

The conversation continues with Julia telling a little about herself and her plight raising her siblings.

Treeva looks at Julia admiring her, and soon he tells her stories about himself that he rarely shares with anyone.

"My best days is working for the railroad. My job is important. I'm the boss."

"Sakes alive! Yur the boss?"

"Well, I am what they call "the call master" for the gang."

"You mean the other rail workers?"

"Yeah! We called Gandy Dancers. We straighten the tracks on my word and beat. It's a special talent comes by nature, in born to me."

"Land sakes. You think mighty prideful of yurself?"

" I'm good at what I do. I have a mind one day to make a tool that will help the industry. If I'm right, I reckon to be rich someday."

"With God's blessing, I am sure."

"Yeah, but I don't know what God has to do wit it."

"Don't spoil your blessings Treeva."

"Anyway, that's just one of my skills you know."

"Oh! I heard yur the beatenest out there."

"Well yeah, I'm pretty good for makin things outa wood. You know furniture and stuff like that."

"Yur death on. Anything you make I hear sells just like that." Julia snaps her fingers.

"I hope you can do something nice for us some day."

"You neva know, I might just surprise ya."

"Just as long as no problem gets in your way."

Everyone knows Treeva's biggest problem is women. He can't resist them. A good-looking woman could get an entire house full of furniture with a pleasing way about her. Of course, practically every woman in the county wanted him or a part of him, and he was aware of that.

He lives very well, working when he needs to work and on weekends. Drinks from sundown on Friday until sundown on Sunday. Shares himself as much as he can. Julia wants him too; he could feel it, but he knows he has to take it one step at a time.

She is smiling flirtatiously at him and still holding herself back enough so that he dares not bring out his baser self. She is a smart woman; he could see that. They sit talking in the dark, laughing and enjoying each other's company.

He always seemed to know when it was safe to come around. While the girls were at school, he helped at home. He cut the wood for the fire and repaired the furniture that was broken. While working, Treeva remained serious and made no passes at Julia. She appeared to be satisfied with the service he provided.

When the touch came weeks later, she was sitting next to him on the porch. She brushed his hand with hers. Then nudged his shoulder, she laughed heartily at his jokes and delighted in his company.

Treeva sensed her drawing him close during their conversation. When she touched him, he leaned closer to her, but as he did, she moved away. By the time the evening was drawing to an end, he was sure he could kiss her. Now sitting close enough to put his arm around her shoulders, she flinches and pulls back in alarm. He takes his arm back down. She does not reveal the shivers that run down her spine. Once more Treeva attempts to lean closer. Julia rises from the swing to stand in front of him. She cannot let anything go that far, knowing the children are not far out of sight. Her exposure by them would doom her if they revealed what was happening between her and Treeva.

"It's getting late, you should be leaving. I have a busy day tomorrow. I'll be getting up early."

"I'll be getting up at dawn myself, good evening." Treeva stands up and rushes down the steps. He jumps on his horse, tipping his hat as he rides away.

It had been so easy with the others. Now this walnut-brown woman, this big, fine woman was offering herself yet holding back and making him crazy.

Whenever Treeva leaves after a time of near closeness, Julia would fantasize about being in his arms and how it would be to make love with him. A desire to be close to him conflicted with her fear of losing herself. In her mind, Treeva was a catch for any woman. She had to tame him somewhat because there was still talk about him and other women. He still played at the joint and would not come around for weeks at a time. Julia is patient; she will make him into the husband of her dreams.

Treeva is carousing around with other women. This is true, she admitted to herself, and it had to stop. She clung to the belief that once they committed to each other, the matter of outside lovers would take care of itself. Julia assured herself that making love with the blessing of God would be all-consuming for both of them. When he makes love to her, she knows her love for him would be so strong that he would never want to be with anyone else. This was why she needed to take her time and have him wait so that he would appreciate what she offered.

Their courtship, however, became combative. She accepted his offer to make repairs around the house; although she didn't always express much gratitude. It was hard to please her, as she would stand over him and try to dictate how the repairs were to be done. Treeva, taking pride in his work, was insulted, which caused an argument. He would leave, swearing that he would not return. Reverend Todd, discovering the improvements around the house, would ask Julia how she had the work done. She informed him that a stranger had come down the road and worked for food.

As time went on, Treeva engaged himself with other women on weekends, drinking as much as he could hold. However, he never stopped pursuing Julia. After drinking all weekend, he would show up at the house drunk. He would have his hat in his hand, and Julia would chase him off the porch with a broom. He was not changing his ways, and she vowed not to put up with them. It was obvious Treeva wanted to have Julia because he couldn't. After a big fight about his relationship with another woman, she seemed rarely home when he dropped by. At least no one came to the door when he knocked. He could see the children playing in the fields, but he hesitated to speak to them. Sometimes she would be at home and in the yard washing or hanging up clothes. She would say she was busy and didn't have time to visit.

Some days she would be pleasant, and other days she would greet him as if he were a stranger. They would go on Sunday evenings in his wagon to watch the sunset. She permitted him to put his arm around her and sometimes snuggle, but as soon as he grew relaxed enough to move closer to kiss her, she removed his arm and reminded him she needed to go back home to look after the family. Her behavior kept him guessing about their relationship. Julia set herself up as a model of virtue for him to conquer and, by doing so, she believed him to become the person she wanted him to be. The model was working because he seemed to fall right in line. For as much as she could see, he appeared to change. The electricity between them kept Treeva coming back for more.

Treeva, unlike some members of his family, had a lot of pride. His walk was more like a strut. His build was slight, but he was muscular. The color of his skin was working to his advantage with town folk and with women. It may have been because he saw himself as nearly white and no man, even a white man, had ever challenged him. He never hesitated to speak up to white people when talking, not dropping his eyes in order to appear humble. To have him back down when he confronted Julia was new to him. He was not conforming in his mind. She was just another challenge he would meet and conquer. It was a game he played with her that he would someday win. Although when standing in front of her reinforced how short he was next to Julia's five feet, nine inches; the fact is this made her more desirable; her standing in the community was empowering for him.

Sunday afternoon after Reverend Todd left on his circuit, Julia and Treeva spend the evening together watching the sunset in their favorite spot on top of the hill, just yards away from Julia's house. Julia could see the whole spread in the distance and the road leading up to the house, in case her father returned home unexpectedly. The wagon is parked beneath the branches of the large oak tree, just out of sight from the road. They argue and make up, but always properly with only a hug. After the hug this time, he holds her longer. She can feel him vibrating and when he lets go, there is heat between them. He remains very close and kisses her lightly on the lips. At first, she attempts to pull back, and then she goes for it. Their first kiss. Julia feels embarrassed by her enthusiasm and turns her head away from his eyes. He keeps her close and whispers in her ear, "that's okay, it's good." The warmth of his breath caresses her neck and spreads all over her body, causing the muscles between her legs to flex. He kisses her again; this time his fingers climb up her back to the buttons on her dress. Julia flinches and pulls away. She swiftly extinguishes the burning desires, asserting, as she does, the necessity to return to the kids.

After weeks of playing the game of pretending she is not smitten with Treeva, Julia's resistance has weakened. This evening, after their first kiss, she hurries to Opal's house, Julia's best friend. Her house is within walking distance, and Opal drops in on the children when Julia is on the hill with Treeva. As Julia approaches the door, it swings open and Opal appears with a wide smile. As she walks into the kitchen, Julia heads straight for the nearest seat.

"You been wit Treeva all afternoon?"

"Yeah, hear anything from the kids?"

"No, they alright."

"Girl, this is sooo hard!" Julia falls into the settee, throws her head back and then closes her eyes.

"Hard, since when is being with Treeva hard?"

"When I say hard, I mean holding out is hard."

"You think he fallin for you?"

"He acts like he wants me bad."

"So, what's new? That's what they do."

"Trouble is that's what's getting to me. I want him too. We kissed today for the first time. My first kiss."

"Okay, how was it?"

"I could hardly hold myself together. I have never felt this way before. When I am in bed at night, I pull a pillow close to me pretending its him. I squeeze my legs together pretending his johnson is up there pleasing me. I can't wait to be with him. I almost let him take me right then. I don't know how long I can hold out."

"Then go for it, deal with the consequences later."

Julia frowns, sitting up and shaking her head, eyes barely open. She bends forward as if she is seeing something on the blank wall.

"No, no I can't give in to him. Treeva has his pick of most gals in the county. Why would he stay with me if I'm easy? When we come together, I want to know it's for keeps. I want him to love me and take me away. I want to get married."

"Treeva ain't the marryin kind. He's gone through a lot of gals round here."

"I know, I know, I need to be special."

Julia is sitting up now, spreading her dress across her legs. It has handmade lace eyelets with pale blue ribbon intertwined. There are tiny pleats sewn together with pearl buttons, not the ordinary country girl's dress. As she lifts the dress, admiring it, she says, "I'm Reverend Todd's daughter. I can't let him play with me."

"I understand you've got a plan. So far, he keep tryin to get you and you don't give him nothin in return. How long you think this gonna last?" Opal sits down next to Julia, placing her hand over hers.

"Last til he can't do without me."

"You keep messin wit Treeva, suppose you get pregnant?"

"Lord help me if I do. I can't let that happen. I would be disgraced. I want him to be in love with me. I don't want him to feel trapped by having a baby. Can't have a baby with no father, it's not a part of my plan."

"But if it happens, then it happens. He's a right smart man. He light skinned, looks white, you'll have pretty children too. But what's gonna make Treeva want to marry you?"

"That's why I don't give in you see. Once he gets a taste of me, he won't want another woman. I will put so much love on him, hmmm."

Julia is closing her eyes again, moving her head slowly, musing. After a long pause, she looks at Opal and says, "I need to take my time to have him appreciate what I have to offer. I need to string him along."

"You betta think of something soon before Reverend Todd catches up to you all." Opal gets up and heads for the door.

"Yur right and I betta get out of here and go home to see after the family." They hug each other as Julia hurries out the door.

A figure in black is barely discernible against a dirt cloud billowing around him. The rider and the horse are sweating, as the gait is faster than the rider and the old horse are accustomed to. Reverend Todd cuts across the horizon toward the farm with a grim expression on his face. He heard rumors about his daughter. She has been seen dancing and carrying on at that joint outside of town with that crowd, folks who don't attend church.

"This can't be true. No child of mine is gonna scandalize my name this way. She's been seen with that Roarke scum. He's a bad egg. He suppose ta visit da house Sunday evenings while I'm out on the circuit. She knows dat I'll beat the devil outta her. She's not expectin me tonight. I'll get there befo dark and ketch em."

He speaks out loud as he swings the strap back and forth on each side, slashing the horse's body. He stands in the stirrups and leans forward in an effort to push the horse faster. His old mare has pulled this wagon across the county for years, from Chippawa County to Bowie, twenty miles each way. This new pace is hard on the horse. All the horse has pulled in the wagon all these years have been the pastor's robe, his Sunday suit, a bible, and a change of underwear in his carpetbag. When Reverend Todd is not traveling, he carries food supplies, which are not very heavy. He arrives at Deacon George's farm, which is five miles from his home. Deciding he could make the best time without the wagon. After borrowing a horse from the deacon, he strapped his shotgun to his side. He yelled, " Giddy up," swinging the reins across the horse's neck.

Reverend Todd left Gate City this afternoon, which was about ten miles from his farm, right after Sunday service. He was passing up a fried chicken dinner and a promise of jugging sister Bell. The failure to take this opportunity escalated his rage, exacerbated by the idea that Julia could shame him. The worst course of action was putting herself in the position to leave his home and the care of the younger children. His purpose today is to put a stop to his daughter's carrying on before it gets out of hand. Just one more mile and the Reverend, although tired and knowing the horse is giving out, pushes forward with the urgency of a surprise arrival. The harder he hits the horse, the slower the pace gets as the animal winds down, snorting hard, giving in to fatigue. Soon the farmhouse is in sight and there appears to be a strange horse tied to the fence. He let the reins slacken to slow down and stopped at the barn, out of sight from the house.

He dismounts and ties the horse in the back of the barn. With his rifle in hand, he heads for the house sneaking up the porch stairs and pushes the front door open, causing it to slam against the wall. This alarms the two people and the children sitting at the kitchen table. Assistant Pastor Barnes jumps up, knocking over the chair he is sitting in. Julia looks up startled at first, but seeing that it is her father, sighs and shakes her head in acceptance. She had been on the lookout for him to sneak home, trying to catch her now that she and Treeva were meeting.

"How ya do, Rev?" Pastor Barnes blurts out, half frightened and looking to Julia for support. "Miss Julia invite me to dinner."

"Barnes!" says Reverend Todd, stopping cold in his advance toward the supposed intruder.

"What's the matter Papa? You look like your scared or something." Julia is smiling as she speaks. The children looked at their father in terror. He was not expected, and the interruption came during the quiet conversation between Julia and Pastor Barnes, which had their attention.

The sight of Assistant Pastor Barnes caught Reverend Todd off guard, leaving him momentarily unable to speak. This is the man he hoped would someday court and marry Julia. Prepared for a fight, he stands there, huffing, puffing, and sweating. He gathers his composure, straightening his stance and points to the chair on the floor. He lowers the shotgun as he reaches into his back pocket and pulls out his handkerchief to wipe the sweat from his face.

"Have a seat Pastor Barnes, pay me no mind, make yurself at home."

Pastor Barnes collects himself, sets the chair upright, and sits down again. Julia smiles in relief. The children, recognizing a strained situation, cannot finish their dinner. One at a time, they quietly get up from the table and head for their room. Seeing Papa this way could mean they were going to get a licking for something. Even watching Julia get it was hard because then she would take it out on them later.

"Dija eat Papa?" said Julia. "Can I fix you a plate?"

Reverend Todd is not looking at her as he tries to calm his shaking hands. He set the rifle by the door, pulled up the chair and dropped his hands by his sides to steady them.

"Yeah, I'll have a bite ta eat."

Pastor Barnes warily looks at the Reverend, noticing the sweat drip from his brow as drops form on the end of his nose. Reverend Todd continues to wipe his face and under his chin. Julia walks over to the pot on the fire and fills her father's bowl with a stew, humming softly to herself. She had planned this scene right. She was proud of her timing. Her gut feeling had told her that the rendezvous with Treeva on Sundays had to cease. Pastor Barnes was working well as her cover today. He had approached courting her, so she invited him to dinner. This was the second Sunday to have him over, only to slip out to see Treeva later that same evening. This charade with Pastor Barnes can only go on for so long. She would not be able to hide the truth about her relationship with Treeva much longer.

The following week Reverend Todd is riding around with his shotgun handy to known hangouts for Treeva and his kind. He still believes the rumors about his daughter and the man he considers a scamp are true. Although so far he could not catch them. He showed up at the juke joint on Friday night to see if Treeva might be there. The hope was to see if he could catch Julia there too, but he didn't see her. He makes his way through the crowd, following the aroma of the ribs. He finds a barrel to sit on near the makeshift bar. A young man is chopping off slabs of ribs, and they are disappearing as fast as the knife completes the slice.

"How much for a coupla ribs?"

"Twenty-five cents." the young man replied without looking up.

"Kinda expensive ain't it?"

"Yah don't hav ta buy any."

"Ya got a name youngin?"

The young man looks up now to see who he is talking to. He recognizes him as Reverend Todd but turns his gaze away. Deacons come to the joint often expecting anonymity. The word was out that Revered Todd was looking for his daughter and trying to find Treeva, maybe to kill him.

"Call me Junior," he replied.

"Most youngins aroun called Junior, what's your born name?"

"They call me Junior." He said again, not looking at Reverend Todd. He sliced off three bones in the slab and passed it to the Reverend.

"Here, thisn on the house."

Junior turned his head and went back to chopping.

It was obvious to Reverend Todd that he would not get any information from him about Treeva.

"Thank you, son, God bless ya."

Not getting any proof of the gossip did not spoil enjoying the ribs. He didn't succeed in finding Treeva nor catching the two of them together that night. Confronting Julia at home resulted in wide-eyed and open mouth denials of not knowing what he was talking about. Other than that, they seldom spoke to each other after the incident with Pastor Barnes.

As long as she kept the house clean and the children fed and satisfied, he would grunt after her meals, move his plate, shove his chair back, and exit the room. He continued to arrive days before he was expected and making rounds to the juke joint; the rumors remained intact. Reverend Todd finally ended his vigil. He had to tend to his needs and the needs of his flock, which were suffering from neglect.

Treeva looks forward to the game he and Julia are playing. Since flirting was over, he has been concentrating on how to get next to her. He thinks to himself that she sure is fine. She not like the other country women. When I see her, she always looks good, smells good too. She dresses daintily, but she ain't dainty. A preacher's daughter and thinkin she better than most. She a strong woman. Don't fear a man. Right up dere in my face. Talk sassy to me, too. She needs to be taken down a tad bit. I'm the man to do it. Only woman I know who hasn't give in to me after some sweet talk. She don't shine to sweet talk. Says I'm tryin to get over on her. That's true too, but I say that I ain't. I do want to get next to her. Now that we see each other friendly-like, it feels good. She lets me put my arm around her and hold her when she's not sassin me. Last Sunday we got real close. I cud feel the heat tween us. She let me stroke her arm and rub her back. Our kiss was somethin special. Then she say it's late, and she needs to get home. We getting there slowly. If she just wouldn't argue so much. I never get to have the final word. I wonder if she on fire inside like she be on the outside. She got spunk alright. Just like I like it. Taming her is gonna be fun. I'm gonna go see Letty this evening ta get the fire put out that Julia done set on me. This is the best I can do til Julia and I get it on. This Julia been keepin my nose open. We need to make haste with this courtin.

It has become harder after all this time for Julia to continue to resist Treeva's affections. So far, her plans for the budding relationship are working. Tonight, while they are looking over the horizon, something about her softens. Her mood is warmer. Their kiss is gentle, almost tentative, but it deepens quickly. Treeva's hand moves along her back, steady and sure. He slips the shawl from her shoulders; she pulls it back up, but he only smiles and lets his hands rest beneath it, his fingers tracing the line of her spine, unbuttons her dress.

When he kisses her again, she doesn't pull away. The shawl slides to her lap. He draws her closer, brushing her bare shoulder where the moonlight glows against her skin. A shiver runs through her, but she closes her eyes and lets the moment carry her. His breath warms her neck, his touch slow and deliberate as he eases her dress aside just enough to expose the smoothness of her back. She trembles, inhaling sharply, surprised how natural it feels to lean into him.

The scent of cinnamon lingers in the air as he presses soft kisses along her skin. When she doesn't retreat—then instead, a quiet sound escapes her. He is surprised that she doesn't pull away but moans in response. Julia turns toward him, seeking his mouth with her own, no longer hiding what she wants. As they kiss, her dress drops exposing her breasts. He cups them in his rough hands as his tongue licks the nipples.

They fall back on the padded blankets in the wagon's bed. Their kisses urgent, their hands tearing at their clothing. While he kisses her harder, stronger and deeper they both realized it was happening. Julia is out of her dress in a flash. Treeva out of his pants. The competition and combativeness they have shown toward each other become the fire that consumes them as they fight to be close.

It has been a long time coming for Treeva and so anticipated by Julia that neither is sure how long to embrace and kiss or how soon he should get inside her to savor the juiciness that the heat of her body is generating. Entering her gently, the sacred space between her legs is tight at first. The artist seduces her the way he seduces the music of his hand harp. He is confident in his rhythm, tender in his touch, skillful and responsive to her joy, he is full of stamina. It is good for both of them. Very good. All Julia had imagined.

The lovemaking lasted long into the darkness of the night. Julia is the strong woman he wants, and her desire matches his energy. He's worried he'll never have his fill of her, as he climaxes again and again. Her response to him is to grip him tightly and dig her nails into his back. After that night of intimacy, lovemaking replaced the spooning.

Arguments are frequent between the lovers. Julia has strong opinions. Treeva, from experience, is accustomed to having his way and the last word. The passion between them is constant in their speech, in their disagreements, and in their desire for each other. The combativeness of their relationship often diminishes to a barb of words that ends with laughter between them. Lately, it is usually during the week just before sunset when she sees Treeva ride up the path and Julia has many chores to do, but, the excitement of spending some time with him takes precedence over her sense of duty for the family. She scurries the children into the house and forbids them to speak of his presence to their father. This is not a problem now because now that she is seeing Treeva, her moods are better and life is easier around the house for them.

Even though she pretends not to care whether she is number one on Treeva's list, she is preoccupied with ways to attract him and keep him interested in her. When Julia decided to pursue her relationship with Treeva, she understood she was in forbidden territory. She outsmarted her father during their courtship and is living in fear of the repercussions when he finds them out. Nevertheless, she maintains she is acting in a way that benefits her the most. She is getting close now to escaping. The girls can look after the house better now because she is kinder to them. Her relationship with Lawrence is better; he helps by taking care of the garden and the few animals. She shows her improved demeanor by disagreeing less with Treeva. Her attitude and tone are conciliatory. Delectable leftovers for the family's meals are shared with him when they were not offered before. His favorite pie is the special offering one night instead of a night of passion.

When Julia becomes pregnant, she appears to cool down in her passion. When she tells Treeva she is pregnant, he is not surprised, since in their passion he has not pulled out to prevent it. Julia decides it is time for them to make plans to marry. Both understand that Treeva would have nowhere to hide and Julia would not escape Reverend Todd's retribution for tarnishing his reputation, should she become pregnant and unwed.

Within the next five months, she will bear their first child. She can no longer hide her growing figure. This pregnancy is the jumping point to her new life. It is time to move. Reverend Todd will not be happy to see his first grandchild. She is terrified of the prospect.

5

Julia's Surprise Marriage

"Well, I done it." said Treeva.

"You done what now Treeva?" replied Joe Cochran.

The four friends who gamble together in Cochran's barn are studying their cards. Gambling is serious with Treeva winning when he is sober.

"I got hitched."

"No lie man. You marry Trina?"

"Naw man, I married up Preacher's daughter." Treeva sticks his chest out at his accomplishment.

"Reverend Todd's daughter? Gimme five." said Shaw. All three men rise to high-five Treeva's hand.

"Rev Todd's gonna kill you man, ya know."

"He'd kill me if I didn't, she pregnant."

"Whoa! You got that right," said Joe. "Aw man that's messed up. What you gonna do about Trina and the kids?"

"They will keep. She knows I wasn't gonna marry her. I will take care of the kids."

"Where you gonna live, not wid yo Mama?" Israel is frowning.

"For now we gonna stay wid her and my sistas. She gonna need help wid the delivery. She be safe from her Pa out dere. He mad enough to come afta her."

"Some come down for her don't you think?" said Shaw.

"Well, she need ta come down offa her high horse. She needs taming. You saying I'm not good enough for her. Shit man, who's betta? She wild, you don't know her. No other man can handle her. I can have some control out dere. My family can back me up. Besides, Reverend Todd's not going out there afta her."

"I guess you right. You gonna need help building a house soon?"

"Man, I'm not sure I am ready to settle down. This is new for me. I never thought I'd have ta marry somebody."

"That's true. You the first now, but we seen that you were getting whipped." Said Joe.

"Hell no, I ain't whipped! Least not altogether. I admit its been good and I guess I lost my head a little, but it ain't over jus cus I married her. I'm still the man." Treeva struts in his chair.

They slap hands and laugh while his friends don't look at Treeva but look at each other. They nod and roll their eyes. The cards are now shuffled and dealt. The game continues with some serious play.

Reverend Todd returns from his circuit and stops in town to pick up a few supplies. The usual crowd, Jackson Smith, Joe Cox, Elias Bloom, and the old man Tucker, is hanging outside the community store. The player's attention is on their game of checkers. They are laughing as Joe Cox, a younger man, is bragging about trying to get dates with women who are out of his reach.

"I also got my eyes on Julia Todd."

"You never get nowhere wit her, she wit Treeva."

No one seems to notice Reverend Todd as he approaches. He steps closer when he hears Treeva's name.

"Dija hear the news?" says Elias, sitting up excitedly.

"What's the latest?" asks Jackson.

“He done got hitched?” Elias sits back and takes a pull on his pipe, blowing out the smoke confidently.

“Who got hitched, not Treeva nooo,” all three players speak at once.

“Shonuff, he did?” said Joe.

“He and Ms. Julia got married down at da courthouse. Just the two of ‘em. I saw ‘em myself.” Elias said with pride.

“I though he was livin’ with that woman who had his kids,” says Jackson, who does not take his eyes from the board.

“He been messin’ around with Miss Julia for awhile now.” Elias says with confidence.

“They gone and got married. Do you think her father knows about it? Old man Tucker speaks and makes his move picking up Elias’ checkers.

“He’s been tryin to ketch them together, but he’s never done it.” Elias says, caught not watching his moves, frowns as his checkers disappear.

“I bet he’ll kill him when he do.” Says Joe.

“Too late now, they’s married.” Jackson smiles as he picks up two more of Elias’ checkers.

Reverend Todd did not stop to question the men as they sat, unaware of his presence. He steps back to head toward his wagon, forgetting his necessity for supplies and heads home.

“Dern that gal. She done messed up shonuff”.

He pulls the reins back so hard that the horse’s front legs go up in the air as he slaps him hard with his whip. The wagon cut through the dirt road, sending a dust cloud wildly as it rattles down the road.

Neither Julia nor the children are in sight when he rides up to the house. He enters, slamming the door behind him to find the house neat and picked up. The children are still at the schoolhouse. The pot over the fireplace is empty and cold. No dinner prepared for the night. Reverend Todd heads into the bedroom Julia shares with Lizabeth. He snatches the door of the chiffonier open so hard that it rocks. There are just a few garments Julia left in it. He gathers them with a fury, puts them in a trunk with any toiletries he thinks she would return to retrieve, and drags the trunk out into the yard. It lands hard on the ground, the lid flying open and many of her items fall out in the dirt. No need for her to go in the house to retrieve any other items of hers. He climbs back into his wagon and heads down the road.

When Julia arrives later that day in a wagon she had borrowed, she could see her trunk lying in the dirt. She rides up to the house; her baby sister, Laura, is with her. The children had come home from school and seeing the trunk in the dirt decided not to go into the house. They walked over to Opal's house, where Julia found them. She and the girls manage to get the trunk of her belongings onto the wagon. Laura starts crying at the prospect of Julia leaving and not being there to care for them, but the other girls are quite indifferent, maybe a little happy that she is going.

Reverend Todd did not return that night, and the girls had to fend for themselves. Julia didn't dare stay the night for fear her father would return. He returned just before dawn to find the children in their beds asleep.

It has been three years since the death of their beloved mother, and the children feel starved for the tenderness and loving care she had given. They survived with Julia as their caregiver, but the resentment she had for the duty wore on them, and they felt the full measure of what they had lost.

They sewed and cooked together, and sometimes when Julia was in a good mood, she played the piano and they sang. There was no time provided for music lessons. Gradually, they were learning to take care of each other and avoided depending on Julia, who was yelling at them so much of the time. Although things got better once Julia started spending time with Treeva. They kept their promise not to tell on her, and she, in turn, was not as hard on them. She assigned duties to each of them, and woe onto anyone who failed to get her job done. She did not hesitate to use the strap on them, having learned this behavior from her father. Julia is gone now. Lizzie, now fourteen, is in charge of the house. Another child is in charge of the family. She is the product of Julia's training, which means she knows very little about caring for the household.

It has taken a few years for Reverend Todd to see himself at home with another woman in his wife's bed. He kept a picture of his beloved in his handbag and pulled it out often kissing it. Privately, he cried not knowing how he would get on after her death. It had occurred to him that he neglected his home and children. The idea of staying around to see the rapid changes in the home and the children was not what he thought he needed to do. Providing for the household was his duty. He did not know how to cope with anything else.

Unlike her mother, he knew Julia wasn't capable of running a household or being the caregiver the children needed. Emma's only failing was not preparing her oldest daughter to know her duty. Julia's upbringing made her self-absorbed and unaware of her role. Nevertheless, he felt they had managed somehow. God knows he tried to beat some sense into her, but she got herself pregnant now and ran away. It is time to get some supervision for the other three girls. He is beside himself, realizing Julia will not be back.

Not too long after burying his wife, Reverend Todd had little difficulty making alliances en route to his revivals. He has a long-standing relationship with Sister Bell, a widow in Dodge County. He often stops by her place to enjoy fried chicken meals and her warm bed. Several souls he sought to save have offered him solace, as he is a handsome man. He has been careful to select only one woman from each county visited so as not to foster gossip about his relationships. Having a number of women in his life is not unusual in those times, and according to the Bible, this behavior is acceptable.

Sister Bell had grown children who had left the nest long before. She is good-natured and aims to please him in so many ways. She often asks about how the children are getting along at the loss of their mother. Her voicing concern sits well with him. With Julia gone, now is the time to ask her to marry him and come to Bowie County to complete his household. She accepts, and now Lizabeth could see the wagon coming in the distance with her father and his new wife.

It is Sunday afternoon, and one would expect the house would be in order, but the girls are not expecting company. Lizabeth is rushing around trying to pick up the living room and kitchen and shouting at the girls to make up their room. She suspected he had married someone, although he had yet to tell them about it. Gossip was rampant out in the country, and news traveled fast about their marriage. His arrival, although unexpected for today, is not a surprise to the children. However, there is no time for them to make a good impression as they run around getting the house straight. When the wagon stops out front, they are standing together, waiting for their father to enter the house. When Reverend Todd and Sister Bell step inside, the state of how they have been living is clear. Articles of clothing are still on the floor of their room. They have not washed the breakfast dishes. With Julia gone, the girls enjoyed the opportunity not to clean their rooms or any part of the house. Lawrence Jr. has not picked up his pallet. His dirty boots and farming tools are scattered by the fireplace. On the hearth, drippings of food are sticky on the floor. Food remains in the pot. Reverend Todd is furious as he follows behind Sister Bell as she surveys each room, trying to explain to her why the house is in such a state.

After the inspection of the house is over, Reverend Todd introduces the girls to Sister Bell and informs them they have a new Mama. Without hesitation, Sister Bell, a heavy-set woman, without a word, removes her cloak, takes charge, and assigns tasks to each child. She is a no- nonsense person and the children could see she means business. Not hearing a word of protest from their father about her takeover and to see him walking out of the door is a sign that a new woman is running the household. There will be rules now for the Todd children.

Julia has been hiding out at Opal's, out of sight from Reverend Todd. Opal's house and her family of several relatives that come and go frequently, was a good hiding place. There were grown-ups and children pouring out daily, and Julia was able to disguise herself as one of them.

The two of them are packing her trunk. Opal hesitates as she takes Julia's hand, "You sure you want to do this?"

"What choice do I have? I can't stay here. The baby is comin soon."

"I know, but out there with the Roarkes. What do you know about them? Have you met his mother?"

"No, I seen one of his sisters at the community store. She didn't say anything. It's possible she has no idea about me."

"They have little to say and they ain't friendly. She look like a poor, white woman. She don't even seem to have much pride in herself." Opal remarks, folding a garment and placing it in the trunk.

"Yeah, she lighter than Treeva. Looks like she never been in the sun." Julia closes the trunk. "I'll be alright. I'm Treeva's wife. They will accept me."

"Anyway, yur pa can't get to you out dere."

"I think he would beat me and I'm showing." Julia sits down on the chair and folds her hands in her lap. "Thank you for letting me hide out here."

"He showed up looking for you. Being in the barn was a good idea because he come bustin in the house. Surprised at not seeing hide nor hair of you. He didn't say nothing to me. After checking every room, he was satisfied you were not here. Then he just left."

6

Meet the Roarkes

Treeva's whole family resembles white folks living in the community occupied by Negroes. His sisters, olive in coloring, have telltale features that identify them by other colored folk as having Negro in their blood. It is the shape of their noses and a frizz of curly hair in the girls. The mother has the same sallow complexion as Treeva and his brothers. All three boys in the family are slim in build, with shoulders slumped as if they don't want to be noticed and no pride in being almost white. They have large, bulging eyes, a feature common to each member of the family. Their eyes appear shifty, darting around as they walk, looking everywhere and in all places at once. They are quiet folk and appear in places around town and in the field quite inconspicuously. The whole family, lacking a father figure, most times stay to themselves.

Treeva arrives at Opal's house and loads the trunk onto the wagon. It has been a couple of weeks since Julia moved in with Opal, but he has been away working on the railroad. He doesn't say much on the journey to his house, and Julia is unusually quiet. When they arrive, its pitch-dark as the wagon pulls into the fenced yard. The house appears to be spread as far as her eye can see; the scale is overwhelming. Candlelight flickers in the windows. Treeva drags her trunk up the steps and through the front door. Julia, left behind, follows on her own. The door opens into a large room, not unlike the home she had left. Rocks form a raised platform for the hearth in the center of the fireplace. There is a small fire in the fireplace; a chill is in the air.

An old woman, dressed in a nightgown, stands in the living room with her arms folded and a blanket over her shoulders. Her cheeks are hollow, and a stain on her lips reveals that her mouth is full of snuff. The lines on her forehead accent the frown her face is making as she watches the couple enter.

"Ma, this here is Julia Todd. She gonna need ta stay here wit us. She's my wife now you know."

"How do you do Missus Roarke?" Julia makes a small curtsy, nodding her head respectfully.

Lucy just eyeballs Julia from head to toe. Julia is wearing a gingham, tent-shaped dress covering her full belly. A coat features velvet lapels and velvet-covered buttons that keep it closed. This was well-dressed for a country girl. Lucy does not respond to the curtsy nor does she answer her. She just turns and walks away. Treeva pushes the trunk aside and signals Julia to follow him, leaving her standing.

Julia finds herself impressed. Instead of the bedrooms being right next to the fireplace, there is a sitting area with chairs all around the room. Through a connecting door are the bedrooms. Treeva has designed and built this house for his family. It has features uncommon to most houses in the area for Negros. Building chairs and furniture is his specialty. They arrived in a room larger than most bedrooms. Julia's eyes rest on the huge iron bed in the center of the room, with a slop jar next to it. A bed she does not have to share with her sisters. Just she and Treeva. An elaborately carved dresser like her Mama had is against the wall, with a pitcher and bowl on top. There is a wood and coal stove to heat the room and a built-in closet. The familiarity of the place gives a sense of comfort; despite the chilly reception she received. The attitude of his mother triggers some self-doubt about fitting into this household. Julia is unaccustomed to being disregarded or made to seem unacceptable. She stands in the middle of the room wrapping her arms around herself. She immediately feels resentful and defensive and decides to address the situation later with Treeva.

Once they are secure in the room, Julia whispers, then understanding there was no need for quiet declares: "Your Mama just inspected me, not acknowledging me and making me unwelcome."

"She's just old, pay no mind to her."

"How am I going to manage if she doesn't want me here."

"This is my house, you my wife now. Youre welcome here if I say so. Make yurself at home. I have ta take care of some business. I'll be back later."

“You gonna leave me here by myself!”

“You’ll be fine. Get unpacked, I’ll be back shortly.”

She opens the trunk and takes out nightclothes. There is no opportunity to discuss the situation further.

Julia wakes to open shutters, allowing sunlight to flood the room. A wave of nausea passes over her. Taking deep breaths helps her manage the urge to throw up. Alone again, she’s annoyed. Before dawn, Treeva left, preventing her from discussing their situation and his mother’s attitude further. She did not look forward to getting acquainted with his family all by herself. What about his sisters? Will their attitude reflect their Mama’s? She gets up and makes her way to the great room. The house is cold. The fire is out. Nothing has changed since the night before, she thinks to herself.

“Do I have to gather wood and start a fire for breakfast like home? Surely it will be different here with so many grown people here to help.”

After the greeting she received, Julia knew not getting along with his mother was inevitable. It is clear from the first day of her arrival that she would be on her own. His family never treated her like a guest. Although six months pregnant when she arrived, Julia is required to pull her own weight in chores. The division of labor is between her and the two sisters, with Lucy staying in her room much of the time. Whenever she appears, Lucy finds fault. The old lady complains about Julia’s cooking and criticizes her housekeeping. Gossip had given her all the details of Julia’s past and her father’s preaching. Lucy looks upon Julia as a spoiled preacher’s child with nothing to do but prance around dressed up, discounting the fact that Julia was left alone to raise her siblings.

Although Treeva and Julia argue a lot and Julia is disagreeable with his mother and sisters, the sex with Treeva remained more than satisfactory for both of them. Treeva is gone a lot, and every time Treeva comes home and makes love to her, she gets pregnant.

A pattern of being large nine months out of the year began when she arrived pregnant. The baby was born three months later in the first year. By the end of the second year, she was pregnant again. The third year, nine months again. Since she is pregnant so often, her major chore is washing clothes for her growing family and the other residents too. There was no end to washing, hanging items to dry, and washing again daily.

Treeva isn't home much, claiming he is working. There are times he would be gone for weeks. To make up for not being there, he brings food and gifts for the family when he returns. Julia's complaints would be silent while she temporarily expressed appreciation and gratitude. Julia later bombards him with questions about where he has been and how he has left her to fend for herself with his ornery sisters and mother.

He is called to work on the railroad, and this time gone for a month. Upon his return, his community lauds him as a hero. There was a railway accident. After the freight train hit a barrier on the tracks, it turned over. The crew lifted the car to place it back on track when the enormous pole holding it up slipped and it came down on the workers under the car, crushing them. Treeva was instrumental in helping to lift the car again to free the survivors. Celebrated for his heroism, Treeva came home determined that someday he would be able to invent a method for lifting the cars back on the track safely.

He enjoyed his status as a hero to the community, but the glaze soon wore off at home. New disagreements arose between his mother and Julia, reminding him how fragile famous heroism can be. Julia was very busy with the babies and the chores. Life was not much different from when she was at home with her father and siblings, except for the beatings; she was pretty miserable. Gone was the dream of enjoying a marriage and her own children. The reality of being a wife to Treeva with her own kids differed significantly from Julia's fantasies. The house she dreamed of having shared with his mother and sisters, not her own. She still worked from dawn till late at night, with no end to caring for the babies.

7

Birth of Susanna

Susanna is born with the help of Lucy and her daughter, Bertha. As soon as she makes her way out of the womb, Lucy takes possession of her while Julia lays on the bed, exhausted. Lucy cleans and swaddles the baby, a tiny package that fits in her hand. This could be time for Julia to rest; except she has to recover soon to prevent Lucy from taking over the care of her child. This baby has come so soon after Anna Mae, who is nine months after the firstborn, Cleo. Anna Mae isn't even walking yet. The babies are coming so fast, hardly two years apart.

While Lucy stays to herself most of the time. She is out of her room and involved in the birth of the babies. She believes her expertise is necessary for the successful birth process. Lucy overrules most decisions regarding the babies, telling Julia she needs to take her advice. Her life experience, more valuable than Julia's. With a grim and wrinkled appearance befitting a poor, hard-working woman abandoned by her man, Lucy keeps her hair pulled back in a bun, from which wispy strands fall. She bares Roarke's notable bulging eyes, the red-rimmed lids, making her blue eyes steely and hard. Her voice is coarse and rough. Her manner is demeaning, always viewing her daughter-in-law with disdain.

Lucy is sitting at the kitchen table, sipping from her cup. Her daughter, Bertha, is sitting across from her. As usual, an argument starts the day with Lucy criticizing Julia for any reason she sees fit.

"I'll never forgive Treeva for bringing that sassy black gal into my home. She don't belong here. He should send her back to her family. There's nothing to like about her. She has da nerve to act like she's better than we are." Lucy said aloud to Bertha.

"This house Treeva's too, so we havta put up with her and his kids." replied Bertha.

Julia is within earshot, pretending not to hear the remarks.

"She thinks she's somebody just because her papa is a preacher. I neva attended church and have no respect for jack leg preachers. Her pa ain't nothing but one of them. The uppity ways Julia brang to this house is an insult to decent actin people." Lucy continues.

"You all are a bunch of sinners!" says Julia, walking towards the old lady.

"Watch your mouth talking to my mama!" shouts Bertha.

"I come from good stock. We love and praise the Lord. We don't countenance sinners like you. I don't havta take what you say." Shouts Julia.

"You in my house and you take whatever I give you." Lucy continues with venom towards Julia. "You come in here with your sassy ways. You don't know nothing."

"I had taken care of my brother and sistas and I am prepared ta take care of my own children. You an old woman and your ways ain't my ways. I don't need you telling me what to do."

"Just cause you birthed two scrawny children and now birthed another, don't mean you know what ya doing. You don't know your place and ya speak out of turn when I give good advice. After all, I dun raised five children successfully."

"Yes, and they are gone passing to get away from you. Is that the advice they took from you?"

"You don't know the reason they gone." Lucy speaks loudly as she gets up and walks out of the room. Reminded now of her loss. Her husband, passing as white murdered by the klan after being revealed as colored. Her boys left for fear of the same threat.

"You need to mind your own business ole woman!" Julia yells at her as she carries an armful of clothing to wash.

Even though outnumbered in this household, Julia keeps her combative ways. Treeva is seldom there, and if he is, he doesn't engage in the battles his wife has with his family. He neither defends her nor one of them. They are on their own as far as he is concerned.

Julia is at the hearth, stirring the pot of boiling clothes. The fire is high. A wooden cradle is close by, and baby Susanna is asleep. It is important to keep the baby close while working, so when she cries, Julia will be the first to rescue her. Otherwise, Lucy will take the child and hold her away from Julia while accusing her of not taking proper care of her.

The baby awakes and begins whimpering noises. She cried most of the night because of a slight cold. The stuffiness is apparent from the choking sounds coming from the crib. Julia is wringing clothes from one pot to another, working as fast as she can. When she hears the sound of the baby, it is right then that she drenches the front of her dress, startled by the sound. Lucy is back at the kitchen table and gets up immediately to pick up the child. She is at the side of the cradle, lifting the baby before Julia can get to her. Julia wipes her hands on her apron and reaches to take the baby from her.

"You don't know whatcha doin, I can take care of her." Said Lucy, pulling away from Julia.

"I'm the baby's Mama; I understand what's best for her."

"You don't know what you talkin about. This here baby's been crying all night again. Something ain't right."

"My milk is low is all. If I could get a hold to some alfalfa root, it would make more milk. You'll see. She will stop crying so much." Julia sounds defensive when, in fact, she is rather desperate.

"That baby crying ain't cause she hungry. Something is wrong with your milk. That baby in pain. I heard that kind of crying before."

"Maybe because I been eating cabbage for the past few days. She got gas. But the baby been crying like this since birth."

"You ain't fittin to be its Mama. I take this child to Miss Nan across the way, and she be the nurse maid. You been drinking root tea and that's what's wrong wid this baby." Lucy with the baby in her arms, elbows Julia out of the way. "I have something to quiet her."

Lucy goes over to the jar where she sips all day to sedate herself. She puts her fingers in the jar and puts drops of the liquid into the baby's mouth. Julia hates to have her baby given this granny cocktail. She believes it is sinful. She overtakes Lucy and, because it is a surprise move, she takes the baby girl from her.

"What you doin gal? Who do you think you are?" Lucy growls at Julia.

"I'm takin my baby. You not giving my child that devil's juice." Julia walks away, shaking the baby to calm her as the baby screams.

Susanna's cries reached a higher pitch in keeping with the anger coursing through her mother's body. Before Julia can take steps toward the cradle near the hearth, Lucy grabs Julia's arm and pulls her back. For a moment, they struggle, and the baby is caught between them. Julia has large hands, and when she reaches for the child again, she grabs part of Lucy's dress along with the blanket that is wrapped around the baby. As she pulls Susanna towards her, the bundle slips from her grasp, and Julia finds she is only holding Lucy's dress. To the ground fell the blanket and the baby, striking the edge of the stone hearth. The landing is a hollow thud. The baby's silence is like a tackle in her stomach. Both women are holding their breath, waiting for a sound to be emitted from the tightly wrapped ball that lay silent and unmoving on the ground. The only sound bubbles popping from the boiling clothes in the pot over the fire. Julia picks up the bundle. She unwraps the blanket to reveal the still baby. Distinctly, she puts her mouth over the babies to blow air into the body. Her action continues frantically until Lucy reaches over to take the baby from her. Julia reluctantly surrenders the child. They buried her in the yard. Lucy seldom said much to Julia after that.

8

Treeva and the Chicken

It's near sunset, and the heat on the horizon rises in waves that blur my vision out on the road that leads toward town. I'm shielding my eyes; only the top of the hill a mile away is visible; there's no sign of life. The track is narrow with rocks scattered all around. A small wagon can barely fit on the dirt road. The neighborhood, as far as I can see, is full of blossoms of wildflowers and weeds. The hard, unplowed dirt covering the area around the house has remained untouched for a long while. A shovel and rusted garden tools lay on the ground near rows of plants that are swallowed by weeds. A warm wind blows hard, sending pollen across the field, leaving powdered dust on the porch.

I shake my head in disappointment, turning now to head toward the house.

I have ta get going to make dinner before my energy is gone. This baby is kicking me on my hip and whimpering, urging me to move on. Being pregnant with my sixth child, my body is aching. I'm so tired all the time. If I walk slowly it helps as my body shifts under my weight and this child. The pain subsides a bit. The last time I looked, I had a permanent crease over my brow, a stark contrast to my once baby-soft face. My lips are dry, they used to spread into a beautiful smile, now they turn downward as sweat runs down each side of my face. There's no time to take care of my hair. I need to do something with my appearance before Treeva gets here. I used ta walk proudly but now I'm slumped at the weight of this child who's sitting just above my swollen stomach. Mary is crying and kicking me harder now against the sides of my body. I smack her leg. Her cries turn into screams.

"Hush up, you're gonna sup soon."

She's rocking as if to push me forward. It's time for me to head toward the house; I'll check toward the hill just one more time. I hope to see some signs of Treeva.

Cleo is stirring the clothes in the boiling water over the wood fire in the front yard.

"Watch the fire now, Cleo.

“I’m headin up to the house to feed Mary. Don't lean too close to the fire, mind you. Enough stirrin, call Anna Mae ta come and help you get more water to rinse the clothes. They have ta be on the line so they can dry before nightfall. Keep water handy in case the fire gets too hot."

"Unhuh!" said Cleo stirring the pot.

There is Hannah hitting a ball in the yard with a stick near the fire.

“Watch yourself and don't let Hannah get too close to the fire; mind yourself now, you have to watch her. Hear what I tell you."

"Now don't make me whip your behind for lettin her get burned."

" Oh my look at Frances, Anna Mae, get your sister out da dirt! She needs a bath. Take her to the creek and wash her off. Be sure to carry a stick with you for the snakes."

Just a few more steps up the porch, I have to pause to gather my strength. The sackcloth draped over my shoulder, I’ll use it to wipe my brow. Thank God for these last steps walking through the door. The aroma of the beans and rice cooking on the wood stove reminds me that it is our one meal a day we have had for the past week.

The fatback has run out, and the cornmeal is gone too. I’ve used the last of the flour needed to make hoe cake for breakfast, and only a little molasses remains. The children and I ate greens from my forgotten garden, with no seasoning for the broth. I neglected the garden because of my condition, and the vegetables I planted with loving care in the spring have gone to seed. I’ve felt so weak and sick for the past few months, and the scorching sun has been too much for me to pick the vegetables and preserve them along with the rest of the chores. A neighbor came by on Sunday and brought the beans and rice we are eating. It’s the middle of the week now, and I’m afraid that when the beans and rice run out, I’ll have to take the shotgun and go huntin for an animal for the children to eat.

I'll place my hand on this wall to steady my gait to make my way to the iron bed I've placed straw on and covered with quilts. Finally, I can sit down on the bed and lay baby Mary down; she's still crying. She can't wait for me to reach for the breast that I'm pulling out for her. She's still whimpering long after I give her my breast, she sucks eagerly.

Now she's fallen asleep. I'll ease her into a comfortable position so I can get up to see what the children are doing.

They seem to be playing quietly. Anna Mae is ten years old, and she still sucks her two fingers. She's sitting on a rock caressing a flannel cloth. There's Hannah heading toward the dirt village being built by her sister, Frances. Frances has been working daily on her village, even making stick figures to occupy the houses. Blood rushes over my face as I look at this child being so creative, making dolls and playing with them, even talking to them. As I look up at the sky and take a deep breath, I'm thankful now that it's warm and the children can spend most of their time outside.

I need to watch Hannah since she is eyeing Frances intently. Hannah, my restless child, is always looking for a way to occupy her time. She's not good with her hands like Frances and tries to destroy the creations made by her. I can tell by the way Hannah's frowning, circling at a safe distance, she's up to somethin. Frances's intent on her project not mindful of what is coming. Hannah kicks at the dirt sending dust toward the village. Frances still doesn't seem to notice. I can see Hannah is becoming frustrated because Frances is not aware of her attempts to get her attention. She makes a running jump and lands in the middle of the houses.

"Oh my goodness, Hannah, leave Francis alone. What've I told you about messin with her?"

Now Frances is startled, begins screaming. She picks up a stick, attempting to strike Hannah. After doing her damage, Hannah takes off running as Frances bursts into tears. Oh these chillren.

"Anna Mae go help your sister."

Anna Mae drops her cloth and goes after Hannah. She grabs the tail of Hannah's dress, and they fall into the weeds. Hannah screams, turning over to kick Anna Mae fast and hard. Anna Mae hesitates to hit her long enough for the angry child to crawl away.

"Enough of the fightin both of you are dirty now."

"I'm gonna whip your behin Hannah. I told you to leave your sister alone."

Anna Mae gets up and takes Frances' hand to walk her to the creek for a bath.

I can't leave the children alone for any length of time. Hannah, the little demon, torments the little ones. Anna Mae isn't always reliable; she hides, thinking I don't know she is avoiding her duties. This leaves Cleo to help me care for the babies. Cleo's my angel. She gets up at dawn to gather wood for the fireplace and hikes down to the creek with buckets, so I don't have to collect water for the day's chores. On days when I can hardly manage, she dresses Frances and helps cook the meals. When we have chickens, she collects the eggs without breaking them, which seems too difficult for either Anna Mae or Hannah to do. With Cleo's help, I try to manage, but my frequent pregnancies cause me to suffer from dwindling energy daily. My Cleo is always at my side. I praise her as often as I can, but she's a child, though, and needs chiding once in a while.

I have a little time now to rest before calling the children in for dinner. I'm going to lie down here on the bed. If I close my eyes maybe I can relax and get rid of some of the pain. Oh that Treeva. Remembering the argument we had before he left. Someone saw him shopping at the community store with another woman. I confronted him, but he denied being at the store. I could think of many things I should have said to him then about his worthless, trifling self. At the time I had so many emotions going, scared that we won't have enough food, and how he's going to make out with the device. I can count on my anger and the urge to hit him, but he got away before we had it out.

Now here we are, I've hardly had time to heal before getting pregnant again. I lost some pregnancies four, to be sure. I'm now facing an almost impossible situation, carrying for my sixth child and nursing my fifth.

Sometimes the herbs I prepared worked to rid me of pregnancies, and most times they didn't. One time they almost killed me, but the babies seemed to have thrived despite the toxic effects. Treeva would come home after being away for days. I'd be upset, but he had a way about him that soothed me, and the lovemaking always made our dilemma seem a little less dire. This would last until the sex lost its luster and Treeva would be gone again for a long while. This was the pattern, and I found myself pregnant again and again.

Lucy's interest in caring for the babies slacked after they were walking and talking. She stayed in her room most of the time and carried her special brew in there with her. In the spring after we didn't see her for a day, Bertha, entered her room to check on her. She was on the floor; a stroke had taken her. We buried her soon after while Treeva was away and out of touch. I was alone, struggling to manage the house, chores, and the children. Lucy had been helpful for the sake of the babies. Despite the strife she caused, I miss her presence.

Bertha got married and left the county. Her younger sister moved away, not wanting to be left with me and all of my children.

Very few of Treeva's family members came to visit because of the constant fights with Lucy, Treeva, and me. Lucy's temperament was as volatile as mine. We were the warring Roarkes. Although the arguments between me and Lucy was never worse than that day when Susanna died.

The arguments started early in our marriage and continued whenever Treeva was around for more than a week. It would start with him attempting to show his authority in the home. I challenged him, as I couldn't let him have the last word. No man's going to dictate how I'm gonna live, remembering the way my father treated me. He ruled with an iron hand and left me to care for his children. When he came home, anything I might not have done, even though I did my best, he beat me. I remember the vows once I left my father's house; I will not allow anyone to rule or beat me again. Treeva's attempts to dictate over our household falls on springs waiting to be sprung. I'm running this show, and if there's gonna be any dictating in the house, it's gonna come from me.

My main complaints are Treeva's being with other women, drinking too much, and not coming home for days. He's always played women. It's a privilege, he believes, that he possesses for his talent as a musician and an artist. There's always a woman who wants to feel the fire of the passion he exudes when he plays his harp at the juke joint. He's my man, and I confront him about his carousing with women. He denies having been with anyone, even when I tell him a witness saw him leaving the joint wrapped around a hussy who frequents there. When he can get the best of me in an argument, I push him and attack him with the notion that I could beat the truth out of him. He has to struggle to hold his own because I'm pretty strong, hard to control. He tries to hit me, but I keep him busy. I attack him, and he defends himself by holding my arms and pushing me away. When we fight, the children cry and yell louder than the ruckus the two of us create. The racket from the children sometimes distracts us from the fight.

There are peaceful days when we work together on Treeva's project. His concern about preventing tragedies on the railroad keeps him busy working on drawings of a device he thinks would solve the problems. This device he spoke of from the time we courted. He's spent hours drawing mockups of the ideas he has. I make contributions too, with some refinements to the raw drawings. When he brings home paper to draw plans, he gives the girls some of the paper to draw patterns for doll clothes and for themselves. They're pretty smart for their age. In good times, Treeva brings the end bolts of fabric for the girls. Anna Mae and Cleo sew their creations. They make curtains, tablecloths, and on long days in the winter, they worked with me to make quilts out of the scraps of material. We got along pretty well during those times. His return this time I pray could mean good news about his device.

The sun is going down, and I must get up and attend to the children. Since the baby's still asleep, I'll put her down in her bed. I make my way to the door and see Treeva coming down the hill with the croaker sack, showing that he is bringing food for the family. I put my hands together in praise. We at least won't starve. Now I'm angry because he's been gone for so long.

Here he comes walking, no staggering, into the yard, trying to pull the chicken out of the sack while it's struggling to get out of his arms. I'd be laughing at the picture of him, half-drunk trying to manage the bird, if I wasn't so disgusted.

He's standing there, just before our desperation sets in, with food in his arms as if he was some kind of hero. The chicken is determined to get away as he's taking it out of the sack. Its wings are beating him in the face as he tries to hold them down and keep the chicken tucked under his other arm. He fumbles it, too unsteady to keep control. I shouldn't be laughing at such a pitiful sight.

"There you is lookin like a fool fightin that bird. Where you been all this time?"

"Don't you worry bout where I was, you got something to eat."

"You been gone for more than a week and all you got to show for it is that squawking bird. What happened at the meeting?"

"Take the chickin woman and quit askin questions."

"I have a right to ask questions, where you been?"

"Take the chickin befo he gets away."

Treeva throws the chicken into my arms, its wings arching as if to take flight. I'm fast with my large hands, holding the bird firmly by the breast and pulling it down to the ground with one foot on top of the bird. I put my hands over its head, twisting its neck. I then swing the bird around and around until all I can hear is the snap of the neck as it breaks, leaving the head in my hands. The bird flies through the air and to the ground and begins flopping all over, spattering blood on my dress and over the yard. Once landing on the ground, the headless creature runs toward the field, falling and getting up again. I yell: "go get it Treeva" but the bloody mess repulses him, and he retreats into the house. The children run screaming, not knowing which direction to flee because the chicken seems to chase one or the other as they run into the weeds to get away. The headless body thrashes around, throwing blood everywhere, and soon disappears far into the tall grass, leaving a bloody trail that I know the children won't follow. I'm the one to go after it. It's going to be difficult treading through the high grass, and my search takes quite a while before I find the carcass; it had given up and was lying twitching in a heap.

Cleo knows she better get the water boiling to remove the feathers. When she feels safe, she'll come out of hiding and start gathering wood for the fire. I better gather wood to start it. After I drop the bird into the boiling water, and strip the wet feathers, gut it, I prepare our first meal of meat in quite some time.

After supper, Treeva falls into bed, he appears satisfied that he's done all that is necessary for the time being. Stealing the chicken and bringing it home for me to cook is good enough to get him into the house and make me satisfied for a while. We're going to have it out after the children get settled. We'll talk about what happened while he was away. What happened with meeting the boss? We have devoted much of our time over the past years to his invention. Our entire future has depended on it.

9

The Card Game

Treeva working on the railroad was the best excuse for him being gone for long periods of time, even though he wasn't always at the site. Julia suspected as much, but she didn't have the time or the means to check up on him.

He admittedly was no farmer; she learned to accept it. He was a dreamer for sure, a carpenter for a fact, and now an inventor. Treeva became fascinated by how the rail tracks worked, how they derailed, and how difficult it was to re-rail them. After an accident and subsequent derailment of the train, the act of getting it back on track was dangerous and complicated. The process was lifting the vehicle frame and then allowing it to fall off the jack towards the track to reposition it. This required the use of poles put under the frame. Often the poles would slip, causing the frame to come down, crushing any workmen beneath it. There had to be a way to stabilize the frame to prevent injury and, usually, death. Treeva knew that perfecting this process would be revolutionary to the rail industry and bring a legacy of money to his family. He has spoken of this from the beginning of his relationship with Julia, and how this device could make a difference. Treeva, when sober and at home, spent hours at night working on his invention.

At first, it was just an idea, but after the marriage, he made drawings to show how his idea could work. Early on, they set aside money to buy the materials necessary to put his device together. Any money earned was first gambled away by Treeva and then spent on tools and supplies needed to perfect the device. The remaining money went to the needs of the household. The trial and error became costly as there were sacrifices to be made to afford the added expense. They also promised the children rewards for their sacrifices, explaining that they would receive handsome gifts someday soon for their birthdays and holidays.

Julia supported his efforts and put up with this situation even though the scrimping affected the welfare of the household.

The success of their project was always on the horizon. Whenever times got so hard and their relations were stretched to the limit, the idea of the project's success renewed Julia's faith. They always thought that once they finished and the invention worked, they would have money, and life could become what they dreamed of together.

Treeva left with the plans to present them to the head of the rail company. Now, the anticipation of the results of their hard work has the entire family waiting for Treeva's return.

"Dis the last hand. It's going to be dawn soon." Says Jeb.

"Time for me to git going." Says Isaac as he gathers his winnings to go.

"Just one more hand and we can call it a day." Dooney needs to keep this game going.

They are sitting in a small room at the back of a feed store. They meet here on weekends to gamble. Treeva shows up when he is not playing at the joint. The games sometimes last all night and on Sunday, switching players as some win and others lose. Dooney flexes his muscles and cracks his knuckles. He's wound up tight; the cards have been against him all night. It is important for him to win or to break the winning streak of Treeva. Dooney is a straw boss for the Redline Railroad Company. He heads the group of section hands better known as Gandy Dancers. Treeva, a section hand, does the chant for the crew. Maintaining the tracks is the crew's job, but most of the time, they were simply straightening them. A chant guides the picking up and manipulation of the steel rails, while a more rhythmic one is for spiking and aligning them. Their movements are like a dance as the workers lunge together against the tools, nudging the rail, their actions synchronized by a chant. It is physically demanding, and much reliance is placed on the caller. As they work in unison, Treeva, the best man given such a title in this area, synchronizes the rhythm for the crew in a call and response process.

Treeva had been bragging about a device he designed that would revolutionize the problem of getting the train upright after an accident. Their current methods often injured many of the workers and had been deadly frequently. The section hands of Treeva knew his talent for putting devices together well, as he had worked on his invention for years. He showed tentative plans to his straw boss, Dooney, who in turn showed the plans to his superintendent. After having a higher-up official examine them, the plans looked pretty good. In fact, they could tell that they might be valuable. So, the superintendent made an appointment to meet with Treeva to talk with him about them. The idea of such a device had been kicking around for some time, and the straw boss and the superintendent wanted to have access to these plans, but they had no intention of allowing Treeva to have credit for its development. Their plan, now in place, was to get the schematics and hand them over to the engineers of the company. Dooney was the man directed to get them away from Treeva.

Treeva was a man of many weaknesses along with his many talents, known by all who knew him. Two of the most outstanding weaknesses were drinking and gambling. The idea was to take advantage of both of them.

So far Treeva had been winning much of the day until late that evening. Only until just before dawn had he shown signs of being unable to keep track of the plays.

"One more hand takes the pot." Said Jeb.

Jeb moved the foul-smelling stogie from one side of his mouth to the other and made no hesitation for the next play. Isaac puts his winnings back on the table for one more hand. Treeva nods off for a few seconds but comes to life when the dealer tosses the cards to him. He plays wildly, barely looking to see what he is holding. He seems so sure of his hand; his motions are automatic.

Dooney's hand seems better; he is winning now.

"You sure you can take this hand, Treev?" asks Dooney. "I tell you what, you're down a little. I'm willing to cover you cause you play like you're bout to take all the pot. I need to take some money home this morning. We can split it, I can stake you for double."

Treeva loses another hand. "I'm short on cash, but I'ma take this next hand and the pot. No split, all I need is for you ta stake me." Treeva spoke confidently even as he swayed forward.

"Up the pot, Jeb, you won last time." Treeva says, slurring. Dooney lays his cards down, and the plan is now in motion. Jeb has been watching Treeva and believes his judgment is off. He figures he will take the pot himself.

"Okay, I'ma gonna put all my winnings in this time and go for broke." Says Jeb.

"What sha gonna do Treev?" Dooney says as he observes Treeva sipping on his jug.

"I'm looking good, I raise ya double." Treeva looks at the cards and feels confident. "You say you'll stake me, Dooney." Treeva sits up straight now; this is serious for him.

"Yeah, I'll stake you if you split the pot with me." Dooney smiles as his mind is racing now. "What you got as collateral? You out of money?"

"Lost most of it with the last hand. You know I'm good for it" says Treeva.

"No, no, I trust you man, but that's not good enough" smiles Dooney.

"Since when my word not good enough?" Treeva looks angry.

"Pot is big and you sometimes disappear for days, and I need my money now." Dooney stares right at Treeva. "Who knows what you're holdin?"

"Right now, all I have is my drawings. You hold them til I win and cover my hand?" Treeva seems well awake now.

"Sure, I'll hold your drawings so put em in the pot. How much you want to bet?" Dooney says with confidence.

Treeva takes a quick look at his cards and momentarily closes his eyes. The three guys are looking at him, wondering if he is now asleep or conjuring up something. At least a minute goes by before his eyes open again.

"Two hundred, that's my play." Treeva pats his cards.

"Naw man, them papers ain't worth no two hundred dollars." said Donney.

"You ain't buyin em, just holdin em." states Treeva.

"Awright, awright, let's play." says Dooney.

Jeb speaks up. "Let's do this, I gotta go."

Dooney wins the hand. Treeva falls short.

Treeva

Well, I stepped in it now. I knowed that. I dun fucked up this time. If I wasn't drinking and showing off wit my mouth, I could of thought about what I was doing. Makes no sense what happened. How did I mess up like this? Julia and me been working for years on my invention. I seen my invention as a chance to make good money, maybe become rich. Ever since we had to raise the passenger car on the Redstar line, I had an idea to make something that would brace the car while lifting it upright. We lost about three men last time the train turned over. The log we were using slipped out from under the brace, crushing the men under the car when it fell. I figure there's got to be a way to prop up the car so's we can set it upright. We've been working on it for years and have put all we have into it, and I know it will work. Julia been good about it. Working by my side and sacrificing and all, faithful she is. We figured all the sacrifice was worth it. The children been doing without lots of things so we could get this device together. Many hours and lots of time we been giving to it. I never figured that it would get away from me. It was a misjudgment was all. I had a chance to meet with boss Thompson from the Redline. I was suppose ta see him on Wednesday afternoon, but he got held up and promised to meet me Saturday. Shouda not start drinkin Friday night. Plumb forgot and missed him again on Saturday. Gonna stay til Monday and try to see him then. No point in letting a good game go, so I stayed in town to see what my luck would bring. I just got mixed up with the liker and forgot the plan. My hand was good. I could of taken the pot the way I saw it. We had been playing since noon til that evening. Been steady tastin from the jug I picked up from the still. Winning and losing about equal when I felt a real buzz. Figured it's my night. I hadn't eatin since morning and I could see through the window behind the dealer the black of night beginning to brighten to grey. I was feelin good, a little sleepy, but I could shake it off by just keeping track of the cards as they flowed. The pot was ready for me even though I was down. The cards had been going my way all day, and I was winning for sure. Had the winning hand til late that night. Lost a little and figured Dooney would stake me. I coulda taken the whole pot. Didn't figure on what Jeb had. Dooney was the surprise. No way did I think he would take the hand. I've been talking about this plan for a long time. Had my plans and model wit me. Dooney will get credit for my hard work now. I wasn't thinking. How am I gonna explain to Julia bout losin em? Guess I'd betta find somethin ta take home. Can't show up empty-handed.

Treeva gets on his horse and heads for home to face Julia and the kids. He pulls out his jug, which he stopped at the store-front market to refill. He turns it up to fortify himself for the inevitable battle when he gets home.

10

Hannah and the Tragedy

It's the music he plays on that harp he blows. I love the magic that spins all around the family when we sit around him.

When I was little, a man came by to talk to Mama. He said he was our grandpa. He and Mama talked for a long time while Mama sat there and cried. I've never seen Mama cry like that before. When he came back, he brought the piano. He said it was a gift for her. We never saw much of him after that.

Sunday afternoons are the times when there's peace in our house. It's best when he plays his hand harp and Mama plays the piano. We all sit and listen to the two of them make beautiful music. Daddy on his harp and Mama playing the piano. They smile at each other as their voices come together. The music they play is magical. .For one fun day of the week, they act like they like each other, and we are this happy family.

Mama treasures the piano because most of the time she covers it with a cloth after polishing it so it would last until we can afford to have lessons. She said that all children should have lessons on the piano. Since Mama doesn't have time to teach us, we are not allowed to touch the piano cause she said we might ruin it.

It was a sad day when Mama and Daddy and some neighbors put the piano on the wagon and Daddy took it away. They didn't bring it back, but he came home with lots of food and stuff. We ate really good for a long time. They brought lots of fabric for Mama, Cleo, and even Anna Mae; they got busy cutting out patterns and sewing dresses for all of us.

Mama told us stories of her life when Grandma Emma was alive. She reminded us always that according to Grandma Emma, the sure sign of "refinement" was the ability to play an instrument and appreciate good music. Grandma taught her girls to act like ladies. They were to sit with their ankles crossed, but not their legs. They were to speak softly and never yell. Curtsy too when greeting someone special or older. Mama attended tea parties in Houston before Grandma died and saw her aunts use delicate China dishes. In Grandma Emma's house, there were weekday dishes, Sunday, and company dishes too. We don't live like Mama used to live.

Grandpa is a preacher. The family dressed up when they attended church on Sundays. They were important people. Grandma Emma played the piano while Grandpa preached the sermon. Grandpa also traveled a lot from town to town, having revivals, saving sinners. They were a happy family until Grandma Emma died. Everything changed for Mama. She and her Daddy didn't get along. He beat her. When she got older, she ran away and got married. Our life is not at all how Mama used to live. Mama had planned to go back to Houston; except she had all of us kids. I wonder, is it our fault that her life is so different now?

We did alright for a long while except for the constant arguing between Mama and my Daddy that spilled over and got other members of the family into it. While he was gone, the battles were with Grandma Lucy and Aunt Bertha, and anyone that got in my Mama's way. When they fought with brooms, dishes, and pots, we were scared at first. We all ran outside into the yard when it got bad. It was always about the babies. Nobody seemed to care when we got old enough to walk. They fought about who was in charge of the babies. I don't understand what the fuss was about. It don't make sense cause the babies kept coming and some of them not making it out of the womb before dying. Anyway, this spring, Grandma Lucy died, and Aunt Bertha and her sister moved away. So now it's just Mama and us kids.

Daddy is gone a lot, and he told me the reason he stays away so long is that he is working on the railroad. They call themselves Gandy Dancers. Since Daddy is so handy, he does all sorts of work. His job on the railroad is very important. The men are laying the track the train runs on. After a while, the tracks shift after a certain amount of traffic. Daddy explained aligning the track is difficult because of its great weight, so timing is needed to move it. He says most of the time he is the crew leader. His job is to instruct the crew while he sings a song that helps them be together as they move the track. That's how they get their name Gandy Dancers; he sings, and they move to the rhythm of the song. When he was home, he was busy working on the device that was going to be our legacy. As far back as I can remember, he was working on the device he said, "would revolutionize the railroad industry." I still wonder what that means.

This device would save lives and the railroad lots of money. Sometimes he and Mama stayed up all night taking it apart and putting it together. I could watch as long as I was quiet. Once in a while I asked to help by finding the hammer or a part that was out of Daddy's reach. I was the only child that stayed close while they worked.

In winter, Daddy would work on it in the middle of the floor with sawdust spreading everywhere. It covered the curtains and the shelves that held the cracked and chipped dishes we used and had to wash daily; even our clothes were covered with dust. My Mama just washed them again. She didn't seem to mind.

I remember the happy times when they laughed and joked together, making plans for the money they would receive as the reward once they finished the device. The work on the device has lasted as long as I can remember, and I am eight years old. Whatever this device was, he was making with the help of Mama, gave us some peace despite the fights they had. My only happiness came from this invention and the times our family gathered around the piano while my Daddy played music.

I saw the whole thing while in the corner under the table. I stared at the tiny ball of blood, little like a marble, as it rolled on the floor, picking up specks of dust. There was a long, thin trail behind it, mixing blood with the white grit. It all happened so fast.

Mama is pregnant, and I heard her tell our neighbor the baby was almost ready to come because it had dropped a few days before. Daddy was supposed to bring someone from town to help Mama deliver the baby. That was a long time ago, and Mama had to ask Aunt Opal to come and be with her when the time comes because she didn't think Daddy would get here in time. When it came nighttime and he hadn't come, Mama put a chair to the door and locked down the shutters at the window. She and Daddy had been fighting and arguing every day about losing the legacy. He said he was sorry about it, but Mama said she lost confidence in him. Mama said he took the best years of her life and he lost their legacy. I am wondering what the confidence is that he lost too. It breaks our hearts to know the legacy is gone. Before he left this time after fighting with Mama, he promised to make it up to us when he returned.

I heard Daddy come home and try to get in; it was really late. He banged on the door and called for somebody to let him in, but Mama told us we better not move. He began cussing Mama for not answering. I hoped that he would be sober so that they wouldn't fight again.

I could tell he had been drinking. While lying there, I listened and wished for Daddy to grow weary and doze off on the porch. After a long while, the banging stopped and I finally got some sleep. In the morning, Mama got up and began fixing breakfast. She put on the pot of grits and told us to hurry and get dressed.

While she is busy at the stove, I want to see if Daddy is still outside. Now that he is sober, he could come in for breakfast. I am in my dressing gown, but I put on my shoes. Anna Mae is helping Frances make up their bed. Cleo is busy tending the water that .is boiling for us to wash up with. Baby Mary is whining as usual, and both Mama and Cleo will be attending to her soon. No one notices me when I walk over to the door and pull the chair down and set it aside. I open the door to look out to see if Daddy was still on the porch. The force of the door opening is so hard that it knocks me to the floor. It's Daddy fighting mad.

He starts yelling at Mama for making him stay outside all night. He's calling Mama names and says this time she's going to get it good. Mama is surprised because she didn't see me go to the door. She jumps as she turns around because she's not expecting Daddy to rush in like this. She sees him coming after her with the broomstick in the air like he's gonna hit her. Mama picks up a knife that's on the table and starts toward him. With the broomstick in one hand, Daddy picks up the chair with the other. I scramble down on my knees and crawl under the table for protection. I'm putting my hands over my eyes so I can't see what is about to happen. When I peak through my fingers, I see him grabbing a broomstick and aiming it at her. She throws a knife at him. He backs up and uses the chair to block the knife; it falls to the floor. I see him step back closer to the door as if he knew she was going to throw something else. She picks up dishes and throws them, and each time he dodges the licks with the chair. He is weaving back and forth, dancing around, trying to get close to her, but she just keeps throwing anything that is nearby. After she runs out of objects, Daddy steps toward her. He drops the chair and is still holding the broomstick as he starts gettin closer. The pot on the stove is bubbling over with the grits. She grabs the handle and throws the pot filled with hominy grits at him. He ducks and raises his arm to protect himself. The grits hit his arm, splatters all over it, and down his shirt. He screams, grabbing his shirt as the grits cling to his skin like glue, burning as it drips down, sticking to his skin. This was not enough to stop her as she turned to reach for the other pan of hot water. His head is turning all around as he swings at her, but he loses his footing, slipping on the slimy grits on the floor. The broomstick flies from his hands. Cleo sees the stick headed for Mama and her big stomach. She runs to be in front of Mama tugging on her dress to pull her away from danger. She receives the blow in her face. She puts her hands to cover it but makes no sound as she slowly slumps to the floor, blood oozing between her fingers and down her arms. I watch the bloody mass fall down the front of her dress. It rolls on to the floor, moving toward me under the table; the gray ball barely showing through the dust. It stops in front of me.

I heard Mama's moan as she reached down to cradle Cleo in her arms. She rocks Cleo in her arms, saying, "Lord have mercy," over and over again. Daddy is staring at the bloody mess that spreads over Cleo's dress, then looks at Mama bent over her. He looks like he is stone-cold sober now, and he doesn't seem angry anymore. He let out a terrible yell, steps toward Mama and Cleo, but he stops. He backs up towards the door, turns and runs down the stairs and out onto the road. I crawl out from under the table, as all is quiet now except for the sound of my Mama praying. I'm going outside to the chicken coop.

She done it this time. She sure did. The stick landed directly in her eye. Protecting Mama from Daddy again, as she always does. I noticed him take hold of the broomstick, and I realized he was not the same this morning. He is always drunk .anymore since he went to get his legacy and lost it. This time, he was attacking Mama for real. I never saw him so mad at her. They fight all the time and make up, and then he would play his music. He no longer plays his music; I guess he lost that too, since nobody plays music in this house anymore, not since he came back without money or legacy. Whatever legacy is must be mighty great to cause so much trouble. Mama stays mad all the time since then, and she cries when he's gone and fusses at him when he's at home. Cleo and Anna Mae take her side. Maybe one day he will work on another device, and I can help him make it. Well, Cleo put herself in the middle again, and she got what she deserved trying to come between Daddy and Mama.

11

Julia's Choices

Julia sits on the porch swing, watching the sunset explode into glorious colors. When the color is gone and it becomes gray, her gaze changes to the Bible she is holding in her lap. She has been reading Psalm 23 over and over again. Her heart is heavy as the pain surges through her body. She looks up at the gray sky. "God is going to punish you for your sins." Now, a punishment is here that makes her suffering hard to bear, because it did not visit her, but her vulnerable child, Cleo. A child who always wanted to please her mother and put her life in jeopardy trying to protect her. God is showing her he will punish that helpless part of her in the form of her child who is least capable of coping with life. The child who most resembles the Roarke clan, her firstborn, is in pain; this child is quiet, shy, and delicate. The one child destined to succeed for sure. To see her now, she is tall and painfully thin. While brushing her hair the other day, Julia could see how limp and stringy her hair is as she lay her head in Julia's lap for comfort. Her skin so pale that it appears almost transparent against Julia's dark dress. Her former two eyes were large and beautiful, now that light in them has dimmed. This once dutiful child is now silent and hiding behind the patch covering the side of her face.

"The Lord is my shepherd; I shall not want." Tears not shed in a long while are flowing. She turns to look at the baby lying next to her in a basket. With a smile, she draws the blanket higher around him while he slumbers peacefully. At last, a boy out of ten pregnancies. He is the one bright spot in her life.

Her best friend, Opal, is visiting and sitting across from her in a chair while knitting a sweater for one of her children. Julia wipes a tear from her cheek and blows her nose into a cloth.

"Do you believe God will ever forgive me? He's punishing me for my sins, striking my poor child," says Julia.

"Why you think what happen to Cleo is from God?" Opal responds.

"I am being punished for the choices I made after my Mama died. Forgive me, Lord, for my actions these past years. Forgive my hatefulness when my mother died. Sassing my Daddy, deserting my family, fighting my in-laws, and with Treeva."

"That's a pile to forgive, I guess so."

"He's caused my child to suffer for my sins. God brought this down on me because of the choices I made. Punished with all these children, and no father to help raise them. Treeva is gone. I don't have a place to turn."

"Don't be foolish, you can't blame God for what happened to Cleo. Some of it has been from yur choices," declares Opal.

"My choices! My Mama died and left me with her children to raise. Those were not my choices. I couldn't do it. It was too hard."

"I understand, of course you couldn't. You needed help and your aunties let you down. Treeva is gone now; it's goin to get better."

Julia raises her voice. "How is it better he's gone?"

"You can stop fightin and you won't have no more children."

"Praise the Lord for that," says Julia.

"The devil taken hold of me and controlled my life." Julia began sobbing again.

"It weren't like you to be mean, like you been," agreed Opal.

"I'm being punished because I deserted them."

"They fine now Reverend Todd married and a new Mama for the kids." Opal nods.

"I was so sure life would be better once I married Treeva."

"You knowed he was many things, but not marriage minded."

"I trusted my love for him would keep him, make him happy."

"Love being all that is necessary, huh?" Opal looks at Julia with disgust.

"He come to me with his story you know and promised to do right. I always forgave him and then we'd make love. Our passion for each other was so strong. Our love making would last for days and then he'd commence to gettin restless, in a short time he would be gone. After a few weeks I would find myself pregnant. You'd think I woulda known better, but I was fooled time and time again. I believed in him because he has so much talent. He's so good with his hands. We worked on his invention and sacrificed so much, we came so close to having success. That invention would have changed our lives." Julia sighs and starts tearing up again. "Those were our best years."

"We've talked about this before. Nothin new here. Can't keep relivin the past. It's a shame a man with all that talent and ability goin to waste. Did he lose it or sell it?" Asks Opal.

"He lost it gambling."

That's what I surmised. What a shame."

"He threw away ten years of my life working on a device that is somebody else's good fortune. I have wasted my time with this man and now look what he done to our child. He almost killed us, and now he's gone."

"Good riddance I say." Opal sighs with relief.

"We loved each other, our love was so strong."

"Yeah, I know you loved him. You had ten babies to prove it."

"Only six survived. I've had to go to Reverend Todd for help to feed them. You know how hard that is for me?"

"You are blessed he forgave you for getting married and leaving the family to fend for themselves." Opal looks at Julia sternly.

"I have surrendered to God. Since Cleo lost her eye, I realize I need to stop fightin. God sent babies who came for a while and then he taken them away. Not even the death of Susanna have I seen the error of my ways. Only when my best child is injured have I questioned my choices. I need to ask myself why. Why is my life so hard?" Julia drops her head into her hands.

"You did the best you could. You followed what you knew then." Opal reaches over to touch Julia's shoulders.

Julia leans into Opal for comfort. "I believed with all of my heart that I was destined for a good life. I had been promised a great future and I trusted in it. How could my choices be so wrong? It's true what my daddy and my aunts said that God was going to punish me for not properly grieving the loss of my mother. And then hatin havin to care for my sisters and brother. Deserting my family has weighed heavily on me. Sometimes I miss them. Now with my own children, I come to understand what family is all about."

Julia covers her eyes again to hide new tears. "I must stop fightin. Everyone is gone. Since old lady Roarke died, the burden of caring for my family has got me down. I pray every day for God to deliver us."

"You ask God, but you got to do for yurself. God don't work by hisself. Answer to prayers come in yur doing." Opal leans forward for emphasis.

"I know, I know. I need to make up for my bad choices. It's too late for tears cus now my poor child is paying for my sins. She's almost blind."

"She can see out the other eye," states Opal. "She gonna be alright, just be support for her."

"She got a hole in her head, no eye there. She must wear a patch for the rest of her life."

"Dat baby boy was saved by her. Be thankful for that blessing"

"Yes, Lord! I named him after Reverend Todd. He gonna make us proud someday. I been reading the Bible and Psalm 23. I believe I will be delivered!" Julia takes a piece of paper out of the Bible.

"I got a letter from Aunt Lily. They moved to California you know."

"They been sendin you money every now and then?" asked Opal.

"Just on holidays, but it helped some. They bought property out there, some place called Redonda Beach. Way out in a small town near the ocean."

"You think you might be able to take the children out dere and get more help?" Opal's face lights up.

"Reverend Todd's working on it. Life will be better there. I'm going to pray on it."

The news about Treeva and what happened to Cleo is the talk of the county. Reverend Todd, content in his new marriage, heard about the tragedy and shows up to visit Julia and the children.

"It's been awhile daughter. Yah holdin up?"

"Yes Papa, we survivin God willing."

"Brought a few chickins and some feed for em. Some corn meal and fat back. A basket of apples I knowd you'd like."

"Thank you Papa for thinking about us. Praise the Lord."

"How many youngins you got?"

"Three babies, two on the tit. Named one of them my only boy afta you."

"He will be blessed."

"You saw the two girls in the yard. Cleo is in the room, sitting in the dark."

"How she makin out?"

"She's ashamed of the patch. Stays to herself most times. She's a daily reminder of how my choices have brought us down. I need your prayers. I need yur forgiveness.

"Ask God for forgiveness."

"He's merciful. You're goin to be alright."

"Thank you Jesus."

"Think maybe you and the chillren can pack up and go to your aunties?

"Yes, praise the Lord. I am writing them a letter to accept their offer. I will help them with their properties and provide some care in exchange for a small salary and a place for us to live."

12

California

Lily graduated from Normal Teachers College at an early age. After teaching school for three years, she decided being in the classroom was not her calling. Mabel followed a few years later in the college graduating with honors. Mabel had an eye for business, and the sisters soon established themselves as businesswomen with a shoppe providing beautiful hats to be worn by the fine ladies of Houston society. They were members of the African Methodist Episcopal Church, whose congregation drew from the well-to-do Negro families of the city. The sisters wore their styles to church and became the envy of many of the congregants. Some of the white ladies of Houston regarded their designs with favor as well. The Jennings girls succeeded in their business, and their natural high yellow beauty attracted many well-to-do men who sought their hands in marriage. They both married well.

During the early 1900s, a significant number of Negros were migrating from the South to cities like Detroit and New York. The two families wanting a warmer climate heard that there were great opportunities out west, so they packed up their houses and sold them to go far west to California. Mabel and Lily, along with their husbands, arrived at Redondo Beach among the early Negro settlers coming out of Arkansas and Texas. They bought property and built rental houses for visitors to enjoy the area near the beach. The house rental business did very well, and they amassed several small houses and a few buildings. The men took care of the maintenance, and the accounting was the job of the women. After twenty prosperous years, Mabel's husband died in an accident. Some years later, Lily's husband died of a heart attack. The women had to manage the properties and collect the rents on their own. As they grew older, these tasks became more difficult, not only collecting rents but fending off con artists who would prey on them to acquire their valuable properties. The idea of a family member coming to help greatly appealed to the women, and they gladly paid for the travel expenses of Julia and her children. Reverend Todd helped them pack up, and Julia and her children took the train to California.

The adjustment to living in California came easily for the children, but it was more challenging for Julia. Aunt Lily gave Julia and her six children a two-bedroom home, which crowded them. The house certainly was not as large or as well put together as the house Treeva built. Julia shared her room with two of her youngest daughters, and the other three girls shared the second bedroom. Todd made his bed on the floor in the living room. The best part about this house was the inside toilet, which they did not have in Texarkana. Because the weather in California allows for year-round activities, the family loved it there. The winters were warm and public transportation was available. Since the house was owned by her Aunt Lily, for the time being there was no charge for rent. Life was still not easy, as Julia had to find work to feed her family. Day work was plentiful, and Julia engaged in a number of jobs trying to make ends meet. Even though not having to pay rent was the least of her worries, keeping the children warm in winter, however mild in California, was still costly. In California, as well as other parts of the country not a part of the South, colored women faced significant racial and gender barriers, but not as strong as she would have faced had she stayed in Texarkana. Julia at first found work as a housekeeper or maid, but her temperament was not suitable for taking orders. She found a job washing streetcars, which worked for a while; less supervision suited her.

Anna Mae, Frances, and Hannah attended school, leaving Cleo to care for the younger children Frances, Mary and Todd. The problem was that Cleo was no longer reliable because they usually found her sitting in dark places. She had spoken very few words since the day of her tragedy. Mourning the loss of part of her traumatized her into silence. No longer clinging to Julia, she sat alone, away from the activity of the house and children. The family role she used to perform was beyond her ability. She avoided being seen as much as possible. She worried about how others would perceive her, and she felt vulnerable.

The other children had mixed reactions to what happened to Cleo. They responded according to their age, personality, and relationship with Cleo. Since Cleo was always at her Mama's side, Anna Mae had avoided being around her mother. Cleo, no longer the handmaiden of her Mama, Anna Mae, had a new role to play. She felt a mixture of guilt and pressure, especially since she must pick up the caregiving Cleo had left vacant. She could no longer hide behind the soft cloth that comforted her.

Mary and Frances were so young that they did not see what happened to Cleo. They acted frightened and confused, unable to understand the physical and emotional changes in Cleo. Her injury's appearance disturbed them.

Hannah, having witnessed the tragedy, isolated herself from the family, playing by herself. At times, she felt conflicted between sympathy and irritation. Cleo's suffering seemed to draw more emotional attention to her from Julia, which sometimes caused Hannah's anger. Since her father was out of her life, she had only her memories of the past to draw emotional comfort from.

Time moved on, and now that the family was in California, some of the past faded slowly, and the older girls had their attention directed toward goals outside of family life. They attended school and made friends.

The Roarke girls were outstanding in their appearance. All the siblings were attractive but bore the signature bulging eyes of the Roarke clan. Anna Mae's noticeable feature was the overbite caused by constantly sucking her two fingers clinging to her blanket as a child. She was tall with a full, shapely figure. Anna Mae alone, among the Roarke girls, bore the luxurious milk-chocolate complexion which was smooth as silk. Her skills were of a talented young seamstress; she designed and made her own clothes. Anna Mae sold her designs, using some of her money to help with household expenses. Once seeing an advertisement for Madame Walker in a magazine selling her hair products, she bought a straightening comb to press out her tight curls. She enjoyed the attention brought on by her sense of style, unlike many of the students her age whose interests were other than fashion.

Anna Mae, who turned sixteen, and Hannah, fourteen, took the streetcar to the one high school in the area. Both girls were quite enthusiastic about attending school and made every effort to attend their classes regularly. Anna Mae's favorite course was home economics. She loved showing off her sewing skills. Securing a part-time cleaning position at a textile shop enabled her to get leftover material for her dress concepts, a significant benefit for her and her sisters.

Hannah preferred physical education. She was an athlete, spending hours on the tennis court at the park in the neighborhood. She approached puberty with aggression, a real tomboy among the siblings, training herself to compete in tennis tournaments sponsored by the YWCA. Her short, tight, muscular body was in constant motion. Quite the opposite of Anna Mae, she cared nothing about style. Her auburn waves, which rarely saw a comb, were tied with a rubber band. The sun's rays often burned her buttercup complexion. Her efforts to gain attention from her siblings and Julia had shifted to sports as she grew older. She had excelled at track, and her first-place ribbons hung over the fireplace. She believed her dad would find the family someday and they would be together again. In her mind, working toward a goal of admiration and praise, like her father, kept her hope alive. When he came home, he would see her accomplishments and be proud of her. Driven by the promise her father made about creating a device to make them rich, she believed in her heart he would not have left but for Cleo getting hurt. She had not forgotten the day her father left and blamed Cleo for setting off the circumstances that caused him to leave. If she had not interfered when her Daddy and Mama were fighting, she would not have lost her eye, and her Daddy would have returned like he always did after he and her mother fought.

Frances at twelve was in middle school and traveled alone walking distance from home. She sometimes sewed with the two girls, but she was not as creative in her designs. Of the four girls, she was the most attractive. Her long, flowing, wavy hair highlighted her soft, tan complexion. She was striking even at such a young age. The attraction she got from the opposite sex did not turn her head because she was shy. Her mother had a rule: no boys. So, she kept her head down most of the time.

Mary was still in grade school. She was painfully shy and played quietly with her dolls. Cleo walked her to school. When the other girls argued and fought like girls do, Mary, being so small, found a corner and stayed away from them. Her frame was slight; her complexion was soft brown. Her hair was always in pigtails. Mary got very little attention. She seemed content to just talk to the dolls she made.

Julia pampered Todd and kept him close to her. He bore no resemblance to his namesake, Grandpa Todd. His complexion was soft brown and very much a Roarke in appearance with his large eyes, but he was destined to have the height of the Todds.

Cleo slept late most of the day, and the family's effort to get her engaged ended up in frustration for all of them. When she was awake, she was silent and withdrawn, ignoring her sisters and brother even when they tried to taunt her. Julia felt stressed because Cleo, once her helper, was now the child she worried about. Julia feared Cleo was not present enough to handle life's challenges. When they were all together, Cleo stood in a corner, facing down. There was no word in their world called depression. She was just down and out, as the family described her condition. Cleo also refused to go to school. She was too shy to speak in class and found it hard to keep up with assignments, having only one eye. The worst times were when her classmates made fun of her. Julia complained to the teachers, but they didn't help, and the bullying continued and worsened. She took pity on her silent daughter and just let her have her way.

Sometimes Cleo accompanied her mother to Aunt Mabel's, and other times she just stayed home by herself. The only time Cleo came alive was when Anna Mae came home with scraps of fabric. This was the time Cleo took an interest and sat with Anna Mae to put together patterns for making dresses. It was amazing how her one eye saw well enough to make patterns and sew dresses on the sewing machine.

The one trip Cleo truly enjoyed was when she and Anna Mae took the streetcar to the downtown Los Angeles garment district. They visited all the warehouse outlet trash bins looking for fabric and clothing discarded by the shops. They took readymade garments apart to make new designs or altered others to fit one of the girls. When a few yards of fabric were available, they made patterns from brown paper bags and made dresses that were quite fashionable. Anna Mae was out and about collecting Ladies' Home Journal and Cosmopolitan magazines. The two of them cut out pictures of fashionable dresses and created patterns to make them as well. Otherwise, they used flour-sack cloth for dresses, which suited Cleo as her joy was in making them and not wearing them like Anna Mae.

After a period of time, Julia felt at peace leaving Cleo at home alone when the other children went off to school. Cleo looked after baby Todd and faithfully picked Mary up from school.

Julia was still barely able to make ends meet with the small sum she received for taking care of her aunts. Julia also took in laundry, but it fell short of providing food, clothing, and supplies. Many days Julia and the girls climbed in the trash bins behind the grocery stores to get wilted vegetables that the stores had thrown away. It was humiliating, but provided many good meals, as Julia was skilled at making what should have been garbage into nutritious meals.

As Julia's aunts showed signs their age was hindering their ability to care for themselves, it was important for Julia to give them more of her attention. Mabel was the first to show signs of senility. Julia, who visited her once a week, found it necessary to pay closer attention to her. There were days that Mabel had forgotten to eat. She failed to shop, so her house contained very little food. There were no homes for the colored elderly, so Julia had to find a way to care for her. It was difficult for her to get up at dawn to get the children ready for school and then walk the three miles to Aunt Mabel's house.

Julia arrived on this day to find the front door ajar. She stepped inside to look for her aunt. As she entered, the lady who lived next door hurried from her house to greet her.

"Hey there, are you Miss Mabel's niece?"

Julia turned to address her. "Yes, sm. What's going on? Why is the door open?"

"Well, yes, it's Miss Mabel you see. She was wandering along the boulevard in her dressing gown and bare feet. Some man brought her home. I was hoping somebody in the family would come along to see bout her. This is the second time this happened."

"She was wandering on the boulevard bare foot? Sakes alive, why would she do that?"

"Sometimes she seems to take on a spell asking questions like she has forgotten where she is. I try to check on her when you aren't around. You haven't been here for a week or two."

"Well, I have a family to take care of and I'm not able to come that often."

"Yes, I see you with your daughter and the little boy. Take a look in the house. I don't believe it's been cleaned since the last time you were here."

They both entered to see the cluttered dining room table. Unwashed dishes in the sink. Clothes littered the room. Aunt Mabel was sitting in the chair, holding her head in her hands. She looked up and recognized Julia and the neighbor.

"There you are Julia. Where have you been? I was looking for you. I hope you didn't bring those children with you. They get on my nerves. Where are they? Are they outside? They need to stay out there. They'll make a mess of the house."

Mabel looked disheveled. Her nightgown was thin, and one could see the outline of her breasts hanging on her chest. Although her hair was on top of her head, held in a bundle, wispy strands were hanging all around her face and ears.

"You're lucky I can get here when I do. I didn't bring them today. I can't always leave them at home you know. When the weather is nice they stay outside when we are here. Anyway, why were you out on the boulevard, and why aren't you dressed?"

Mabel does not respond to Julia's questions and seems to be disoriented.

"I know Aunt Mabel sometimes has her spells. I had no idea she was leaving the house." Julia walked the neighbor to the door.

"Thank you for looking after her."

"I'll do what I can. Why don't you' all move in here with her? She seems to have plenty room."

"We can't move in here with Mabel; she won't tolerate children since she and Aunt Lily had no children."

"Well, something must be done. It's dangerous for her now to be alone. She's not even able to dress herself. I don't know how long she has been in that nightgown. If you look in the icebox you can see, she had very little to eat. I'm not sure the last time she has eaten."

"I need help with her. Can I depend upon you to see after her a little each day until I figure out what to do?"

"Well, I don't know. When I see your girls, they always look so nice and well dressed. Can't you pay somebody to help you?"

"Oh no, I don't have no money. I work hard every day. My girls are seamstresses. They make all of their own clothes."

"I see, they make nice dresses."

"If you'd like, they could make some dresses for you."

"No, no, not for me, but how about they make some clothes for my granddaughter. She would need them."

Julia made a deal with the neighbor to assist her aunt for her, and in turn, clothing made by her girls for the neighbor's granddaughter. The dresses the girls made were plentiful, and sharing them was a delight for Anna Mae and Cleo.

Julia prepared Mabel for bed before leaving to go home to prepare dinner for her children. The neighbor looked in on Mabel to make sure she was in bed and locked the door to make sure Mabel would not leave. It didn't always work out well, but there was no choice but to leave her alone many nights when Julia could not stay.

Sometimes Julia arrived to find her aunt soiled in bed. If Mabel got up during the night, she often did; she would fall and be on the floor the next day when the neighbor checked in on her. When Julia came to find her lying on the floor, the first thing that Julia had to do daily was to clean up the mess when there was one, bathe and then dress Mabel. She prepared breakfast of oatmeal and toast. On the days when Julia walked to the grocery store to shop for Mabel, the neighbor watched Mabel.

She was very hard to manage and became angry and attacked Julia. Often Mabel didn't recognize Julia and screamed for help. Even though Julia was strong and able to contain her, it was frustrating trying to control the old lady. The days Julia brought the girls, she didn't understand why the family was there and their presence created unrest for her.

On the properties Mabel owned in the area, the tenants took advantage of her inattention to repairs and, as a result, they had stopped paying rent. Mabel had hired a storefront attorney to manage the properties and collect rent. His poor supervision of repairs and lack of response to tenant complaints did not help the money situation. The money he collected for rent mostly went to pay him, debts, and court costs. The cash flow to pay Julia came from a dwindling bank account.

Her Aunt Lily, who was younger than Mabel, in her eighties, lost some of her other properties, was living off two buildings for income. Lily had acted uninterested in details about money and bills and appeared to be forgetful. She could still take care of herself and even perform some small chores around her house. The two women were in separate houses a mile or so apart. The burden of looking after both of them was great, as Julia eventually had to care daily for Mabel and tended to Lily's needs when she could.

It was not long before trying to care for the two women living apart was much too much for Julia. While the two sisters had always gotten along over the years, they steadfastly remained in their own homes. Julia finally convinced Lily to allow Mabel to live with her. There was no other choice. This move was necessary because the bank had taken over some of Mabel's properties, and there wasn't enough money to place Mabel in a home, even if she could find one willing to take her. Times were not as hard there in California as it would have been in Texarkana, but there would be no mixing of races in homes for the infirmed. Although there were many colored families in the South Bay area, resources were few. There were practically no homes for the aged colored people in the Los Angeles area either. It was up to Julia to make do with whatever few resources she had.

When Julia arrived from Texarkana, the sisters tried to depend upon her for help with the properties, considering her youth and ability to get around. The sisters did not consider that Julia had not completed middle school and knew nothing of the business world. She was also busy trying to make a living and taking care of her children.

No one helped Julia, and the legal system exploited her. People knew that the area was growing and beach property was valuable. The acquisition of Mabel's home was a gold mine for the investors. Many people approached her to sell at a very low price, not at all what the property was worth, and Julia hired a lawyer whom she trusted to handle the business. In reality, she could no more trust the lawyer than the buyers. The properties sold for less than market value. After paying the bills, the sales yielded very little profit for her. Julia had to sell the furniture and antiques collected by Mabel over the years. The money earned helped to pay for the move. Although many of Mabel's antiques were rare, as she travelled the country to find them, they had to be sold at a pittance since Julia was ignorant of their value. Time was not on her side either, so she took what she could get.

After five hard years had passed, Julia continued to struggle to keep the two properties Aunt Lily owned. She had difficulty finding someone to make repairs. Monitoring the apartments was something she could not do. She could trust no one to collect the rent, and she could not do so herself. Eventually, the tenants stopped paying rent, and she had to turn over the titles of the properties to lawyers to pay the debts.

When the aunts died, Mabel first, then Lily, Julia was able to get enough money from the sale of Lily's house to buy a one-bedroom house in the Los Angeles area. It would be many years later before Julia realized what they had lost. The legacy of wealth from the valuable properties of Redondo Beach had slipped through her fingers.

All of Julia's children showed signs of the trauma and desertion by their father. For sure, the anger and fighting by their parents gave them deep emotional wounds that shaped their behavior in complex ways. Frances and Mary stayed to themselves and avoided social interaction and were emotionally distant. Todd got into a number of fights on the playground and had been dismissed from classes in high school. Hannah, even despite her sporting accomplishments, had low self-esteem and feelings of unworthiness.

Anna Mae had left home by the time Julia purchased her home. She married a young construction worker. Frances got a job dancing at a club and had to leave home because Julia disapproved. Cleo came out of her solitude and became a flapper. The dresses she made were high fashion and popular for the era; her hair was marcel-styled short and wavy. She was taller than the other girls and presented herself glamorously with a black patch over her eye. She married a young man who was a carpenter and an artist. Hannah remained at home along with Todd. Mary, the youngest girl, who had been most ignored as she grew up, was still a quiet child who spent time making dolls rather than sewing with her sisters. As she got older, she ran away and was gone for days. No matter how Julia threatened her, she could not control Mary's behavior. Eventually, Mary left home for good. Frances found solace in the favors from men and lived with a man who became her pimp.

While Julia was struggling to care for her aunts and providing for her children, her focus was also on gaining redemption for her sins. Keeping it all together was so hard that she felt she had reached rock bottom. Into her life came Sister Gray, known for driving her huge Lincoln Zephyr, a member of an Evangelical store front church. Their revivals baptized sinners; once attendees declared their devotion to Jesus Christ, they were saved. Worldly sins were no longer something they would take part in. They wore long grey dresses and black high-top shoes. The church forbade wearing colors. There was no drinking and no dancing, no gambling, and no joy. No longer concerned about how they lived as long as they followed the rules because they were saved and guaranteed to go to heaven.

Sister Gray strongly influenced Julia's life with her strict code of living. Although Sister Gray saved her congregants, they had to keep a vigil against worldly activities. So strict were her dictates that both Todd and Mary soon left home to fend for themselves, as Julia was intolerant of most of their choices of living. Only Hannah remained until she was eighteen.

13
The Langoires

Thaddeus Alphanso Langoire waited through six girls and three boys before the child that would bear his name was born. When he saw the scrawny, dark red infant shaking his fists at the world, he said, "At last, this one will have my name. He is going to be black just like me." Sure enough, little Thaddeus didn't grow very tall for youngsters his age, and unlike the honey-browns of his brothers to the high yellow of his older sisters, Thaddeus was blue-black just like his father.

As a full-grown young man, he referred to it proudly on one hand and cursed the disadvantage of such blackness on the other. Nonetheless, he was Clara's brightest boy and Thaddeus Senior's spitting image of spunk and get up, the five-foot six-inch stature did not limit his son in the least; as a matter of fact, he gained the advantage by being very handsome, witty, and comedic.

Thaddeus Jr., in his heart, considered that good looks gave him an advantage, and by all means that asset served whatever the occasion merited; nevertheless, he considered himself the underdog, having to scheme and feign for every right or privilege accorded him. His father favored him, and his mother and sisters pampered him, because the family endeared Thaddeus more than any other child. The deep hue of his skin was, for him, the bane of his existence, as he noted the references to the dark side of anything were proof that all the world was viewing darkness as evil or ill-fated. Beneath the shine of his looks, internal conflicts churned within him; he felt a pride in his identity but frustrated over how others perceived his darkness. He was often in trouble, pilfering fruit from neighbors' trees as a youngster, stealing liquor as a teenager, then performing a skin game while gambling when he was older. He was charming and clever, as he used his otherwise good looks to his advantage.

Despite the shenanigans, he had experienced the minimum amount of punishment, even though his mischief-making was the topic most discussed regarding the family unit.

Mostly, the Langoires had the respect of the community, which included any whites who lived in the city of Dade County, Florida.

Thaddeus senior was the personal valet to the local judge, a position of much honor and respect. He carried himself with great pride as he walked the five miles daily to and from work. Coloreds could not ride in the streetcar's front and were removed from the rear if crowded to advantage any white person needing a seat. His personal protest to this condition required that he not use the service, so he walked. This act of his spoke volumes about his moral compass. He refused to accept the indignity imposed upon him, even at personal cost. Living in a racially stratified society, he challenged the norms of racism without confrontation.

When his favored child, Thaddeus Jr., had to appear before the magistrate for minor infractions of the law, the magistrate set him free with a lecture because of the respect for his father and notwithstanding his service to the Judge. His companions received harsher punishments. The reaction at home was of greater concern, as these snags in the law reflected badly on what his father considered his untarnished character and that of the family before society. They were all glad when Thaddeus Jr. graduated and went off to college at Fisk University in Tennessee.

There for only six months, he persisted in his defiance, leading to his expulsion from the dormitory because of his possession of an iron and a hot plate. He used the hot plate not only for meals, as he disliked the food provided for the students, but he also cooked a mixture of flour and water to make his white shirts stiff. He was an immaculate dresser, with his pants pressed to perfection so that the creases aligned with his big toe. The ironing of his shirts and the creasing of his pants were a daily ritual. He spent hours getting a spit shine on his shoes and slicking his hair down. His body shone from his head to his toes when he attended classes. The young girls loved him.

After getting his Bachelor of Science degree, Thaddeus Jr. served the two years required in the army. He later ventured to California to complete his education at the best school of dentistry. After making inquiries, he soon learned that they were not accepting Negroes in their dentistry program. Undaunted, Thaddeus Jr., who now preferred to be called Thad, no longer under the shadow of his father, discovered that being colored was not the problem if he could pass himself off as anything other than an American Negro. With the help of some students from India for his wardrobe, he put on a turban and introduced himself as Abdul Mohammed from Egypt, accent included. He passed all his entrance exams with excellence and attended university, graduating with honors. He was the first Negro to graduate from this private university in 1929, but nobody knew it. Thad did not just play the hand he was dealt; he reshuffled the deck to get what he believed he deserved.

Thad was a party animal and spent evenings and weekends gambling and escorting beautiful women. He married three of them, too. Subsequently, he was never without action. The local Negro paper's gossip columns often featured his name and picture, making his reputation known throughout the City of Los Angeles.

Fortunately for him, on the few occasions he was in contact with the law for his gambling, a friend was always there to cover for him.

After graduating, he and a fellow student who had graduated college and passed the bar for a law degree rented space in a building on Vermont Street, the heart of what was known as Sugar Hill in Los Angeles. The building provided space for offices across from one another. Thad lived above his office for a number of years and kept a space for crashing even after he married and owned a home.

He is one of the most prominent dentists in the Negro community. He will play an important role in the life and future of Julia's family.

14

Hannah and the Dentist

The only child remaining at home was Hannah, whose athletic participation kept her busy. Hannah finished her senior year, graduating at eighteen. She was excited about being in a tennis tournament sponsored by the local YWCA. Lately she had complained to her mother about a tooth that caused her headaches. Julia has been very protective of her girls, her spiritual beliefs prevented her seeking medical attention, but Hannah's situation would need a doctor's attention. Hannah was showing promise unlike Frances and Mary; she modeled the behavior much approved by Julia and was active in the church community.

Her minister, Sister Gray, provided Julia with Doctor Thaddeus Langoire's name when she asked for a dentist referral, adding a caution about his liking for young women. Julia took her daughter to his office despite what she knew of his reputation as a player. She will guard her daughter's honor.

Julia opened the door and saw several people waiting for the dentist, which surprised her. She immediately approached the window and picked up the bell, shaking it to announce their arrival. The sparse waiting room felt crowded even though there were a few seats that were not filled. The one table had outdated magazines scattered on it that partially covered a pad and pencil used to sign in the patients as they arrived. Julia put her name on the slate and placed it next to the bell and rang it again. She and Hannah waited rather impatiently, but no one responded to the ring. Recognizing that she wouldn't be announced, Julia scanned the room for a seat to join the others who were watching them.

One could not help but stare at the two of them when they entered the waiting room. They were in complete contrast to one another. One appeared to be almost six feet tall. A few grey hairs sprinkled her black hair, which was pulled back severely into a bun at the back. Though her walnut complexion was clear and smooth, her mouth was turned down in permanent sadness. Her dress was grey, plain, well-worn around her ankles. Although she seemed older than her years, washing street cars and carrying heavy loads of laundry while walking many miles had not bent her posture. The girl with her, Hannah, was short and stocky with curly auburn hair-streaked blonde, bleached by the sun. Her complexion was bright, the color of cocoa butter. She was also dressed plainly.

Julia was wearing a pillbox straw hat and white gloves, which she used to wipe the seat of the chair before sitting on it. An imposing person while seated, she was even taller as she pulled her shoulders back, crossed her ankles and made sure her dress lay over her legs. She looked up to see if her daughter had found a seat. Hannah waited to ensure her mother was comfortably seated before she dropped her shoulders and eased into a seat on the other side of the room. Julia nodded with approval of her daughter's actions and then gazed around the room to survey the others who were waiting. She folded her arms across her chest and looked disapprovingly at the man seated across from her, as his gaze was intent on Hannah. It was the way she held her chin; she seemed to look down on everyone, not just that she towered over most of them. She had no particular expression on her face as she looked around, but anyone who felt her gaze knew she was judging them. Each felt compelled to change their position to either uncrossing a leg and sitting up straighter or shifting from one hip to another. One man coughed and cleared his throat under her watchful eyes. Hannah sitting across the room, tucked her feet under her chair and tugged at the hem of her dress.

Their wait was significant as they watched one after another disappear behind the door, accompanied by a man in a white coat. When it was their turn to enter the inner office, Hannah sat in the dental chair, while Julia explained the reason they were there. The look on her face belied a woman of no nonsense. Hannah remained quiet but was sheepishly looking at the doctor. He was quite dashing in his white coat. His good looks were not lost on Julia either.

"This is my daughter, Hannah. You can see she is youthful and strong. She will be in the tennis tournament next month."

"Congratulations," says Doctor Langoire, looking at Hannah.

Hannah just shrugs her shoulders and smiled.

"She is a good girl, a virgin you must know, and does not consort with men. She is saving herself for marriage." Julia says.

"Okay! And what is her complaint today," asks Doctor Langoire, ignoring this comment.

"It is important that she is accompanied by me or her brother so that she is protected." Julia continues.

"Uh huh! So, let's take a look in your mouth to see what is ailing you." Doctor Langoire chuckles to himself quietly at the comment about her needing to be protected. He turns his attention to Hannah, who opens her mouth obediently.

"I will sit right here in this chair while you attend to her," says Julia as she pulls up a chair in the room's corner designated for the doctor.

"You might be more comfortable waiting in the reception room," he says looking at her.

"No, I shall sit here where I am comfortable," replies Julia.

Doctor Langoire frowns in wonder at this woman but turns his attention to his patient. He examines her teeth and determines that a decayed tooth needs removal. He starts to write a prescription to deal with the infection and aspirin for the pain.

Julia rises from her seat and appears at his side, saying, "Hannah will not be needing anything for pain or infection, she will be healed for that. I am saved and my prayers will conduct her healing."

Dr. Langoire frowns, saying, "I can't pull this tooth until the infection is cleared. You will have to go somewhere else for treatment if you cannot follow my instructions."

Julia considers this threat and relents, saying, "She will take the prescription for the infection but not the aspirin as we do not use drugs of any kind."

Doctor Langoire shakes his head and gives her an appointment for her return visit, saying, "She will need to come in to have her teeth cleaned and another appointment for me to fill some cavities."

Whether Julia takes Hannah to this office with the notion that Hannah would attract this young doctor, exemplified by Julia's behavior. Indulging in a quiet unspoken desire for something more to unfold, or she was just super cautious to protect Hannah, this was unknown, even in the mind of Julia.

Hannah

Mama took me to the dentist's office because my tooth had been bothering me. She doesn't believe in doctors, but the pain was so bad, and my face was swollen, so we had ta do something about it. I never saw such a beautiful man. His jet-black skin glistened on his handsome face. He looked so important in his white coat. He promised me he was going to fix me up just right. It was easy to trust him because he looked me straight in the eyes and smiled. Warmth rushed all over my body when he looked at me. I knew he would take good care of me, and he promised Mama he would. When I returned to his office for my teeth cleaning with Mama, everything was all proper and he didn't say much. It was the same when he finally pulled my tooth. He put me to sleep while Mama had to wait in the other room. She did not like it, but he insisted he would not pull the tooth with her standing over him. I felt nothing after the shot. But when he touched me, I almost jumped as it sent lightning bolts through me.

After my gums healed, my appointment for the check-up and cleaning required me to go on a day Mama had to be at church. By now she seemed comfortable with the doctor. Todd accompanied me and he stayed in the waiting room as I entered the office for the treatment. Mama told him to stay in the treatment room with me, but the doctor said to stay outside, and Todd did what he said. As he prepared to clean my teeth, he asked me about my tennis tournaments. His taking time for me to talk about myself made me feel important, knowing he was interested in me. A long time passed as he shared stories about the time when he was a young man. As I sat in the chair, I looked forward to his soft hands on my cheeks. When he put his fingers in my mouth, it caused a tightening between my legs, a quiver to my thighs, and warmth that rushed through me. No one has made me feel this way. I looked forward to the next appointment to spend time with this man. I continued my appointments accompanied by my brother. We arrived after hours and my brother remained in the waiting room. When I could no longer make excuses to my mother about being absent certain times during the week, I no longer visited the doctor's office. No one was more surprised than me to find I was pregnant.

Hannah, frightened by the consequences from Julia, denied knowledge of how this happened to her. She was surprised as she did not associate a pregnancy with what transpired between her and the dentist. She remained silent while she processed her condition. Her silence was an emotional shut down for a long period of time. Pregnancy was overwhelming for her; it was as if her body betrayed her. Her sports were curtailed and the weight of carrying the child made her tired all of the time. Finally, after threats of beating and being put out of the house, she claimed that while she was getting treatment, the dentist put her under anesthesia, and it was then the dentist took advantage of her. She had been sexually assaulted.

This situation may have been the consequence of ambiguous intentions by both Hannah and Julia. A thin line between care and neglect, between protection and projection by Julia. At any rate, one can only imagine Julia's outrage upon finding out Hannah was pregnant.

Julia's first reaction was disbelief, refusing to accept the possibility of a connection with the doctor, clinging to the idea that Hannah's visits were innocent and purely medical. Julia was unaware of the many visits that were not accounted for. She mentally replayed every moment, trying to convince herself she hadn't encouraged anything inappropriate. She was only protective. Julia's reaction oscillated between anger at the doctor herself, and the situation. There was sadness for Hannah's lost innocence or future as an unwed mother, but there may be a future in it for Hannah. There was resentment because Julia felt manipulated by the doctor and hoped privately that something good would come out of this situation. Sadly, there was no answer. Hannah was pregnant, and the doctor was to blame. She reverted to the defense she felt appropriate: the fault was only with the doctor, and he would pay for this.

He must be informed of the pregnancy and take responsibility for this child. Julia contacted the doctor. The first call was to inform him of the pregnancy. He denied any knowledge of Hannah other than as a patient. Then the calls were no longer answered and not returned. Julia, very frustrated, visited the office.

After several visits in which Julia could not see the doctor, she remained in his reception area and yelled for all to hear that her daughter had been taken advantage of by the doctor and was now pregnant. The police responded and they removed her. They also stated that they would arrest her if she returned. By now, extremely frustrated and angry at how they treated her, Julia returned to the outside of the office, displaying a sign stating that her daughter had been raped. She told anyone who would listen about the situation until the police came to remove her again. For weeks later, she returned daily.

Doctor Langoire told himself he could have been one of many young men who slept with Hannah. The ease of the encounter encouraged this belief, despite what Julia had said about how chaste her daughter had been. There was no proof that he was the father of this child. Most importantly, he could not have this woman parading outside of his office with such a sign; something had to be done. This situation was embarrassing for him and hurting his practice. In order to stop Julia from protesting in front of his building, Doctor Langoire had to take her to court. Julia was glad of the opportunity to have a day to be heard.

The best advice the dentist received from his lawyer before his appearance in the court was to find a way to prove he was not the father. He consulted a friend who was a surgeon, who advised Thaddeus to have a vasectomy and predate the surgery a year before he treated Hannah. Proof of this procedure was presented in court, and any accusation of paternity was impossible. Julia's voice was silenced, and any further cries of rape would cause her to be punished under the law.

Meanwhile, the child was born in Los Angeles County Hospital. The sad story of Hannah's plight was the talk of the floor in the ward. A prominent doctor had raped this poor girl. He used his influence and power to deny touching her, and now he has left her to raise this child alone. Convinced of Hannah's story, in retaliation for this situation, the nurses named the child after the dentist so that he could no longer deny him. Thus, the child was named Thaddeus Alphanso Langoire.

Meanwhile, Hannah had a visceral reaction to having this baby. She refused to nurse it or care for him in any way. Once all the paternity accusations were silenced and since Hannah refused to mother the child, Julia put her daughter out of the house so she could, as a good Christian, raise this boy properly.

The doctor had no desire to father a child. He had two other marriages and no children. A few years later, he married a beautiful woman from a professional family who was aspiring to be a model. Her family was rich and prominent. When his wife learned that the child he vehemently denied fathering was named after him, she tried to convince him to go to court and have the name taken away. He was now five years old, a very damaging course for the doctor to take against an innocent child. Doctor Langoire gave the idea much thought, and in his heart, he knew there was a possibility he could be the father. It would be so cruel to take this child's name from him. Julia was told about the possibility of a name change. This kept her silent for a while.

Thaddeus decided to let the child keep his name, thinking maybe this decision on his part could mollify this woman and stop her from publicly harassing him. It worked.

Later, after word of the child's name became society news, Doctor Langoire's wife left for Europe to pursue her modeling career. He later divorced her.

Despite her harsh Christian upbringing of little Thad, he thrived from the love and support of his aunts Cleo and Anna Mae. Julia persistently fueled the boy's disappointment over his absent father by expressing her daily anger toward the doctor. For years later, under the direction of Julia, he made calls to his father to threaten him.

When Thad was twelve, the dentist invited him to visit his office. This was an attempt by the doctor to start a relationship with the child, since looking at him, it was hard to deny that he was a Langoire. He could have been the offspring of the doctor's older brother, William. He had his fair complexion and Langoire's sharp features.

Of course, Julia accompanied Thad Jr. to the office, as she would supervise all communication between the two of them. The dentist offered some hand-me-down clothing, which was vigorously rebuffed by Julia and by the boy. He made no other attempt to start a relationship. This contact just reinforced Julia's campaign to get financial support for the boy. She began calling his office, which was to no avail. For years later, the dentist received calls of silence or hang-ups. Although Thad Jr. wanted so much to connect with his father, he had no clue how to make it happen.

Thaddeus's half-hearted gesture of offering old clothes and failure to build a relationship further reinforced to the Roarke aunts his unwillingness to connect meaningfully with his son. They in turn harbored bitterness toward him, as none of them ever contacted the doctor, not traveling in the same social circles as he.

Doctor Langoire kept tabs on his son throughout high school. He attended football games where Thad Jr. was team captain. Showing up never letting his son know he was there. He seemed to take pride in this boy and a mixture of remorse, although he would never admit to this inner conflict.

The fact that he kept track of Thad Jr. didn't change his desire not to be a part of his life. Not making any contact may have been out of fear of restarting the conflict with Julia. She showed great tenacity in getting recognition and support for this child. There was no point in the Dentist opening that wound again; his reputation was also at stake.

Thad Jr. saw very little of his mother as he grew up, just visits on holidays and his birthday. Public transportation to their area was poor, and she didn't drive, so her visits had to be infrequent. He bore resentment toward her for not taking him to live with her and away from his grandmother. Julia's campaign against the dentist and her daughter, combined with their coldness toward the child, made a genuine connection between Thad Jr. and his parents impossible for the next twenty years. Her determination to be the sole steady presence in his life risked undermining her own intentions. In the end, neither Julia, the dentist, nor Hannah gave thought to the young man's needs.

15

The Wedding

The upbringing of a young boy was challenging in the big city, and Julia had her arms full with Thad. She aimed to have him present at the church on Saturdays, Sundays, and during Bible studies on Wednesdays. Hoping he would develop into a minister, much like her dad, she had to keep him free from sin. This presented a hardship due to the allure of Los Angeles' streets and friends not aligned with her faith.

He had to testify before the congregation during childhood church services. He was called up front to the podium. The season had turned to winter and he had on the brand new wool pants his Aunt Cleo bought for him. He hated wool next to his skin. It itched between his legs. He felt shame at the impulse to scratch. He stood looking out over the congregation of old women all dressed in gray wearing old fashion hairdos. They sat waiting in anticipation for him to say something about Jesus or about being saved. His palms were sweaty, his hands trembled. He wiped them on his pant legs. He started to speak, nothing came out. He had no voice. Now his whole body became damp with sweat. The itch between his legs became intense. His eyes bleared, he could no longer see the congregation, he might faint. Sister Gray saw his dilemma walked over to him and gently guided him to a seat. He did not become captured by the spirit, and this was necessary if he were to become a preacher. No amount of coaching from Julia over the years made it possible for Thad to testify in front of the congregation because he had nothing to say.

The concept of committing a sin remained foreign to him. He saw none of his activities as sinful, even though Julia declared them so. Fear of punishment from the Lord did not move him to obey. When he failed to do as he was told, his Uncle Todd delivered his punishment. Julia would call him over to beat Thad when corporal punishment was deemed necessary. As a result, Thad developed two personalities. One represented the choirboy before his grandmother and her companions, and the other embodied his self-perception among his peers at that moment. When he became a teenager and went out with his friends, Julia waited at the door when he returned to require him to show his underpants to make sure he had no sexual relations.

This lifestyle resulted in the exact reverse of Julia's aim to raise her grandson as a devout Christian minister. He hated the church, and anything associated with Christians and being saved. There were other humiliating experiences he had to bear. Instead of grocery shopping in the store, he had to dive into the dumpsters for vegetables and fruits discarded by the store. The thought of his friends seeing him there or knowing about this activity was a source of embarrassment. Despite the excellent and wholesome food his grandmother made, he couldn't stand vegetable soup or any type of stew.

Thad endured so much unhappiness residing with his grandmother, and apart from his Aunt Cleo and Aunt Anna Mae, he thought he had few connections in Los Angeles and needed to depart from her dominance. At twenty years old and attending junior college, her constant monitoring of his comings and goings became too oppressive. The humiliation could not go on. Her possessiveness strangled him. He concluded that by joining the service, he had the greatest chance to get away from her. He enlisted in the U.S. Air Force; his test scores qualified him as a pilot. He said no because picturing himself in flight seemed impossible, so he opted for a radar school, a similarly distinguished choice. Before accepting him into the school, he had to be seen by a psychiatrist. It is uncertain whether this became a requirement for all applicants. During his meeting, they asked him many questions relating to his life with his grandmother.

"Who were the main people who raised you growing up?"

"My grandmother was the only one to raise me."

"What was a typical day like living with her?"

"It was hard, she criticized me a lot. She wanted me to be religious. But she made sure I was well fed. She was hard to please and made sure I did the right thing."

"How did family disagreements usually get handled when you were growing up?"

"My grandmere always had her way. There were fights all the time with my mother and aunts. I stayed clear of them."

"How did her beliefs influence your own views on life?"

"I'm not religious. I'm not sure there is a God. It's important to do what makes you happy."

"How would you describe her in three words?"

"She's domineering, controlling, and religious."

"How do you feel about leaving your grandmother to be on your own?"

"I am happy to leave. I needed to leave."

"What best describes your feeling toward her?

"Sometimes I hate her, but I'm also grateful since she was the only one who wanted to take care of me."

"How do you feel towards your parents?"

"I hate them too."

He made no effort to hide his unhappiness growing up. They concluded that while he fit the profile of a potential serial killer; they decided he showed no obvious criminal tendencies. The program accepted him and sent him to Colorado for basic training. Upon arriving at Lowry Airforce base in the spring of 1955, steering his brand-new Chevrolet, he inquired about the Negro community and took part in the society's functions. He attended social functions at the University of Denver and met several young ladies who asked him to be an escort in a fashion show sponsored by their sorority. It happened here that he found his future wife.

Laurie Smith and her close friends LaVon Taylor, Winifred Jones, and Betty Jo Brickler, sat together at the fashion show which the popular local sorority organized. They found the young men who took part as escorts impressive. One in particular, Thad, new in town. When the show ended, Laurie invited the new man to join them at her house to get better acquainted with her friends.

Initially, Thad did not select Laurie for a date, but after Winifred, the person he asked on a date, rejected him, Laurie became his second choice. Thad definitely caught Winifred's eye, however, she had a relationship and became with child by the minister of her congregation. A very unfortunate circumstance in the life of a young college-bound girl. Her friends had no knowledge of her circumstances. She eliminated herself by turning down Thad's invitation to go out with him. LaVon made her desire to spend time with Thad known, but Thad seemed to ignore her offers.

Although he had many telephone numbers of prospects, he called Laurie for a date. She found Thad attractive, and even though she knew she was not his first choice; the girls had discussed openly who he called and asked on a date. She said yes. They had their first date in a movie theater. Thad fell asleep, disappointing Laurie; he was forgiven, and soon they were a couple. Seven months later, Thad proposed, and they decided on an April wedding date.

Thad got ready to marry one of Denver's young debutantes. Her family enjoyed widespread recognition in town, and this wedding promised to be one of the most significant and widely discussed events within the colored community.

The Smith family lived in East Denver, a neighborhood of single-family homes with duplexes and bungalows side by side with two-story homes. It housed Ted and Beatrice Smith, a son serving in the army based in Germany, their daughter Laurie, nineteen, her sister Patricia, fourteen years old, and their nine-year-old son Trent. The three-bedroom brick bungalow on a corner sat on a hill, surrounded by grass and a backyard in full bloom with fruit trees and a sumptuous garden.

People in the community knew Ted as a house painter and Beatrice as a housewife who stayed home to care for their children. Beatrice, considered the social maven, sponsored formal parties and soirees for teenage youth, teaching them social graces. She organized a marching band whose many trophies sat on the mantle in the living room. The young participants later became pillars of the community, including a mayor, lawyers, and political representatives, crediting her program for encouraging them to strive for success.

Julia arrived a week before the wedding with her two daughters; both Cleo and Anna Mae had quite an effort exiting the vehicle because they were enormous women. Laurie and her mother stood by to extend a welcome. Laurie pictured these seamstresses to the stars as glamorous, and their appearance surprised her. Once out of the vehicle, Beatrice and Laurie extended hands to the very tall woman, their mother, Julia.

"We are so pleased you ladies have come to participate in my daughter's wedding. We're so excited to meet you."

"Happy to be here," says Anna Mae.

"Where is Thad's mother? Her name is Hannah I believe. When is she arriving?" Beatrice asks.

Julia, looked quite stern at Beatrice, and after composing herself, announced: "Hannah will not be attending the wedding."

Both sisters echoed the same answer "No, Hannah will not be here."

"I thought she would come. She provided a very nice engagement ring. She surely would love to be here," says Beatrice.

"I raised Thad. I'm the only mother that should attend this wedding," said Julia.

All three faces had a look of finality. The issue concluded.

Neither Laurie nor her mother could understand this conundrum concerning Hannah, but they didn't feel comfortable discussing it further after witnessing the dynamics between mother and daughters.

After the family established itself, it became clear that the three individuals had friction. Julia seemed to be the instigator of the difficulties.

Their arrival had not been long past when Julia began awful quarrels. Once the women got their passions stirred, Julia sat back and laughed at their tirades against each other. Laurie worked during the day and did not witness this behavior. Her mother could not wait each evening to tell her about the arguments. The Smiths and Beatrice's siblings had disagreements for sure, but nothing like what she witnessed between Julia and her daughters.

The wedding dress comprised of a joint present to the bride from Cleo and Anna Mae. Cleo's husband, the jeweler, made the wedding band. The family certainly showed generosity towards the bride. The three of them, Cleo, Anna Mae, and Julia arrived early so that they could make any alterations to the dress in plenty of time before the wedding day. It seemed a good idea since Laurie had gained weight subsequent to her fitting several months prior. Creating this dress required a significant amount of time, and it appeared stunning with voluminous lace and embedded pearls that Julia had attached herself. The dress and the ring were a substantial contribution to the wedding. The Roarkes reinforced these facts upon the Smiths, often reminding them, with Beatrice dutifully praising their efforts. After all, one must acknowledge that they were somewhat famous individuals who owned a shop in Beverly Hills, California, and are known dressmakers for Hollywood stars. They have closed their shop to attend this wedding. Laurie was impressed.

Additional evidence pointed to this being a family situation alien to the Smiths. Beatrice felt driven by her capacity to handle interactions with Julia. She found herself refereeing their battles. She had to console Cleo when the mother and sister seemed to pick on her. Criticism persisted among them. They disagreed about everything, shouting at each other. A look of contentment washed over Julia as she stirred up her daughters' emotions.

In the evening, when the family watched television, Julia sat in the living room with them, her chair facing the television, a focal point in the room. Beatrice also favored this location. Julia's religious beliefs did not allow such depraved activities as watching television. She sat in this chair with her hand covering her eyes so that she could not see the show. All the time talking loudly condemning those who insisted on viewing it. She could potentially have a place to sit without needing to shield her eyes, but she was adamant about positioning herself solely in this spot, which drew all focus. As the others attempted to view the performance, she found fault with her lodging; notwithstanding, her lodging incurred no charge, and she stayed as a visitor at the home of her prospective parents-in-law. Although Julia's behavior flustered Beatrice, she maintained her calm and conciliatory demeanor as the gracious host.

Julia's youngest sister, Laura, along with her daughter- and son-in-law, arrived from San Francisco for the wedding. They stayed at the home of Beatrice's sister. Laura's grandchild, a three-year-old boy, would be the ring bearer. They brought silver and crystal gifts for the bride and groom. The family kept their distance from Julia and her daughters and did not correspond with them upon arrival.

A dinner occurred to unite Laurie's aunts and cousins with the Roarkes and the San Francisco family. Ted, quite the chef, prepared all the fixings: fried chicken, his famous rolls, macaroni and cheese, green beans, greens and cornbread dressing, and peach cobbler for dessert. Regular-sized plates sat with gold-plated platters beneath them as decoration. The Roarke sisters filled the two golden platters each, eating from them at the same time, an enormous amount of food. Laurie could now grasp the reason for the ladies' considerable size. They ate their pain, having to deal with their mother.

After observing Julia and her daughters having vicious arguments, and Julia being the instigator of most of them, along with Julia's behavior in general, Laurie and her mother seriously doubted the wisdom of marrying into this family. Alas, they invited over one hundred people, purchased six bridesmaids' dresses, and prepared the church for one of Denver's biggest weddings in the largest African Methodist Church. Beatrice told Laurie they could not back down now and be disgraced.

On April 21st, 1956, Laurie Smith married Thaddeus Langoire Jr., the same day Grace Kelly married Prince Rainier of Monaco and Margaret Truman, President Truman's daughter, married Clifton Daniel.

Near disasters are common at weddings, and this bride encountered two. Everyone hurried about, confirming all wedding attire accounted for and boxed the gown intended for donning before the ceremony. Because the Roarke women possessed such large sizes, Ted needed to transport the Roarke clan and the clothing on his own initially and subsequently return to bring his family. In their rush to get everyone to the church on time, they forgot the bride. They had all departed. Silence permeated the house. When would they discover the bride's absence from the church? It became impossible to inform them of her predicament; Laurie went to the street to thumb a ride. Fortunately, a young man, a member of the church who had not been invited to the wedding, happened to drive by. He smiled as he delivered Laurie to church; he knew her and her family well.

Upon everyone's arrival at the church and the commencement of the ceremony, an usher guided Laurie's mother to her seat. She had on a lengthy turquoise gown adorned with pearls and rhinestones. Lemon-yellow and white flowers lavishly covered the altar area. A white trellis adorned with blossoms occupied the middle space for the bride and groom to stand beneath. The bridesmaids proceeded down the aisle wearing short, yellow silk dresses, garlands of yellow flowers in their hair, and white leather gloves. Julia, dressed in her usual grey dress and white pillbox hat, stood in the church's vestibule, behind the doors leading to the auditorium. She observed Thad had not appeared up front by the altar.

A young man opened the door and took Julia by the arm to escort her down the aisle.

She didn't move. He whispered to her, "It's time for you to be seated."

"Oh no, I can't be seated. My grandson's not up front. He may have changed his mind."

"No maam, he'll be there just as soon as you get seated."

"I'm not going until he is up there in front. I know he's changed his mind."

"I am sure he hasn't changed his mind. He is waiting for you to sit down. Can't we just have you sit down front so we can start the wedding?"

"No, he's probably changed his mind, Not till I hear from him. I'll wait right here."

Julia now spoke rather loudly, and the ushers felt embarrassed and did not know what to do with her or how to silence her. Her voice reached inside the church, and some people attending began to turn around to see what was happening. The wedding planner tried to assure Julia. It became evident that Julia's actions could not be managed.

Finally, Thad appeared with his best man. Thad stood five foot seven, muscular, stoutly built, with a honey complexion unlike his father's blue-black skin, but he had his father's good looks. It appeared that all was in order. Two young ushers escorted Julia down the aisle, this time holding each of her arms firmly.

After the ceremony, the bridal party and a select group of guests arrived at the home of the bride's aunt and uncle for the reception. The families of the bride and groom mingled while waiting for Laurie and Thad to arrive in a black Cadillac provided by her godparents. The groomsmen and bridesmaids arrived soon after.

A young man, DeVern, employed by her father, who spent five years in a relationship with Laurie, attended the reception. He stood five feet eleven inches, just under one hundred forty-five pounds, and sported thick black wavy hair. His skin tone so white it prevented him from ever being mistaken for a Negro. People believed that he and Laurie would eventually marry. Prior to her departure for university, they ended their relationship, it occurred approximately twelve months preceding meeting Thad. Coincidentally, the young man rented a room in the house belonging to her aunt, where the reception took place. He did not attend the wedding, but since he lived at the house, he appeared at the reception. He mingled with a few friends, filled his plate with food, and left. Julia realizing who he was observed him as he climbed the stairs to his room. Laurie had gone upstairs earlier to one of the bedrooms to change out of her wedding dress. Julia found Thad and alerted him to what she pictured unfolding upstairs. Julia caused quite a stir with this occurrence for Thad, and Laurie would recall this situation later in their marriage.

16

Moses Lake

The couple settled into an apartment close to the family. As a result, there were frequent, unannounced and unexpected visits from her siblings and parents. The situation at times became embarrassing for the couple since he was at the base all day and Laurie was working. Her father would make early morning visits on weekends when the couple were still in bed. He would bring her favorite pie or his famous rolls; these visits were every weekend. They felt they had little privacy and little time to spend alone. Toward the end of his classes at Lowry Airforce base, Thad could now select his permanent Air Force Base. Both he and Laurie, now pregnant, decided they did not want to be stationed near his grandmother, so California was out of the question. Laurie did not want to be near her family either; they selected Washington state.

They packed all their possessions in their Chevy and left on their journey. On the way, they stopped in San Francisco to visit Thad's Aunt Laura, Julia's baby sister. Laura, who attended their wedding, behaved pleasantly with everyone. Laura and her daughter, however, remained reserved around the Roarkes, especially Julia. There seemed to be some tension between them. Laura welcomed the bride and groom to stay with her, although she required them to pay her for their stay. Requiring a payment was appropriate under the circumstances. She had a large house, and she lived alone with a limited income. The time there was interesting for Laurie since she could learn from Laura about Julia's life with the family.

"How is it going with you youngsters in your relationship with Julia?" asks Aunt Laura.

"She was hard to deal with at the house and the wedding," said Laurie.

"Did she argue with her girls?"

"Oh yes, my mother and I could not believe the fights. She embarrassed us at the wedding also when she refused to be seated until Thad appeared."

"I am so sorry. I heard about that. She is very protective of you Thad, you know. Julia has had it hard. I find myself feeling sympathetic to her. She had the job of raising us when our mother died, you know. It was hard on her trying to care for us all by herself. She got beatings from our father. This drove her away, you know. She left after she met your grandfather, Treeva."

"She was beaten?" asked Laurie.

"Oh yes, you know getting beatings was the only way to get obedience when parents had to use brute force you see. During slavery, that was what they did, you got beaten. The slave master's taught us how to get obedience."

"That's horrible," says Laurie.

"Life didn't get better when she married Treeva. It didn't turn out the way she planned. You see. She had all those children and again she had to raise them all by herself he was gone all the time."

"Is he still living?" asked Thad.

"Yes, I heard he had another family and he's with them. He was responsible for putting out Cleo's eye, you know. A terrible situation."

"My grandmere told me all about it," said Thad.

"I can't imagine a father doing that to his child," says Laurie.

"He and Julia were fighting as usual. Wasn't done on purpose, you see."

"I hear that is when he left and never went back," says Laurie.

"You know I kinda felt sorry for Julia overtime. She's had it hard, you know. Julia and I had our differences, and we still do. You see she was always envious of me, my color, my hair and my looks. When I was young, I was lighter than I am now. Grown brown in my old age."

Laura's fair complexion, now darker from her childhood yellow tone, had brown spots splashed over her face and arms. She tied her long, wavy hair back in a bun. There was no way Julia had to envy her now, thought Laurie, since Julia had a very clear, smooth brown complexion free from blemishes. It felt strange for Aunt Laura to be talking about small differences such as these after all these years. Such petty acrimony for ladies in their 60s. It was in the 1950s, and skin color and hair still divided the race and culture. Laurie noted her mother, Beatrice, had similar beliefs, so she was not alone with her skin tone preferences.

Their short visit ended, and they were back on the road.

Thad and Laurie arrived in Moses Lake, Washington, their new home at Larson Air Force Base. The couple found public housing in Ephrata, Washington, five miles from the base, and settled in.

Their housing was in the welfare section of the city. Upon entering the two-bedroom shack. Laurie saw when the front door opened it was a direct path to the backyard exit better known as shotgun housing, meaning one could shoot through the front door and out the back door all at the same time. It was Fall, and the wind blew through the cracks in the wall of wooden shack. It had a wood-burning stove in the center of the living room. Inconvenient for Laurie, because she had never struck a match to light a wood fire in her life. Because the shower had aluminum walls, while she showered, her arm bumped into the wall causing a ringing sound in her ears that resonated throughout the house. Separated floorboard joints made the rug on the floor float up and down due to the wind. Thad rigged up a wire to the outside clothesline in order to get reception on the radio. The allotment for living was less than two hundred dollars a month; it was vital for Laurie to find employment even though she was five months pregnant.

Laurie worked at the airbase in Denver.. She also found employment at the Airforce Center here on the base soon after arriving, and Thad began radar school.

When they lived in Denver, Laurie started work after the wedding and enrolled in college again. The couple had a one-day honeymoon celebrated in Denver, since the Air Force paid so little to its servicemen. Now, in Moses Lake, it was important for her to support the two of them, and there was no school available for her to attend. Her five-month pregnancy did not stop her from getting a job at the base, even though she felt she was hiding it with her clothes. She later learned that they hired her despite her pregnancy.

Although the Smith family was average and not regarded as affluent, the lifestyle foe the two of them was much lower than the standard either of them had been accustomed to. This was how they must live now they have decided not to be near family for help. They accepted the situation as temporary until he served his allotted time. There were no plans for him to stay in the service.

Once Laurie's pregnancy showed, Thad was distant. When he dated her, he could hardly keep his hands off her. Lately, when they walked together, he walked three feet ahead of her or behind. It annoyed her, and she didn't understand his actions.

Thad observing her sudden large bump once they got settled wondered at whether there were even three months left in this pregnancy. She could have the baby any day now as far as he could see. When did nine months start?

When baby Michael arrived, he was tiny, merely five pounds. The doctor required the baby to remain in the hospital for two weeks to gain more weight.

The nurse knocked on the door of the hospital room. The room, more like a barracks was dimly lit as the nurse entered. The mother had her eyes closed and barely opened them as she received her baby bundled tightly in the blanket. She prepared to offer her breast for feeding when she paused not seeing the small red spot she remembered near her baby's hairline.

"The red spot seems to have disappeared," she said looking up at the nurse.

"What red spot? This baby had no red spot." The nurse said bent over to look at the baby in its mother's arms.

"My baby had a red spot just above his temple." The mother said this as she unwrapped the bundle to get a better look at the baby. She held the tiny hands and while caressing the miniature fingers she could see the beige nail beds common for Negro babies, not pink like white babies.

"Oh my God, this is not my child! This is not my baby. Where is my baby?" She pushes the baby into the waiting arms of the nurse who quickly looks at the bracelet on the baby's wrist.

"I'm so sorry, this is not your baby. I'm so sorry." The nurse quickly rewrapped the baby and turned to leave. "I will get your baby, my mistake. It's gonna be okay. I will bring him to you right away." She rushed out the door with the baby.

Word was out all over the hospital about the mistake. The nurse who brought Laurie's baby to her apologized to her for the error concerning her child. Laurie accepted the apology as she was familiar with this kind of mistake in the birth of her baby brother.

"This was a common mistake experienced in our family. I thought all babies are born with a neutral color," said Laurie.

"No, some babies are very white, some are born red and some are born very brown."

"The babies I have seen in my family have been born very light, not brown," said Laurie.

The nurse left and returned with a baby. She unwrapped him from his blanket. He was like the doll she received as a child. A mass of cold black curly hair covered the top of his head. His body a smooth dark chocolate. He waved his little fat arms and legs even though he made no sound. Laurie was surprised to know the baby was not Negro.

After three weeks they finally were able to bring the baby home. The couple decided not to give their baby the name Junior Number Three. Neither wanted reference to the father who had no contact with Thad and, as far as they knew, still disowned him. They named him Michael Langoire.

Thad's attitude, now that they had the baby home, seemed cold and emotionally distant.

"Would you like to hold the baby?"

"No, I don't know how to hold a baby."

"I can show you, I need your help can you just hold him for a minute while I prepare his dressing?"

"No, put the baby on the bed. I don't want to hold him."

When Laurie finished changing the diaper, she wanted to talk further about his attitude toward the baby and her concerns about nursing him.

"Why are you so distant from the baby?"

"I'm not distant. I know nothing about babies. It's better if I wait until he is bigger and can sit alone without support from me."

"That will be quite a while from now. Do you really want to wait that long to hold him?"

"I don't need to hold him. You are the mother, you hold him. Besides, I need to get back to the base. I will see you later tonight."

Thad was relieved to be walking out of the door and getting into his car away from the house, Laurie, and the baby.

Michael was still so small, only six pounds, when released from the hospital. He was a quiet baby, not prone to crying as much as some babies at this age. He was also not a particularly hungry baby. It was beneficial, given Laurie's nursing challenges. She feared for his well-being if she didn't resolve his feeding issues. The subject came up the next morning when she and Thad were talking while she attempted to feed the baby.

"The nurse said I should try to nurse him. It's been so painful, and the baby hasn't responded to me."

"He's so small, you should give him formula. Don't try to nurse him."

"I want to nurse him. I'm supposed to nurse him. The women in our family always nursed their babies. We never heard of using formula."

"You don't need to nurse him. You know he's too small. Don't keep trying."

Thad's tone was gruff, almost angry. It was obvious he didn't want her to keep trying. He didn't want Laurie to nurse the baby. He handed her the empty bottle and pointed to the formula on the table.

"Don't keep trying. We got formula, just use it."

Thad's attitude was a little threatening. There was something about it that made Laurie uncomfortable. She could not figure out why he was so determined for her not to nurse the baby.

The argument continued, and since the baby was so small, rather than jeopardizing his welfare, Laurie relented and used the bottle to feed him. With her mother expected to arrive shortly, she possessed a firm belief in her capacity to manage the delicate baby's care.

Beatrice's plane landed in Spokane. There was no public transportation between Spokane and Ephrata, one hundred miles from the airport. She found a gentleman who was driving his truck in that direction to give her a ride. She arrived at the community, and to her dismay, it was shabby; she was taken aback. If being disappointed with the housing in the area was not enough, the worst was yet to come. She thanked the driver, paid him, and headed up the wooden steps to knock at the door. Thad abruptly opened it.

"You might as well tell that driver to wait cause yur not welcome here, we don't want you here, and we don't need you," shouted Thad.

Overcome with astonishment, Beatrice let her bag fall to the ground. Laurie pushed her way out of the door past him.

"I am so sorry Mother, I don't know what has come over Thad. Of course I want you here."

Thad waited until this moment to express his feelings about her mother coming to aid Laurie. Both Laurie and her mother were stunned by his behavior. Laurie reached for her mother's hand to help her up the stairs, but Thad pushed her aside.

"I said we don't need you here and you can't come in."

Beatrice was no pushover, even then taken by surprise, said, "You are going to stand aside and let me in to sit down. I have traveled quite a long way to get here. You can't refuse to let me into your house. What is wrong with you?" She walked past him and into the house.

"You don't have my permission to be here," he declares walking behind her as he picked up her bag to take it into the house.

"I don't need your permission to be here. This house is my daughter's house as well as yours and she invited me here."

Beatrice looked around at the bareness of the room as she spoke. One drab couch covered with a blanket, a lamp on a table, and one chair. She hid her disappointment at the spareness, she sat on the couch, and Laurie sat next to her.

His mother-in-law's boldness surprised him. She didn't appear to be intimidated in the least by him. She looked at him squarely for a moment and then asked: "What is going on here? Why are you acting this way?"

"I don't know what has come over Thad. He's been acting strangely ever since we got here."

Beatrice states sternly, "Sit down Thad and tell me what's going on. I'm not going anywhere today. You have some explaining to do."

Thad doesn't sit but paced around the small living room. Anxiety filled him, and he was stymied on how to deal with the two of them. Laurie sat next to her mother; their presence was a force together. After the two of them kept asking him to give a reasonable response, Thad finally sat in the chair facing Beatrice.

"My grandmere, uh…she says uh…that the baby is not mine."

"What! Have you lost your mind?" Both mother and daughter declared at the same time.

"She saw you, she says she saw you at the wedding reception going upstairs to be with your old boyfriend and the two of you got together then and the baby is his."

"You both are crazy," declared Laurie. "I did no such thing. How could she say that?"

Beatrice was quiet and sat there thinking for a moment before she spoke.

"May I remind you, young man, you got married in April and this baby was born in March. Babies are born nine months later. This is almost twelve months after the wedding."

"Just nine months?" asks Thad.

"You can look that up if you can't take my word for it." Beatrice shook her head at his gullibility.

DeVern left town right after the wedding, almost a year ago. How could he be the father of this child?"

Thad was stunned by this information; he had just taken his grandmother's word for this accusation. In the daily conversations on a pay phone with his grandmother since arriving in Moses Lake, the discussion about the incident at the reception became the focus. Julia had decided there were sexual relations taking place between Laurie and her former boyfriend, DeVern while they were both upstairs. Once the baby arrived and it was not red as Julia said it should have been, but white like the other babies in the nursery who were, of course, white. Unfortunately, according to Thad's estimation, baby Michael was white like DeVern.

He drew his hands into a fist because it had to be true what his grandmother said. His not knowing anything about babies, together with not taking the time to check how many months had passed since this so-called relationship occurred, made him seem foolish. By all accounts, Julia failed to calculate the months either because she believed this baby was not Thad's child, or she knew better and wanted to cause this problem in their marriage.

"The baby looks like your old boyfriend. He is white like him, not red like Black babies," he said.

"Oh, my goodness! Who told you Black babies are born red or brown? Our babies are born white. Lots of Black babies are born white. He will turn brown in time."

"My grandmother said…"

"Your grandmother doesn't know what she's talking about. Don't listen to her," said Laurie.

Beatrice became quiet and held her head in her hands. There was terrible news she had to bear, and now this misunderstanding. Laurie's favorite aunt, who hosted her wedding reception, had died just a day before baby Michael's birth, and she had not yet told Laurie. She was grieving the loss of her sister, and this rejection by Thad was heartbreaking. She hid how overcome she was at that moment. This behavior was not what she expected of her son-in-law. She wanted to break down and cry, but she couldn't. She had to remain strong.

Meanwhile, Laurie walked to the bedroom to pick up their baby to show her mother. She could not believe that Thad had been keeping in touch with his grandmother, who had fed him this lie all along. The worst part of it, he believed it. After a day passed and tempers calmed, Thad talked about how his grandmother convinced him of Laurie's affair with DeVern, which caused his poor treatment of her, her mother, and the baby.

Beatrice had been pleased with this marriage to a man whose father was a prominent dentist in Los Angeles. She expected that the strained relationship with his father would become less so with this new family. She had only the side of the Roarke's story, and she could not imagine he would not be happy to meet her daughter and now a baby boy. A further connection to the Langoire's was the discovery that the dentist's sister Danielle had lived in Denver and was a piano teacher for Laurie when she was little. The Smiths and the Bryants ran in the same circles before Danielle and her husband moved to California. This could have been a positive start to an improved relationship. It was quite a shock to be treated this way by Thad. He eventually relented and let her stay. Laurie and her mother called the doctor and made Thad talk to his nurse, and she explained the impossibility of this child being DeVern's.

17

Edwards Air Force Base

They paused Thad's training at Larson Air Force Base to continue it at Edwards Air Force Base in California. Larson's purpose was to have World War II pilots receive advanced training on radar systems. Thad's training continued temporarily at Edwards for hands-on with the F-104 fighter jet made by Lockheed. The base was over 100 miles from Los Angeles. They packed up to make the trek back to stay with Thad's grandmother, even though they both dreaded this circumstance. Staying on the base was not possible nor could they afford to live in the town nearby. Julia beamed with joy as she welcomed them warmly. Her joy was evident upon the baby Michael's arrival. Since it was a one-bedroom house, Julia gave the couple her bedroom. She made a bed in a room next to the kitchen, which was in the living room. Most living rooms were where one would receive guests and have tea, but Julia did not have guests. The house, on a deep lot far back from the street, was overgrown with flowers and fruit trees. Despite the house's cramped state, they would manage.

Thad dropped Laurie and baby Michael off at the house and left for the base. Laurie had had several discussions with her mother on how to cope with Julia. They both remembered how difficult it was to get along with her when she attended the wedding. They also discussed the lie she told Thad about the so-called tryst upstairs at her aunt's house. There would be no mention of these circumstances. Beatrice encouraged Laurie to maintain respect for Julia, despite her own lack of regard for Laurie. After all, she was an elderly lady and deserved to be given some leeway for her behavior. These admonishments had been driven into Laurie by her mother, and she was going to try to remember them.

All was well for a few days after their arrival, with Julia offering help but not insisting. At least once a day she was on the phone with her pastor, Sister Gray, giving an hour-by-hour account of what occurred in the house. Days later, this conversation became an open criticism of how Laurie tended to the needs of the baby. Julia didn't hide what she was saying to Sister Gray, nor did she seem to care that Laurie heard what she said. Laurie pretended not to hear the negative comments and proceeded with caring for her child as best she could. Sometimes Julia took charge of the baby and expressed to Laurie that she didn't know what she was doing, and that she should leave the care of the child to her. Laurie, as gracious as possible, declined her help. Now when Julia talked to Sister Gray, she called Laurie incompetent and berated her. Laurie still tried to remain calm and ignored the comments since Julia was talking on the phone and not to Laurie's face.

Julia didn't limit her claims of Laurie's incompetence to phone calls; she claimed the formula was not adequate, that the baby should be given cow's milk heavy with cream like she fed Thad as a baby. She even substituted the formula when Laurie had an occasion to leave the baby in Julia's care. The baby suffered from severe diarrhea as a result. This brought on a big argument and threats from Laurie. Thad even called from the base to rebuke Julia.

Caring for a baby was not foreign to Laurie. She had fed a bottle to her baby brother Trent and even changed his smelly diaper when she was only ten years old. As other babies arrived in the family, she was a babysitter for them. Even cared daily for her niece as an infant who lived with the family. Despite having this experience, Julia's constant criticism made her doubt what she thought was in the best interest of the child. She worried that she indeed was not doing a good job with him.

The baby ate rice cereal that morning and suddenly he broke out in a rash. This gave credence, according to Julia's claim, that Laurie didn't know what was good for the child. Thad was home on a weekend visit. They took the baby to the base to see the doctor and were told the rice cereal was the culprit. When they returned home confident in how to proceed with Michael's care, Julia met them at the door and immediately took the baby from Laurie's arms. Julia's swift action surprised Laurie. Once the baby was in Julia's arms, she began her tirade about how it was Laurie's fault the baby had the rash. She had refused to follow Julia's advice. While holding the baby away from Laurie, she declared she was taking over the care of him from now on. Outraged by Julia's actions, Laurie reached for her child and tried to take him back. A tug ensued. Thad, seeing what was occurring, got into the fray. Julia was determined to keep the child and backed away from Laurie near the bed. Thad then grabbed Julia's shoulders and pushed Julia against her bed, catching her off guard, as she fell on it. Laurie grabbed the baby, rescuing him from her. Laurie shivered at the resemblance to the tragedy of Susanna's death, Julia's third child, a story that was by this time well known.

Thad's brute-force tactics were ultimately what caused Julia to stop trying to control the babies' care.

The weather in Los Angeles was like heaven compared to Moses Lake during the fall and winter months. Laurie and Thad tried walking while in Moses Lake, but the temperatures were as low as thirty degrees below zero at night and below zero on some days in November and December. The autumn weather in Los Angeles averaged temperatures of eighty degrees during the day. It was customarily warm and Laurie took advantage by walking daily. These were the early stages before smog covered the city, and most days had clear blue skies. The air smelled fresh and felt damp from the dew still on the sidewalk and covered the trees early in the morning. Laurie, after bathing and feeding the baby, then putting him down for a nap, took her long walks and returned braced for the day to deal with Julia. It was a consolation for having to live with their less-than-desirable circumstances. After she left for her walk, the neighbor next door left his house also, he was a gentleman with whom Laurie was neither acquainted nor was she aware of his leaving his house after she departed. His house was also at the rear of the lot. Many times, he returned right after she did or much later. Julia noted these coincidences and discussed this daily activity with Sister Gray. She described how many women she saw following him into his house on some days. They talked about how sinful that behavior was. Julia approached Laurie about the similar occurrences of her leaving and his departure shortly after and only hinted that Laurie should have known about this timing. Laurie answered she was not aware of this man and didn't see him leave.

Laurie had her walk as usual on that day, and as she returned, approached the house and saw Thad's car out front. She was overjoyed that he had arrived for a visit, since it had been three weeks since she had last seen him. Because it was the middle of the week, it was unusual, since he should have been in class. When she entered the house, Thad and Julia were standing together. Julia had her arms folded across her chest with an angry expression on her face. Thad was sweating; his face was red with anger, his eyes flashing.

"Where have you been?" Thad says angrily.

"I went for a walk. Why are you so angry?"

"You've been with that skag next door every day since you been here," declared Julia. She can't wait for Thad to interrogate her.

"What skag? What are you talking about? I just took my daily walk."

"Let me handle this, grandmere," said Thad, taking over. "She knows you are leavin the house every day and she thinks you're meeting with the man next door."

"Are you kidding me? What man next door? I don't know anything about a man next door."

"She thinks you're meeting with someone."

"I'm not meeting anyone. Your grandmother is always accusing me of something. This is ridiculous. I take a walk every day to get away from her. I'm not meetin with some man. Who is he anyway?"

"Don't try to fool me. I see it every day you leave here, and then he leaves his house shortly after you. You come home and then he returns right after you. I've seen him marching other women back there in his house. His behavior is disgraceful."

"Have you seen Laurie going into his house?"

"Well, no, but they must be meetin somewhere else."

"Have you ever been to his house?"

"Absolutely not. I've never even seen this man to know him. Not more than the top of his head when he leaves his place," declared Laurie. "Your grandmother asked me about him, and I told her I didn't know him. You know she makes up stories. She's done it before."

"How long is your walk?"

"About 20 minutes, maybe half an hour."

"Grandmere, you told me you had proof that she was with him."

"I've seen them almost every day, she leaves and then he leaves."

"How's that time to meet with somebody and to do what? "Says Thad.

Thad's agitation caused him to break out with hives. Laurie could see the red welts on his neck. The exasperation with his grandmother for her daily calls reporting on his wife's activities had to be affecting him.

In order for Thad and Laurie to talk and for him to get to the bottom of this situation, they had to go outside into the yard. They couldn't talk inside because of the interruptions by Julia.

After talking privately with Laurie, Thad said he believed her; she was not meeting with the neighbor. Thad monitored the neighboring dwelling for the duration of the day, and when the man returned home at dusk, Thad approached him for a discussion. Thad got proof his wife was not having an affair with the neighbor. The rest of the time now they spent trying to calm Thad's nerves. He returned to base the next day.

While Laurie continued her daily walk, Julia usually headed for the mailbox near the street. It never occurred to Laurie to pick up the mail. She found this to be a big mistake on her part. She received a letter from her mother and realized it when she heard Julia reading it out loud to Sister Gray.

"Is that a letter addressed to me?" asked Laurie.

"Yes, I was reading it to Sister Gray."

"You opened a letter addressed to me and you are reading it to someone else!"

"Of course, any letter coming to my address in my mailbox, I'm entitled to read it."

"You can't read other people's mail. That is a letter addressed to me from my mother. You have no right to open it."

"Calm down child; I'll read it to you."

"I don't want you to read it to me. Give me my letter."

Laurie reached for it, and Julia held it high in the air out of her reach. Julia insisted she would open and read any mail that came to her address. Laurie couldn't snatch it from Julia. She stood there while Julia read the letter aloud. When Julia finished, she handed the letter to her. From that day forward, Laurie made sure to check the mailbox daily. She also called her mother to tell her what Julia had done. There was no way to control Julia's behavior. Laurie had a cousin who lived in Los Angeles, a short distance away. She picked Laurie up occasionally to visit with her. Laurie directed her mother to send mail to her cousin's address in the future.

When Julia was not on the phone with Sister Gray, she worked in her garden. The flowers were beautiful, and her fruit trees produced baskets of fruit in season. Everyone knew Julia was generous with her neighbors. Flowers and fruit were sent to homes for the aged and the sick in the hospital. She always fed beggars, and some came often, knowing this.

All was not unpleasant between Julia and Laurie because some days Julia told stories about her life. They even had a laugh or two about Julia's life at the juke joint. But thankfully there were just a few more short weeks before the couple and child must return to the base in Washington state.

18

Thaddeus Meets His Grandson

Thad and Laurie prepare to depart Los Angeles following the completion of his tenure at Edwards Air Force Base.

"We'er leaving in a few days, what if we call your father to see if he would like to meet his grandchild?" asked Laurie.

"Whoa! I don't think that is a good idea."

"Why not? Surely by now he should be ready to accept you as his son."

"That's not my impression. He's never approached me to start a relationship."

"According to my mother, we have a basis to believe he may be receptive."

"You mean just because his sister Danielle used to be your piano teacher. That's hardly a good intro."

"It's a start. Mother said they were quite friendly. She also said that your father kept up with your progress growing up by going to your football games. Mutual friends have filled her in on how he was back then dealing with your grandmother."

"He never let me know he was keeping up with me."

"This is a golden opportunity to get to know your dad without the interference of your grandmother."

"I've wondered how he'd react if he didn't have to deal with her."

"Babies have a way of bringing people together."

"He's never been interested in seeing me. What makes you think he'd be curious about this baby?"

"He's older now. He will be thinking about who will come after him. You know his legacy."

"He has a legacy. He's known as a prominent dentist and a playboy."

"Seriously, let's give it a try. You know you've said you wanted to get to know him. You've tried calling and then hanging up. Let's call and at least see if you can get him to answer. What have we got to lose?"

"Hm, I don't know. I have nothing to be ashamed of. I just graduated from radar school. I'm one of the first persons to work on the new F104 airplane and its systems. He needs to know about that."

"Yes, he would be proud of you."

"I don't know. Maybe I can try. Nah, I don't think so."

"Come on give it a try. If he doesn't want to see his grandson, it will be his loss."

They found a phone booth to make the call. Julia was unaware of their plans. The two of them squeezed into the phone booth, with Laurie holding the baby close to shield him from the biting cold. Thad perspired even though it was fifty degrees that evening. It represented his first phone engagement since his adolescence, a time when he dialed his father for the purpose of harassing him. He wanted to call to share the news that his father had become a grandfather. Should he ever gain insight into his father, this present time and justification served as the occasion. Thad wiped his sweaty hands on his jacket and dialed the number.

He recognized the sequence of numbers because he had initiated calls to it many times over the years, intending to get in touch with his father, not understanding how and utilizing the misdirection from his grandmother.

The aggressive nature of his calls in the past wasn't conducive to the communication he desired. They actually consisted of threats of harm and pleas for money. Given Doctor Langoire's denial of paternity, Thad should have known that this man certainly would not offer him assistance or want to talk with him. He didn't as a child and not when he grew to be a young man. Thad Jr.'s reflections on calls caused his hesitation at this time.

Over the years, Thad's resemblance to the Langoire family was so striking that denying him now was ludicrous. What was once just an accusation was obviously now a fact. Thad Jr. was indeed a Langoire. He remembered some requests had been civil enough years ago for Thaddeus to invite him to his office to offer him some hand-me-down clothing. Julia was naturally insulted and didn't accept them. The acrimony ensued from then on. Will he even now continue to deny him? These thoughts and feelings ran through Thad's mind as he listened to the phone ring once, and then twice, and then a woman's voice said: "Hello."

Thad had to struggle to get his voice out; he was unprepared for this.

"Hello, who is this?" said Rowena.

He hesitated before saying: "Uh...this is Thaddeus Junior; I uh...want to speak to my father."

"Thaddeus Junior?"

"Yes, I'm. I'm here in Los Angeles with my wife and baby. I was wondering if he'd like to meet them?"

He blurted all of it out at once. Before he could say more, the woman shouted, "Oh my goodness! Thaddeus, it's your son, Thad Jr. on the phone, he has a baby."

You could tell she was excited as she spoke back on the phone to say, "You have a baby?"

Back away from the phone she shouted to her husband. "He wants to come over so we can see them." Without hearing a reply, her voice was now clearly talking to his son.

"Of course you can bring them by. When can you come over?"

"We can come tonight if it's alright. We leave town in a few days to go back to Washington state."

"Yes, yes you can come now?"

The two of them stood at the door as Thad rang the bell, the baby held close in Laurie's arms. The door opened immediately as a short, well-dressed woman wearing an apron smiled brightly and greeted them. Before they could cross the threshold, she wiped her hands on her apron, a gesture to cleanse them, as she reached for the baby, taking him out of Laurie's arms. Once inside, it was all about the baby and the excitement of it all.

Thad didn't look at his father upon entering the house. Their eyes didn't meet. He stood aside once inside to have a view of all the activity without being a part of the mix. He watched his father's reaction to what was going on as the dentist who also stood in the background, observing the enthusiastic conversation and his wife, who was animatedly discussing how happy she was to finally meet his son. Thad was aware his father had married beautiful women, three of them. Rowena was no beauty, he could see that, her personality and apparent devotion to him according to gossip made all the difference in his life. Rowena was the dentist's fourth wife, some twenty-four years his junior. Dr. Langoire and his wife were often featured and followed in the gossip section of the newspaper. Thad had read all he could about them.

It was a long time before Thad saw his father join the conversation while, perhaps remembering the many threats he had made to him in the past.

Although the evening went smoothly, Thad found it hard to relax until he saw his father bending over talking baby talk to his grandchild. Still no word between them. He was surprised after he and Laurie spoke about how difficult it had been living with his grandmother, Rowena said they were welcome upon their return to stay with them.

19

Return to Los Angeles

Back in Moses Lake, the family settled into another welfare community. Thad continued his radar training and Laurie acquired a job on the base again. They put little Michael in the base nursery. He, a very talkative little tyke, was very much a mama's boy. There were difficulties, as the child struggled in the nursery. Laurie found him well at home on weekends with his parents. But during the week, she received calls daily about her child's low-grade temperature, which made her leave work to take him home.

Laurie arrived at the nursery after a call to pick Michael up. The person on the phone had said that her son appeared to be listless and running a mild temperature. She needed to take him home. Laurie entered the playroom full of children with toys spread about and miniature chairs with children sitting in them in a corner. Two children were banging little hammers on blocks, and one child was pushing a red truck around in a circle. They all seemed busy, as children do, occupied by the various objects provided for their entertainment. The air felt humid as the odor of freshly sprayed room deodorant assaulted her nostrils. Laurie almost sneezed but restrained it by taking a deep breath.

The children in the circle of chairs were white, as were the ones playing with various toys. Michael was not one of them. She looked around, almost panicked until she saw him sitting on a rocking horse, lazily moving up and down. His head hung down, and he appeared to be asleep. Disturbed by what she saw, but before she could say anything, one of the staff appeared behind her and called out, "Andy, your mother's here." Michael didn't look up or respond. Laurie looked behind her, expecting to see another mother approaching.

The staffer repeated herself, "come on Andy, your mother is here to pick you up" and looked directly at Michael, who then looked up to see his mother. Seeing her, he scrambled off the rocking horse and ran to greet her.

"Did you call him Andy?"

"Yes, that's what we call him."

"That's not his name. His name is Michael."

"Oh! Some of the children have nick names and that is the one for him."

"His name is Michael. Don't call him Andy. I would prefer that you call him Michael. He doesn't need a nickname."

"Yes, of course."

Laurie arrived on another occasion to pick him up at the request of the staff who referred to him again as Andy. She told her about Michael's lack of response and quiet, detached demeanor. He did not interact much with the other children either. This seemed strange because Michael was a cheerful eighteen-month-old child at home, moving and speaking well for his age. Additionally, Laurie looked around to see that Michael was the only colored youngster in the nursery. She corrected them once more and wondered why they kept making that mistake. Meanwhile, she took Michael to the doctor to diagnose the cause of the temperature. They found no reason for it.

At eight months into her pregnancy with their second child, Laurie quit her job. Once at home caring for Michael, he retained his joyful self, with no trace of the low-grade temperature. Both parents wondered if the staff at the nursery constantly calling Michael by the wrong name caused him enough stress to make him respond the way he did.

The Air Force offered Thad one thousand dollars for him to sign up for another four years or take the early out. He took the early out which would come shortly after the birth of their second baby.

On December twenty-fifth, Laurie gave birth to Antoinette, and five weeks later the family left Washington state forever and headed back to Los Angeles.

The couple arrived in Los Angeles with two babies, only twenty-two months apart, strapped for money with only a small savings and the last allotment from Thad's service. The only alternative for them was to live with Julia until they secured positions and accumulated adequate funds for their own place. Julia, overjoyed at the prospect of having babies in her home, greeted them warmly.

Thad sought jobs immediately upon arrival. Their baby, merely a month old, Laurie would not leave this child and Michael with Julia to take care of them. It was going to be challenging; Julia, ready as always, to take care of both children, believed that Laurie would not be capable of the job. The arguments began right away with the myriad of responsibilities that came with caring for an infant and a toddler. Julia resumed her daily phone calls to Sister Gray to criticize Laurie and her care for the babies. Laurie declined to nurse this baby, like Michael, and this became a point of contention with Julia. This baby was born a lot larger than Michael, six pounds at birth, a healthy crier for sure. Laurie acted with confidence. The preparation and choice of formula became a battle for them, as before. Julia insisted that the baby should get cream from regular milk, like she fed Thad some twenty years ago. She reminded Laurie how Thad grew to be a healthy, strong, stoutly built young man. Never mind how sick the milk made baby Michael. However, Julia did not try to take over feeding this child. Laurie insisted on following the guidelines given by the pediatrician for the baby's formula. Julia lost this battle.

There were good days too when Julia shared her life story about the promise made to her and not fulfilled. The disappointment of her dreams denied and the way she acted after the death of her mother her favored topic. Speaking tearfully as she spoke of the way she treated her siblings and all her regrets. She spoke of the beatings from her father. The beatings accepted as a normal circumstance of living, although she hated her father for them. And yet, she had a sense of pride in his being a preacher, and in how classy the life they lived before the death of her mother.

Julia's stories about her life with Treeva fascinated Laurie. It also helped Laurie understand why this old lady remained bitter and angry. Her telling of the story went from anger and disappointment to musing on how good it was when things went well. She had spoken on the previous visit about the death of Susanne and her regrets of fighting with her mother-in-law. She related again how Lucy made her life miserable while she struggled to raise her babies. Julia made Laurie's life miserable at times, too.

One day Anna Mae joined them as Julia shared tales of her life with Treeva and her escapades at the juke joint. She pulled out a picture of herself sitting on the lap of a man, a pipe she smoked in her hand. Julia laughed as she related the scenario, showing the picture to Laurie. Her children had never seen this picture. She did not seem to be ashamed of herself as she related some details of that time. Anna Mae's reaction shocked them both by grabbing the picture from Laurie and tearing it into pieces. How disappointing and sad for more than one reason. Anna Mae was ashamed of her mother's actions and did not want the picture to be seen, but also a loss of the opportunity to see how beautiful Julia was at that age. It turned out to be the only picture they had of her as a young woman.

Many stories were told about the life Julia led and losing her babies. The invention she and Treeva had worked so hard to create was one of them. His foolishness in gambling away what he called their legacy, another. The fight that robbed Cleo of her eye became the final straw in a harrowing marriage full of love, joy, strife, and sadness.

There were other times when it seemed impossible to stay in the house with Julia, like the time Laurie was sitting in her room looking through a magazine. The proximity to the room where Julia sat, just a few feet away, although she could not see Laurie because of the wall between them. Julia raged at her for playing cards in her house. Julia interpreted the sound of flipping magazine pages as shuffling cards. Of course, Julia and her congregation considered playing cards a sin. Julia would not tolerate this kind of behavior in her house. Once Laurie showed her the magazine, the truth mollified her.

20

Laurie Meets Mary

The final straw living with Julia.

The county hospital called Julia to inform her that Mary, who had not been seen for a few years, was quite ill. Mary had been the favorite aunt of Thad.

"Aunt Mary appeared off and on to visit. I always loved to see her."

"Was she the aunt who made dolls, puppets in the world's fair in San Franscisco 1915?"

"Yeah. She was always making dolls. We laughed at her for talking to them. She didn't have much to say to anyone, but me. She and I used to sit on the curb in front of the house and identify every car that passed. Traffic was heavy in the evenings when the sun started to disappear just before dark we had contests to see who named the most cars. I have had a love of cars because of her."

"Did she live nearby and visit often?"

"No, Mary didn't get along with my grandmere. Visiting with family members wasn't her style. As a matter of fact, she avoided her sisters. She came early in the morning, stayed a day or two, got in an argument with Grandmere and then disappeared during the night. Not to be seen sometimes for years."

"Wow! that must have been hard on you. She just disappeared?"

"It was. She was the only one I could talk too. She understood how I felt living with her mother. It was hard you know. Never knowing if I would see her again."

"I would love to meet her. Do you think I could go to the hospital to see her."

"Let me ask grandmere to let us go tonight to see her. She can go tomorrow. I'm really anxious to see her."

Against Julia's better judgment, she let Thad talk her into letting Laurie go just this time to see Mary, and she would go the next day since the hospital only allowed two visitors at a time.

Arriving at the hospital, the antiseptic smell along with musk prevailed as they walked through the corridors. The hospital founded in the early 1900 hundreds showed its age with old chairs, tired equipment, and cracks on the walls. After Thad identified himself at the desk as Mary's nephew, the staff guided them to the ward and bed where Mary lay. They found her curled in a small ball uncovered on the white sheets. She immediately rose to greet Thad. Her thin nightgown made her look childlike as she beamed with delight at his arrival. He introduced his wife, and Laurie shook her hand. Mary sat up pleased to have met her. The conversation was lively and they even joked and laughed together. Even though she was frightfully thin and tiny in stature, she didn't appear to be too seriously ill. The nurse allowed the couple about thirty minutes, and then she informed them that visiting hours were over. Thad hugged his aunt, so did Laurie, and they turned to leave. As they walked down the hallway, Laurie turned to look back to see Mary clinging at the end of her bed. Mary raised her hand to wave goodbye. As Laurie raised her hand for a final wave, a sudden coldness and a premonition washed over her, hinting that this would be her last moment with Mary. She attempted to shake it off. She and Thad got into the elevator and headed home. In the car, the peculiar sensation lingered, and she confided in Thad about her unease.

Upon their arrival at home, Julia was at the doorway, anticipating an update on Mary's condition. They informed her of the visit's success when the phone rang. Julia answered it and then yelled, "Lord have mercy!" Mary had passed. Julia would not see her daughter again. She forfeited her opportunity to spend time with her child to an outsider. She would not forgive Laurie for this missed opportunity. Julia spoke with Sister Gray, as they shared their disdain for Thad's wife. Consoling Julia proved impossible. She placed her anger over missing her last chance to be with Mary on Laurie at every opportunity. Hannah, Anna Mae, and Cleo, the three sisters, united in accusing Laurie of causing their mother's suffering after their sister's death. Laurie's guilt and the family's vilification created a strain. The badgering continued for days despite the family not having an internment service for Mary. The county laid her to rest. Julia had no closure for the death of her child. The regret regarding Mary's death was a daily recrimination now of Laurie. Her every action faced scrutiny and criticism from the family.

Rowena, the dentist's spouse, informed about the death of Mary and during a phone conversation told Laurie that she was welcome to contact her if she needed any help as she understood their struggles in cohabiting with Julia. On the occasion of their arrival for a visit, Rowena observed how upset Laurie appeared, and she noted the weight lost on Laurie since their previous encounter. They received an invitation from both her and Thaddeus to come live with them, a chance to escape the family environment so burdened by discord.

Thad's family arrived at the Langoire's, a two-story house with two bedrooms upstairs and one bathroom. They would occupy the guest room that had twin beds. Along with the enormous master bedroom, the guest room, kitchen, and sunroom were on the second floor. Downstairs the living room, the full length of the house served as a perfect party house. The Langoires entertained frequently.

As the young couple settled in, it was surprising that Thad and his father seldom said more than hello or said only what was necessary. They didn't seem to be able to have a conversation. They had nothing in common. Thad went to work each day returning in time for dinner. Thaddeus worked at his office came home had drinks and ate dinner with his wife. Neither Thad nor Laurie drank alcoholic beverages. There were no family dinners. Thaddeus spent time with his grandson it was obvious he appreciated the child's presence. He spent less time with baby Antionette said she was too young.

After a time, Laurie complained of nausea and later realized she was pregnant again. It was unexpected, since she thought she had been careful. Her preventive measures had not worked. It was a challenge for her to look after two babies. Rowena criticized her for having babies so fast. Laurie showed her irritation, as though she would intentionally conceive again in this situation if she had the power to prevent it.

The pregnancy was full of challenges. A tooth had been bothering Laurie for a while. She woke one morning in pain and a swollen jaw. Even though Doctor Langoire practiced dentistry, it proved inadvisable for him to tend to her, particularly given her pregnancy.

She decided to trust the Army dentist on a nearby base. Lucky for them, his benefits were still in place for another two months before his final release from service. Doctor Langoire indicated that the correct approach would have been to first administer an antibiotic for the infection and subsequently, if needed, extract the tooth.

The base dentist dismissed the recommended treatment and chose instead to pull the tooth he believed was causing the problem. The moment he began, it was clear something was wrong. Every attempt he made sent a bolt of agony through Laurie. He shifted his grip again and again, searching for leverage, but nothing worked. The pain was blinding, and Laurie could barely breathe through it.

When she saw him lift his leg and brace his knee against her lap, terror shot through her. She was pregnant, and he knew it. She couldn't scream; she could only clutch the chair and brace herself as he forced more pressure into her jaw. The final wrenching pull tore through her, and only then did the truth emerge: he had extracted the wrong tooth.

Laurie was shaking, half in shock, half in pain. The dentist offered a mild sedative but no apology. Thad helped her out of the chair and took her home, where the dizziness and pain only grew worse. From that day forward, nothing felt the same. The pain of that day remained in her memory. Any confidence she had in the medical profession was diminished.

Doctor Langoire and Rowena, outraged, discussed suing the dentist. The challenge stemmed from Thad's lack of standing to sue since military personnel or their kin were barred from initiating legal proceedings while serving. The dentist who pulled the tooth, a trainee, would not be held responsible for what he did to Laurie.

On the third day, Laurie sat in the kitchen when water from her body began to flow to the floor. She was again vulnerable to the expertise of a man in a white coat. Thad rushed her to the hospital. Upon arrival, doctors explained that Laurie's water had broken, leaving a sac not conducive to the growth of a child. She had a choice to make. She decided to abort the fetus. Promptly thereafter, being sensible, Laurie implemented stricter precautions against more pregnancies, in addition, avoided visits to the dentist.

21
Life With the Langoires

Laurie enjoyed a good relationship with the Langiore's, but Thad remained distant from his father. The two men shared no real conversation, trading only the bare phrases required to get through an interaction. When the family gathered and the room filled with lively discussion—Laurie and Rowena offering opinions, Thaddeus chiming in, and Thad adding the occasional short reply—the distance between father and son became even more apparent. Thad found himself tongue-tied whenever he tried to speak to his father. Too much had happened over the years, and the weight of it left them unable to bridge the silence. They rarely addressed one another and exchanged glances only by accident.

Otherwise, the family relations were amicable, as Rowena worked daily and Thaddeus went to his office. Laurie experienced a little difficulty cooking for everyone, and some uncomfortable situations ensued with some preparations, but they eventually worked out a solution. It became cramped too, with two small children, the husband and wife in the bedroom with twin beds.

Coexisting with the Langoires did not protect the couple from the Roarkes' dysfunction. Thad and Laurie still made efforts to maintain relations with the Roarke family for the children's sake. They did not let the children know about any discord if they could help it. Since Laurie seemed to be the object of discontent from the relatives, she allowed the children to visit with their grand- aunties and great- grandmother without her being present. This was the situation at Christmas time. As a result, Laurie spent many hours of the holiday alone while her children visited their relatives. The aunts clearly loved the children, showering them with gifts and treats. How they felt about her did not change how much love they gave to them. Laurie felt the sacrifice was worth it. She didn't have much choice in the matter keeping peace.

Thad took the children over to his grandmother's house now and then, leaving them in her care for the day. All was well until Thad overheard his grandmother speaking disparagingly about Laurie to the children. After addressing this situation with Julia, she did not change her behavior, so he decided not to have them visit alone with her anymore. The only way she could get him to return with them was to call him to come over to get specially hatched eggs. She claimed they would be good for the children. He took them over not believing the ruse for a short visit with him always present.

The Langoires possessed apartments joined to their primary residence, and a casita situated at the back. The casita was occupied by renters, and when their lease ended, the family took up residence. Once living in the casita, phone calls that meddled in their affairs began. This would not have occurred had they stayed at the Thaddeus's residence. To get to the couple, the Roarkes would be obliged to contact Thaddeus or Rowena, given that the house possessed a single telephone. The harassment began as soon as the couple established their own space. Both Cleo and Anna Mae made daily calls to give their opinions on just about everything.

"Now that you two have one boy and a girl, I suppose you are taking precautions after your miscarriage," said Anna Mae.

"Yes, we can't afford to have another child right now. I have enough just dealing with the two of them," said Laurie.

"You know you have to remember to feed your husbands needs to keep your marriage intact." Cleo is also on the line with Anna Mae.

"Thad and I are just fine in our relationship."

"There are many ways to satisfy him other than the intercourse you know," said Cleo.

"We have safe practices that we use. I really don't want to talk about it."

"Is he using his mouth to satisfy you? If he is that's terrible. You can't do that. He will suck you internals right out of you. God has not ordained that way."

"I don't know what you are talking about," said Laurie.

"I don't know what practices you are bringing to this relationship, but my mother didn't condone it to Thad, and you shouldn't be doing it," said Anna Mae.

“Why are you into my sexual relationship with my husband. It’s none of your business.”

“It is our business. He won’t be saved if this continues to go on,” said Cleo.

This kind of meddling continued almost daily.

The situation became intolerable. The couple eventually removed their phone from the listing service and changed their phone number to stop the calls. The couple moved to an apartment later, settling in to raise their children without interference.

The Roarkes became acquainted with the dentist and his wife. Cleo and her husband met them but were not frequent visitors like Anna Mae, her husband, and her brother, Todd. Anna Mae made beautiful dresses for Rowena for every important social occasion. Dresses were made for Laurie also. While Laurie’s dresses were rather plain, the dresses made for Rowena were stylish and very flattering. There seemed to be an attempt to make the dresses just a little larger, not to emphasize Laurie’s figure. They exploited Rowena’s short figure; however. Laurie commented to Thad about the slight she felt, he as usual reframed from getting involved. He at all costs stayed out of any discord within the family.

Todd was a frequent visitor. He expressed his artistic talent by constructing a bar in their living room with the likenesses of both Thaddeus and Rowena embedded in the walls. It was quite a conversation piece. The Roarkes were heavy drinkers, and the Langoires were always up for a party, so they got along pretty well. As time went on, the partying was taking a toll on Thaddeus, and he told Rowena he needed to slow down.

In the evening after a visit from the Roarkes, Thaddeus experienced severe pain in his lower back. The pain usually appeared the next day after dinner cocktails and later drinks before bed. In the morning his ankles and feet swelled making it hard to wear his usual brogans. He resorted to wearing leather slippers which were more comfortable. Rowena noticed the change to slippers, but she did not express concern until he finally complained of sudden pain the morning after partying with the Roarkes. She suggested he see a doctor about the pain to get something for it, and of course, determine the cause.

In the fall of 1966, after Thaddeus complained to Rowena about persistent lower back pain, he sought relief from a doctor friend, a kidney specialist who suggested surgery. The surgery was an exploration in which they found third-stage cancer in his kidney and spreading to his lungs. Thaddeus had been a smoker since his teens. Thad was allowed to visit accompanied by Rowena. He spoke of how much he dreaded being in the room. The hospital room pulsed with the rhythm of the machines exhaling in slow sighs. Tubes threaded into his father's body, monitors on both hands. After the surgery, he wasn't doing well, and a specialist was called in to consult. According to the specialist, short of accusing malpractice, the tubes were in Thaddeus's body just hanging inside for no purpose after the procedure. His survival was less than twenty percent. Specialists followed exhaustive procedures to save him. He was not told about his critical condition. Thaddeus, caring about his appearance, asked Rowena to have his son come to the hospital to shave him. Thad visited his father with Rowena present and the thought of seeing his father alone made him nervous. He entered the hospital room and was reticent. He looked at his father but couldn't speak. His father looked frail, his face narrower. His eyes widened as Thad stood over him. Not until he put the warm cloth on his father's face did his father seem to relax. Thad applied the shaving cream and gently shaved his dad as tears rolled down his father's cheeks. They had never touched. It was a special moment between them. Thad caressed his father's face tenderly. Tears blurred his vision. Finally, all was well between them. Thaddeus made his transition the next day.

Laurie got the news that her father-in-law passed away at 10:00 a.m. that morning, just as they were starting their day. Before she left to take the children to school, Thad started an argument of no consequence and slammed out of the door. He had always taken pride in the quality of his work on his old-world finishes on antique furniture. A business that flourished for them. Since his father's surgery, the projects he started were left unfinished and delivery dates missed. Commentary he sought from her about his work was interpreted now as criticism of it. He became angry tossing his brushes, and tools aside. Today he slammed out the door, got in his truck, and took off recklessly down the street. Laurie couldn't understand his actions under such sad circumstances. His behavior was irrational and hurtful, directing anger toward her for no reason at all. He seemed to act out rather than trying to cope with this news. She did not understand this behavior and was dealing with her own shock and grief.

She had an errand to run and left shortly after him, disgusted at his actions. There were preparations to be made. Rowena needed her help to plan the final arrangements, and she had to prepare the children for the news. His illness had progressed so fast. So little time to absorb the news of cancer, the surgery, and now the death.

Thaddeus was "Big Daddy" they called him affectionately, not only by the children but also by Thad Jr. and Laurie. Big Daddy shopped with little Michael. He took the kids to the park and made paper kites for them. On Sunday mornings he put a stepladder next to the stove as he taught Michael to cook, making a concoction he and Michael called gravy eggs. The children loved their grandfather dearly, and it was obvious that he adored them. Two weeks before the surgery, Big Daddy took Michael to the office with him. This was what he did on Saturdays. Although he still said very little to Thad, he was always present for Michael and Antoinette. Thaddeus at last stepped into a role he hadn't known he would ever possess. Now he was gone.

As she neared the street leading to their home, neighbors were standing near an ambulance with blazing lights in front of their shop. She made it through the small crowd to see Thad being brought out on a stretcher and put in the ambulance. She rushed to his side and asked the EMT what had happened. Thad had taken an overdose of pills when he returned home. He called to tell a friend of his pending demise, who immediately called 911. This bizarre incident happened after his behavior had been erratic for days since his father's surgery. Frustrated and feeling helpless, Laurie felt she needed to be with him at the hospital, but how could she be there for him, look out for the children and tend to the needs of Rowena? This was too much. Fate was moving forward. She had to participate in what she could control. She declined to accompany him to the hospital. She stayed home to pick up the children from school.

After treating Thad, doctors put him under a seventy-two-hour watch in the psychiatric ward and then released him. He attended therapy sessions later. The death of "Big Daddy" was a turning point in the lives of the children as well as the rest of the family.

22

Julia's Children

Cleo and Anna Mae combined their talents to make apparel and exquisite dresses for the wealthy in Beverly Hills. They were designers for the stars in their small shop in Hollywood with famous movie stars as clients in and out daily. They were well thought of for their designs. A glass eye replaced the one Cleo had lost. It was the same grey color as her natural eye, and one could tell the difference by the icy stare of the eyeball. Stylish clothes of the era draped her thin figure; her fair skin and soft, wavy, marcelled hair portrayed her as a flapper of the twenties. Cleo was tall and quite attractive. Silent in manner, she seemed never to get over what her father had done to her. In her mid-thirties, her marriage to the artist now jeweler brought the stability she craved.

After a few years of trying, unable to have a child, Cleo and her husband adopted a biracial child who was born to a white Jewish mother who could not keep her child because the baby was born jet black. Sybil, her name, was a troubled child who possibly suffered a form of mental illness. They spent many days at psychiatrists' offices trying to get medication that stabilized her. She and Thad, the only children in this family, formed bonds that lasted until her death, some twenty years after her birth.

Anna Mae's husband was a skilled worker whose job was preparing materials for use in construction. He loaded and unloaded materials such as bricks and mortar for masons and bricklayers on a construction site. He drank heavily to cover the physical pain he suffered nightly. Unlike Cleo, who with her husband, prospered in later years and bought a home with a pool in Palm Springs. Anna Mae and her spouse never had a child and remained in Los Angeles in a modest apartment, living paycheck to paycheck.

Frances seldom made time to visit her mother; her resentment towards her ran deep. Julia never approved of her lifestyle, even after she settled down with one man. She was known for her temper and was difficult to get along with.

Mary began making dolls and selling them to a street vendor. She was very much like her father in her ability to disappear for days at a time. Her visits were sporadic, only spending time with her nephew, Thad, with whom she could make a connection. She continued to leave often in the middle of the night without a word. The news that she was a puppeteer in the San Francisco world's fair in 1915 was all they knew of her life. A first for a Negro person to do so. She died without the family seeing her for years.

Todd, the only male child, attended high school and played football. He stood six feet tall and was well-developed. Todd's internalization of his relationships with his sisters, particularly Hannah, is not known. Had he felt guilty about her situation? What did he believe about her pregnancy? Did he also believe Dr. Langoire had taken advantage of Hannah? If so, how did he justify his close relationship with the Doc later.

Todd was quite young, possibly fourteen or fifteen during that time. Sexual behavior may have been foreign to him under the religious dictates of Julia. Hannah being pregnant was no longer just his sister, but someone according to Julia carried something forbidden or something to be ashamed of. He had to internalize shame as well as some guilt about his role in this situation. Julia's belief system condemned and harangued Hannah while claiming she was an innocent victim. This had to be very confusing for him. Todd may have had emotional reactions and developed behavioral issues, further and more progressive anger issues with this family drama. He and Thad Jr. were the only men born under the influence of the shattered dreams of Julia.

Todd joined the Los Angeles Police Force after graduating high school. Although Los Angeles may have seemed a mecca for people of color, there was a darkness little known by the many-colored folks who fled the South to find a good life there. Well-educated Negroes in particular found no jobs open to them in their desired careers. Joining the Los Angeles Police Force was one of Todd's goals. After he finished high school, he did not attend college. He must have been very bright because despite his race being a deterrent, he became the first lieutenant, a commanding officer of the police force. Just because Todd was fortunate enough to become a police officer did not immune him from the prejudices that were rampant in the department. Standing up for his rights and probably the injustices he saw committed by the department, he spoke about the injustices and made a number of enemies who later plotted revenge. Subsequent to allegations from fellow officers, he was found guilty of excessive force, and the department suspended him. Whether fellow officers trumped up those charges remained unknown; a year later, authorities charged him as a serial rapist, and he was incarcerated for this crime. Of course, he was innocent, but he remained in jail until they caught the real rapist. The guilty person was a white man; Todd was brown skin and bore no resemblance and was completely innocent of the crimes. The authorities later released him and cleared him of all charges. Todd did not file a lawsuit as a result of this miscarriage of justice. Todd was to live with this taint on him of a rapist, preventing him getting a decent job for the rest of his life. He died from diabetes, leaving a daughter to live with the aftermath shame of such a crime.

Hannah bitter over the years, unable to find solace for her plight. She was relieved when she was banned from her mother's home. Unable to bond with the baby, she felt miserable from being constantly questioned about her part in the so-called rape. She was happy not to nurse the child and found it difficult to care for him with Julia constantly criticizing her. She protested the way Julia took charge, but when Julia decided she needed to leave, Hannah left without any protest. Thad remembered her visits with regret because of the arguments she had with his grandmother concerning his care.

She became a hairdresser and did piecework in a clothing factory in the garment district of downtown Los Angeles for years. Hannah married a man in the Navy who was a photographer. Thad remembered their visits fondly; they arrived in a big Chrysler car. Hannah and Charles had a good ten years before he died. She married again unsuccessfully and divorced. Later, Hannah cared for a young man, a relative of the Roarke family, whom she raised with her son Thad's support. He did not seem to bear any resentment of her caring for this young man but assisted in his development as much as he could.

Thad and his mother never shared a close relationship, even when he reached adulthood. Thad, however, took over the care of her when he received a call one day that she was in the hospital having her leg amputated. It was the same day he received his final divorce papers from Laurie. Hannah had suffered from diabetes for years and had not taken good care of herself. She stubbed her toe, which did not heal. Gangrene set in, and her leg had to be removed to save her life. He looked after her for years as she aged and developed dementia. They cremated Hannah, Julia's and Treeva's last surviving child, and scattered her ashes over the ocean in Camarillo, California.

23

1967

Laurie arrived at the small house located on Las Madras Avenue. It had been a while since she last visited here. Her peace of mind depended on her keeping some distance from Julia and the aunts as well. An occasional phone call occurred, from either one aunt or the other, to Laurie for updates on the children's health and activities now that they trusted their unlisted phone number to the family. Due to Cleo's adopted daughter staying in contact with Thad and Laurie, the families shared a link through that connection.

A few years before he died, Treeva came to California for a visit. He had spent years with another family of his after leaving Julia and their children. The amount of preparation Julia invested in expecting his visit proved surprising. She had her hair pressed, which she rarely paid someone to do. She fussed about the house in a way she never had. The anger and recrimination of the past had calmed somewhat over the past years, but still Julia could not help referring to some of the pain she suffered. Their meeting revealed a lingering tenderness in Julia's feelings towards him. It went off pleasantly, as they were careful in their speech. Talking then to Treeva didn't cause anger; it only led to speaking about the regrets shared between them.

After meeting Julia and before he left to go back to Texarkana, he came to the shop where Thad and Laurie sold objects of art and Thad finished furniture. The usual busy day with customers, but curiosity prevailed to see the grandfather they had heard so much talk about. They closed the shop to prevent interruptions during his visit. A friend had dropped him off.

A short, wiry man stood before them, a cowboy-style hat slouched over long, stringy hair. His suit clung tightly to his small frame, an odd mismatch that made him look even smaller. His complexion matched the dull gray of his hat and jacket, giving him a washed -out, almost colorless appearance. When he settled into the chair and crossed his legs, he seemed to shrink further, as if folding in on himself. Laurie was sitting across from him, and baby Antionette, eighteen months old, sat on her lap. She had yet to take her first steps. Treeva dominated the conversation, speaking of his many accomplishments. Baby Antionette watched him and slowly slipped down from her mother's lap. The child observed him, perhaps owing to his petite stature or his distinctiveness compared to anyone she had encountered in her young life, and approached him. It was an astonishing sight for Laurie to witness her baby's first steps toward her great-grandfather. The distance a little more than six feet. Antoinette, with her arms outstretched, approached, expecting her great-grandparent to pick her up. Treeva, saw the child coming towards him, appeared frightened. He wrapped his arms around his body and lifted his legs from the floor and begged for someone to come rescue him from the child. Laurie, stunned by the unfolding events, swiftly gathered Antoinette before she reached Treeva. She felt surprised, then anger, concerning his reaction to the child. She left the room with the baby in her arms. She did not know how long he talked to Thad, and she did not see him leave. This negative impression of Treeva remained. They never saw or heard from him again.

Laurie's most recent visit to the residence occurred because Julia called, requesting she come as soon as possible. That meeting proved enjoyable, as Julia presented her with two Bibles, one for each child. Dates inside recorded the births and deaths of their ancestors: Reverend Lawrence Todd, born 1820, died 1898; Emma Todd, born 1830, died 1870; Julia, born 1886; Treeva Roarke, born 1883, died 1961.

Julia's health over the years for the most part, was fairly good even though she suffered from diabetes. It was surprising, considering she would not see a doctor. She managed her diet with directions gleaned from knowledge her daughters gave her because they sought medical help for their diabetes. A pimple appeared on her back, ruptured, and discharged pus. Julia cared for it over many years without seeing a doctor. She carefully dressed it; no one except Cleo was allowed to attend it. When Cleo was not available, Thad provided the care. This pimple remained over the years, draining frequently. This worked to prevent infection for most of her adult life.

At eighty-one, the pimple had become infected, and Julia, as usual, hesitated to seek medical attention. She continued to treat it as she had successfully over the years. Cleo, concerned about how her mother was treating her wound kept a close watch on her.

Today Laurie came at the request of Cleo to check on Julia. She walked down the path to the front door and knocked, no response. Knocking again, she heard the radio blasting gospel music inside. Other than the music, the house appeared still. She looked at the yard filled with Julia's pride in beautiful red, yellow, and purple flowers. The plentiful flowers and fruit trees received exceptional care from a woman of her years. Laurie felt immediate awe at the surrounding beauty. She hoped Julia would allow her to take some flowers home with her when she left. She walked up to the front door and saw a note stuck on the screen. It read: "Sorry to miss you. Will call later. Sister Gray."

Laurie knocked again and yelled, "Is anyone home?" No response.

It appeared quite strange, seeing as Julia habitually remained at home caring for her garden. Flowers, probably just picked in the early dawn, filled a basket on the side of the path leading up to the house. Dew still clung to the petals. Julia normally rose before dawn, said her morning prayers and prepared her first cup of coffee with a buttered biscuit and no jelly. Her Christian conviction deemed it sinful to enjoy earthly pleasures at such an early hour. After breakfast, she picked avocados from her tree and fruit from other trees and put baskets of them on the sidewalk in front of her lot for passersby. A young man arrived weekly to help and to pick up flowers and fruit to deliver to the homes of patients who needed assisted care. Julia worked in the kitchens of several assisted-living homes over the years. Faithfully then she brought flowers with her, declaring that she was returning the blessings God had given her for a long life.

Mid-morning now, and the box for the fruit, which hung heavy on the trees waiting to be picked, remained empty. Her peach and plum trees had yields of sweet fruit from her daily watering and fertilizing. On the ground, the strawberry plants had sprouted large, ripe, juicy fruit, also waiting to be picked. Friends and family knew Julia for the sweetest fruit unheard of in local markets. She used her fruit and flowers to bribe her children and grandson's family to visit her. Otherwise, her children seemed to avoid being there for her onslaught of chiding about getting saved and Julia meddling in their personal affairs. The great-grandchildren spared from her rebukes received lots of love and sweet treats. This scene around Laurie now was deserted, missing Julia picking flowers or weeding the garden.

"Is anyone home?" Laurie raised her voice.

She walked to the rear of the house thinking Julia could be there. Why hadn't she responded? This marked the middle of the week. She had no transportation other than her sons-in-law, who worked during the day. Laurie wondered why she was the only one available to make this call. She considered that Anna Mae and Cleo were busy at their shop; they didn't drive; Frances almost never visited anymore. The same for Hannah, who called frequently, depended upon her husband to bring her by. Her son, Todd, deceased, had a daughter who called from time to time, but she didn't visit. Her grandson, Thad, visited only on request and remained at work. The years of trying to balance life with his grandmother and family had been challenging. He soon realized that ensuring his wife remained apart from his aunts and grandmother represented the solution to his mental stability. His son and daughter had not yet reached an age to notice the discord within the family and cherished their great-grandmother and grandaunts. So, Laurie visited Julia because she must find out why Julia had not answered calls since the day before. It's not unusual for Julia to not reply for hours or most of the day. She would be outside in her garden or attending church services. Today, Cleo felt a little anxious about the delay in Julia's response. Not finding her anywhere in the yard, and getting no answer when calling her, Laurie looked in the planter next to the door to find the key. With the key moist in her hand, wishing she had asked a friend to accompany her, she unlocked the door.

The small living room had space for a couch and one chair. A quilt covered each piece of furniture to hide its wear. Religious magazines and a Bible covered a small table next to the chair. On the wall hung a large portrait of Jesus Christ, not in his usual beige complexion with long blonde hair to his shoulders, but jet-black hair in the prevailing 'black is beautiful' full natural. He extended his arms. His complexion ebony, an imposing sight as the portrait seemed to fill the room.

Once inside, the scent of cooked meals, mold, damp air, and floral sprays assaulted her. The air registered in the low sixties, yet a sudden heat washed over her. Her armpits became moist with sweat. She took a deep breath and walked toward the kitchen.

"Is anyone here?" she called. No response.

Julia's body, dressed and in a fetal position, lay on the floor beside a chair. Laurie rushed over, calling Julia's name. She tried to lift Julia's arm to pull her up. Julia remained unresponsive. Laurie pulled back in shock. She grabbed the phone and called 9-1-1. Her voice was hoarse and shaky as she asked for an ambulance. Cleo was her next call. Laurie cried as she ran out of the house down the long path to the street to wait for the ambulance to arrive. She led the EMTs to the door of the house, but she didn't enter with them. She waited outside, pacing back and forth, sobbing. Upon entering the kitchen, the EMTs attempted to revive Julia without success and subsequently pronounced her dead. The autopsy later revealed that she had sepsis. Her infection permeated her blood and her entire body.

Hardship marked Julia's life, yet she moved through it with a fierce, unyielding strength. Her dreams were not delayed; they were denied, her plans repeatedly derailed, and the odds seemed permanently stacked against her. Still, she gave everything she had. Life's blows made her difficult, shaped by loss, disappointment, and a marriage that brought more sorrow than happiness. The death of her mother, the collapse of the promise, her hopes for a better future, and the tragedies that followed left deep marks. The way she carried those wounds—and the choices she made in response—echoed through the generations that came after her.

Part II

24

Living with Thad

Thad is a ninety-year-old, slightly bald man. He sits in his chair facing his laptop. The voice of his therapist coming from the screen is raised to a high pitch to accommodate Thad's inability to hear well. The room, a window for a wall looking out on the forest. Flowered bushes are under the window and the occasional deer prance by as the sunshine breaks through the trees. He's living in his daughter's home along with her husband. The room is large enough for his bed, a dresser and a writing table for his laptop. There are pictures of him standing next to a 1950 chevy truck on the wall. Other pictures throughout the room are of him receiving trophies. His oxygen apparatus swishing noises is the only other sound in the room. He has been seeking therapy for his depression and help in navigating the disabilities that plague him now in the twilight of his years.

"Why don't you start at the beginning and give me a synopsis of your life, in particular with Laurie. It will help me see what is going to be important for us to work on with our sessions." Said the therapist.

"Okay, well, Laurie and I had been together for over thirty years. She divorced me partly because I had been a lousy husband, but probably because I tried to kill her." Thad looks straight ahead to see the reaction to his revelation.

"That must be incredibly difficult to carry. How does this moment in history affect your relationship now? I need to know what led to that moment in your life."

"Well part of my having to see a therapist is how I'm trying to cope and get over what I did in the marriage."

"Let's start with how this act of violence in your relationship began."

"I'm not going to make excuses for my behavior back then; I just acted crazy during those times. Driving back and forth from Ventura to San Luis Obispo County to be with Linda,

Linda being my girlfriend, and keeping Laurie in the dark kept me on edge. I can't imagine what Laurie would have done if she knew what was going on."

"I'm going to need some background to understand what was going on. Can you explain why that happened?"

"I won't even try to account for my behavior over the years. I've never been faithful to our marriage."

"And for what reason?"

"We fought about money, my late nights out, she has confronted me only a few times about other women. She may have been ignorant of what was going on or maybe she just didn't care."

"I am to assume you didn't have an open marriage."

"No, but she had been accused of being unfaithful herself a number of times. Each time it was my grandmere who accused her. We never had any proof, however. Her relationship with Edward appeared innocent enough until I heard he had affairs with several women in town. Surely Laurie could have been one of them. The idea she would be unfaithful to me was more than I could take."

"So, you responded by trying to kill her. Is that right?"

"Well yes. I felt like a fool. They said their affair was talked about around the office."

"Had they been seen together to indicate something was going on?"

"Well, no, he had a reputation for taking advantage of women. Lots of affairs they said."

"So, you acted on gossip about your wife. Despite your infidelity."

Thad moves around in his chair as he speaks. "That's true. After the incident, he found me and threatened my life if I ever hurt her again. Isn't that evidence that something likely occurred?"

"I don't know, the point is, it convinced you. What happened next?"

"His threat was in vain because she left town, she went to her brothers in Connecticut."

"What did she do next?"

"She served me with papers for a divorce. We had court ordered therapy and even received support from friends, but we couldn't put the marriage back together. Laurie was done. She walked away without a word to me and got on with her life."

He looks out of the window. He frowns and slowly shakes his head. There is a silence for a while until the therapist asks?"

"Were you able to move on with your life?"

Thad comes out of his revery. "The day I received the final papers for the divorce; I got a call from the hospital saying my mother's leg had to be amputated. She suffered with diabetes and had no one to look after her. She became my responsibility."

"I'm getting ahead of myself. I need to review the past before going so far forward. So, you can understand why I need to get help from a professional."

"Okay, where do you want to start? I want to hear your story. Start from the beginning."

"Laurie and I got married while I was in the Air Force. I volunteered for the service in California where I had lived with my grandmother all of my life. Getting away from her control was important and being on my own excited me. Shortly after arriving in Denver for basic training on radar systems for the new F-104 Lockheed aircraft, I met Laurie, we got married and right away we had our first child."

"You moved pretty fast."

"To be sure, I was not ready to have kids. Maybe not getting married so soon either. I should have spent more time on my own, but we were in love and virgins and wanted to have sex, so we had to get married."

"Is that what you believed necessary? Was matrimony the only means of having sex?"

"Yes, that's how we were raised. Both my grandmere and her parents would've never gotten over her having a baby out of wedlock."

"Both of you started a marriage under the expectations of your parents. That's a difficult start."

"It was rocky from the start, interference from my grandmother didn't help the situation. We went back and forth from Washington state, my home base, to California, each time staying with grandmere and it was tough."

"I'm sure it was. How did you manage?"

"We stuck together and I kept my peace and didn't get involved with the disagreements she and my family had. I couldn't be a part of the chaos. My solution would have been violence, so I stayed quiet."

"I see, probably a good choice on your part. Did you often think of violence to solve your problems?"

"Hell yes. I've always thought about killing somebody. I've kept the urge under control over the years. My fantasy has been going into a crowd and just mowing them down."

"What kept you from acting on such violence?"

"Fear I guess. The fear of going to jail. Fear of being killed myself. I don't know."

"Have you done violence other than the attempt on your wife?"

"No. Thought about it, but no."

"We will spend more time talking through this. Let's get back to some background."

"I left the service finally and returned to California, then I faced my father for the first time."

"You grew up without a father. How did you deal with him not in your life.?"

"I grew up being told I was a child from rape." This information comes out from Thad in anger. There is silence for a long moment.

"I never had a real relationship with my father. To be sure, I never knew him until my son was born. Because of this start in life, I probably wasn't a good mate, in fact, I know I wasn't."

"How did you react to being told you were a child from rape? Who told you that story?"

"This had been told to me throughout my life. I've had to live with the hate for my father from my grandmother, my mother and the whole family."

"You feel the story set you up for life?"

"Yes. It did. Yes, it did. He denied being my father. He and my mother left me with my grandmother. She remained the sole person who took care of me."

There was silence again letting this thought sink in. Thad seems uncomfortable in his seat. He moves around while speaking.

"You will need to thoroughly examine your emotions and response to being abandoned by your parents. For now, let's get on with your story. I need the complete picture from your prospective."

"Well, Laurie and her mother were instrumental in bringing us together, I mean with my father and his wife. Being in his presence after the fiasco as a child when he called me over to give me some old clothes, it seemed strange. He just nodded when we arrived at his home. It was what I remembered along with phone calls I made to him just to harass him."

"You made calls to harass him?"

"Oh yeah. My grandmere made me call to get support from him. Then, later as a teenager, I called just to hear his voice and I just hung up. It never worked."

"I'm sure it didn't. Go on, we'll deal with that later too."

"In any case, it surprised me how cordial his spouse behaved. She right away took to our baby. I'm pretty sure the baby acted as the catalyst for our beginning a relationship with them. My father and I had little to say to each other even when we lived with them for a while. It wasn't until he got sick and died, the pain of the past of not being wanted by him to the love he showed my kids, shook me to my core. Our time was up; we waited too long to connect."

"It's hard to conceive of the challenges you faced upon his death."

"Yeah, I took it pretty hard. I even took a lot of pills trying to cope. I ended up in the hospital under psychiatric care for three days." Thad teared up and reached for a tissue on the table. He bowed his head and turned away to hide the emotions he stirred up.

"A devastating experience, I'm sure. Would you like a break for a while to pull yourself together?"

"No, I'm okay." He sighs. "Let's get back to my marriage and how it was living with me."

"Sure, tell me what it was like for you."

"I would leave home after work for hours at a time, not accounting for my whereabouts. This behavior became a source of discontent and continued for the duration of our marriage. The worst of it was promising the children their favorite treat of ice cream as an excuse to leave the house and then not returning until long after their bedtime fooling them. It seems ridiculous to me now that the children believed my sincerity about giving them a treat, trusting that I would return as promised time after time, I've felt bad about that to this day."

"The children must have been hurt by this behavior. It's hard to imagine you're doing such a thing."

"Me too, now that I think about it. It didn't bother me then because I wanted to leave without being confronted by Laurie. I spent a lot of my time with friends who raced cars. Many nights I would participate in street races. Once in a while I just screwed around."

"Did you have relations outside of your marriage?"

"Oh yes, I had a few."

"It's possible certain things you did were the only coping mechanisms you were aware of. "

"Probably was. I can't make excuses about it. It was what it was."

"You can get analysis and understand your motives then. We will do that in another session. Let's move on with your background. How did you make a living?"

"My training as a radar technician qualified me to work for an aircraft company when I left the service. I worked there until we had an opportunity to start my own business. Art was my first love, but job opportunities were nonexistent since I had no formal training. We met a couple who offered the opportunity to work with them. Laurie learned to make lamp shades, and I apprenticed for old world finishes on furniture. It came easy for me and soon we were on our own with a shop on a main thoroughfare. Our venture proved quite fruitful until health concerns compelled me to give up the company."

"What kind of issues, can you speak of them?"

"I suffered from sarcoidosis. By taking the prescribed medication, I've had repercussions in my health to this day from it even though I got over the disease."

"The remedy proved more detrimental than the ailment. So, the story goes?"

"Yes, in my case it was." Thad smiles briefly.

"Let's go on to the next chapter of your life. Did you stay in the technical field?"

"My last job was for a fire alarm system company. My responsibilities progressed pretty fast to the manager in Ventura County. I installed the first fire alarm system in the country for this company in a major hotel chain in Los Angeles. The job appeared enormous. The schematics were situated on the huge walls of the hotel's basement. I interpreted the schematics and built the system without assistance."

"That was quite a feat. The hotel stands to this day?"

"Oh yeah. Later, I installed a fire system for a major hospital in Los Angeles, and on a ship in the harbor too." Thad sits up while speaking about his accomplishments.

"Those represented major, consequential responsibilities. The company had to be impressed with your talents."

"I guess they were because a short time later executives flew Laurie and me to the company's main offices in Massachusetts. All expenses paid by the company's account. We attended a party to meet the company's owner and higher officials. It represented a considerable honor. The company saw this future in me and I became supervisor of the entire Ventura County and San Luis Obispo area. I traveled daily, working on alarm systems in this territory and beyond."

"Sounds great. How did you handle so much responsibility?"

"The responsibility was too much. I was also on the spot to perform tasks, solve problems that no one else could solve. The pressure was great. Each day I woke full of anxiety worried I would fail the tasks of the day." Thad begins to ring his hands.

"My stomach churned constantly. My hands were sweating and I had to wipe them constantly in order to work. While working, sometimes I would break out in sweat all over my body. I kept a towel to wipe my brow as water dripped across it. Other times I was nauseous. After a few months, I notified the company that I no longer wanted the job of supervisor and wanted to be demoted back to being a technical representative of Ventura County. I recognized it as a personal failing, and Laurie's disappointment with me was evident. The relief I experienced was worth the loss of confidence she had in me."

"That was a long way to fall from such great heights. The disappointments for both of you had to be tremendous. We'll deal with how that played out for you in your life's journey. Tell me more."

"It was hard, the company continued to expect me to tackle major problems many times for them within Ventura and San Luis Obispo County. They accepted my stepping down. It didn't cost me my job, just the difficult position. It was alright because now in my spare time, I designed and built an engine for my antique truck I purchased years before and I didn't have time to work on it. I must say it is a stunner; I painted it myself. The trophies for it lined the wall of our living room. It sits here in the garage of my daughter's house now."

"Sounds like a good consolation for you. It must have softened the disappointment you felt."

"Yes, it did."

"We will talk more about the repercussions and results later again surrounding this portion of your life. Tell me more about how you got along with your children. What was it like for them growing up with you and Laurie? Tell me about the happier times."

"I recall certain times spent with my family. On weekends I would wake everyone with loud music of artists like Pat Metheny, Sergio Mendes, Herb Alpert, Lou Rawls, and Dinah Washington, to name several of them. Laurie, the kids and I would dance around the living room. The kids kept us abreast of the latest moves to break out with at parties. This love of jazz and R & B music characterized some of the good memories of our being together. For Michael, the car shows and car races he attended with me stand out as some of my fondest memories. He is still part of my life and looks after me in a pinch with my shows up north."

"Shows? You still have car shows?"

"Oh yes." Thad gets excited as he explains. "I still direct car shows up north in California. Every year for fifteen years. It's the pride of the town. They honored me this year with a parade."

"That's astounding for a man of your age. You do this by yourself?"

"Pretty much. Like I said, my son accompanies me and helps."

"That's marvelous, there must be great pride in what you have accomplished."

"The town seems to appreciate what I've done for them."

"And Antionette, tell me about your time with her."

"Admittedly, I've not been a good father. I paid little attention to Antoinette, except to punish her when necessary." Thad looks down as he talks, fiddling with his fingers. He doesn't look up at the therapist.

"Michael got more attention as a companion for me, going with me to car races and shows. During a time when we sought family therapy in heartfelt family discussions, Antionette expressed that she felt her mother had been a single mom raising two children. Michael said he would have been happy if his mother had divorced me. I felt hurt, but they had the right to their perspective." Thad uses his hand to wipe under his eyes. "After thirty years of failed family therapy and disastrous attempts to keep the marriage together, it wouldn't have been a surprise we divorced."

"I see and what was the situation in the following years?"

"Since the day Antionette graduated from college, I've held a grudge against her. She didn't show up for a date with me and Linda on her graduation day. My girlfriend, Linda and I lived in northern California. Me and Laurie, naturally, had divorced by then. We came to Los Angeles to celebrate Antionette's graduation, but we didn't attend it. I wanted to introduce my girlfriend to her. Linda bought a beautiful and expensive multi-decorated sweater as a gift for her. The date, in some way, got mixed up. We learned later once Antionette received the sweater that she said it was gaudy and ugly. She would never wear it. Linda never forgave Antionette for standing us up and not appreciating the sweater. From that time on, she forbade my daughter from visiting me, there was no other choice since I lived in her house. I failed to attend her wedding. I gave the excuse blood pressure meds prohibited travel. According to Laurie, this served as a fake excuse. Thirty years later, whenever a disagreement arises, I'd bring up the graduation incident."

"That didn't help your relationship with her, I'm sure."

"Well, she busied herself at school growing up by becoming a cheerleader and dating the captain of the football team. When the team traveled to Hawaii, Laurie made sure she and Antoinette followed them. She seemed fine."

Living with me was no picnic; you know, I didn't have a model of how a husband should be for his wife and children, and I didn't have a model on how to behave amicably in a relationship. We had arguments all the time. Laurie came from a family that expected long marriages and they believed couples should stay together through thick and thin. 'Until death do us part,' as the minister had us pledge. Her parents fought and still devoted themselves to each other. I believe she thought our marriage could mirror this kind of behavior. It would get better in time as she had observed the devotion in her parents' marriage shown in their later years. She told me this."

"Do you share her disappointment on how it developed and then ended?"

"Yes, I do. I take responsibility for my part in the demise."

"Well, you've had quite an interesting life, Thad. You've been a man of many talents; you've performed exemplary feats in your field of work. Your personal life has been in shambles. We will talk about the relationship with your daughter now that you are living in her house. We will do some work on gratitude and thankfulness to help your depression. We will meet again and deal with some of the most difficult times. Especially your attempt to kill your wife. We will get some resolutions to go on with your life now. Let's make an appointment for our next session."

25

Laurie's Story

I am fifty-one years old, and a crisis is happening now. It has been on the verge and should have happened anytime as early as twenty-years ago. Looking back now, and with the help of therapy, I see that neither Thad nor I could allow this crisis to break us before now. I had never seriously considered not being his wife.

During our many marital upheavals, I would fantasize about the climactic conclusion where I was being forced to make a choice of being taken away from all of my problems in the marriage by a shining knight. I knew I would always choose Thad because I was always going to be loyal to my commitment to him. Through therapy, I saw that neither he nor I was strong enough as individuals to consider moving out of this relationship, either getting together with someone else or accepting a life alone. Now that I had arrived at the state where the crisis presented itself fully, I could no longer deny the reality of it. We had to resolve the conflicts between us now and end the marriage rather than continue to tear each other apart.

Several months ago, the semifinal incident, not so shakingly consequential in itself, brought about the decision to separate legally. A mysterious illness had plagued me, and doctors eventually diagnosed me with sarcoidosis. Thad had become deathly ill with this disease about ten years ago and was in remission after having taken steroids for several years. He blew up, his face round like a ball. I was determined to not take steroids. Although I suffered a great deal, my symptoms were never as critical as his. Meanwhile, I was sometimes bedridden and not capable of handling many household responsibilities. Thad took over paying the bills. I should have known better; he had never shown he could be responsible with money. Soon, Thad failed to pay the electricity bill and they cut off the power. We received notices of payment arrears on the mortgage. I found out we were one hundred thousand dollars in debt. The company had given him a credit card to cover his travel expenses. Instead of paying the bill monthly with the company reimbursements, he spent it, then paid the lowest monthly payment. I wanted to be free from liability for the debts he was incurring. California made spouses equally responsible for community debt; of course, our community property would accept the brunt of his debt, I was to find out later. I filed for legal separation hoping to remove myself from his ever-increasing spending.

Dissolving my marriage was a requirement, and the time was right. It was not a matter to be taken lightly, like separating to get our heads together as we did many times. It was a signal to me. I had given up on the idea of holding the marriage together because it was hurting so much. Thad wasn't trustworthy. He had betrayed me in so many ways. It was time to end this farce of a relationship. There seemed to be no areas of agreement between us either. We could not even agree to end the marriage.

Since then, I have gone through grief and loss of the relationship, the good and the bad. I read somewhere that there were five stages of recovery through which one goes after the loss of love: shock, denial, anger, depression, finally understanding that leads to acceptance. These stages, you understand, are not specifically and always defined. They intertwined with each other over various periods of time. The stage I relate to most is the one about which I read in novels or saw on soap operas. Like those stars kissed lovers, struggling through crisis after crisis, their love deemed not to survive. I am afraid I was in the denial stage for a very long time, maybe various stages of it for many years.

We started out like most young people, in a fantasy state. We thought that despite the problems that surrounded each of us, we would overcome them all and be happy thereafter. Acting without the benefit of guidance, our fantasies were to condemn our marriage to certain instability. The shock set in when we gradually realized how difficult it was to live with another person while wrapped in our own insecurities. Only a neediness on each of our parts, a lack of self-worth, and fear of being on our own, held us together.

I had the challenge of breaking the hold my mother had on me. She had dominated my life as far back as I can remember with all the unfulfilled desires and dreams of her life. I was attempting to escape from her. Loving school and looking forward to a career as a lawyer were my main goals. I also wanted a home, children, and someone deeply and passionately in love with me. Eighteen and Mother just wanted me to be safely married before my sexual energies got out of her control and produced a child out of wedlock.

When I think of the time of being eighteen and nineteen, I shudder at the nightmare of my situation. My social life consisted only of young men my mother might have chosen for herself. This was based on her criteria for good looks, fair skin, and hair softened by nature against the crinkle of kink. My mother insulted and turned away from the house my choices of boyfriends and girlfriends. Her social nonacceptance of their appearances, being a little too dark, rather than the good values she had instilled in me, which I might have seen in my friends.

From the age of sixteen, I dated a young black man who passed for "a po white boy" who had wavy black hair and skin so white and transparent that the blue and purple veins shone through it. My mother and I argued every time she referred to him as my fiancé.

"I don't understand why you refuse to accept that DeVern will make you a great husband," said Beatrice.

"In the first place, I'm not thinking about getting married. I need to finish school," I said.

"You can always finish school after you marry. He treats you like a Goddess."

"DeVern is sweet, but I don't see a future with him. He hasn't even finished high school. Ninth grade was the last year of school he completed."

"He's smart, works hard, he will make a good living."

"Yeah, working for my father. I don't want that."

"What's wrong with that? Your father makes a decent and honest living for his family."

"You just want him to work for daddy because then you have control over him and me."

"That's not true. I don't know what you mean by saying that."

"Let's not go there. I know he loves me, but I don't think I am in love with him."

"It's best if your husband loves you more than you love him. It works in your best interest."

"I know you say that mother, but I want to feel something too in my relationship. Some passion. I don't feel that with DeVern. I only date him exclusively because I don't see anyone else I want to be with."

"You will not do better than DeVern. I can just see the beautiful children you two would have."

"You've got me having babies already, Mother. I don't believe you. DeVern lacks ambition and drive. I want more than just being a housewife. I want a career. I want a husband who has a professional job, making good money."

"It's time you knew when you are better off. You won't find a better man than DeVern."

Upon entering college and just about the time DeVern was talking of marriage and Mother was getting excited about the prospect of it, I broke it off with him.

During the process of breaking away from my mother, I had a good start by refusing to marry this fair-skinned young man she had settled upon. I stayed on campus for the summer school to assert independence. Mother was able to keep me isolated from my friends by not giving me messages and invitations to social events in town. Loneliness, lack of money, even though I worked two part-time jobs off campus, and needing moral support, found me back at home in the fall trying to shore up the love I felt I lost from my parents through my rebellion. Mother retaliated for what she viewed as my disobedience to her command to come home by renting my room. I had to sleep on the couch. Meanwhile, DeVern had gone to the service after our breakup. He returned a year later, wanting us to make up. I refused to even talk to him.

Mother and her sister kept the pressure on me to salvage the relationship. She truly believed this arrangement would be in my best interest. One weekend I came home from college for a visit. Mother and her sister ambushed me one afternoon; they grabbed me and forced an old maid's bonnet on my head to demonstrate what they were sure I was going to end up wearing if I didn't consent to marry DeVern. We argued and both of them took turns trying to change my mind. Their forcefulness and condemnation of my decision hurt and angered me. I left home crying and spent the day in the Catholic church praying, depressed and despairing of my situation. I wasn't dating and had few friends I could talk to or who understood my situation.

Shortly thereafter, I met Thad. The confrontation with my mother and aunt was still looming in my mind. I needed to consider other factors that were important going forward in my life since getting married was a solution to getting the life I wanted and having the approval of my mother. Thad, as an example, his looks, his prospects for making a living because he was so smart worked for me. His father's place in the community was an important determinant from my mother's point of view. It was perfect; maybe this was the answer. I thought about this when I introduced Thad to the family.

He fit all the primary qualities Mother wanted in a husband for me, and indeed his father was professional, never mind the fact that he was an illegitimate offspring and never publicly recognized by his father. His father's position in society, a prominent doctor in Los Angeles, was bragging rights for Mother to pass on to friends.

Thad's challenge was being born to a very unhappy woman who had an affair with her dentist. As soon as he was old enough to understand, he was told this man had raped his mother. This reinforced his obvious feelings of resentment towards his father and family, who on the other hand, refused to have anything to do with him. These were fences that needed to be mended. Mother suggested this was a job for me.

We spent five months together courting and trying to avoid the lust we felt for each other. We talked a lot and many times throughout the night. Thad and I seemed to want the average American dream, and I could continue my education that he promised my father. I was later to learn during the marriage that Thad had no idea of what he wanted out of life. He made deterrents and sabotaged me during marriage to prevent my finishing school or exploring my career that might compete with the time I would devote to him and the children. He said many things during those conversations because they sounded good and seemed to agree with what I said I wanted. Responsibility and obedience from his upbringing made him decide it was right to marry the girl he was to have sexual relations with, especially since he thought he loved her. He had no thought beyond this scenario.

We came together and pledged to love each other forever as we set out on our one-day honeymoon to break the hymen of virginity for both of us. My expectation was that Thad and I would be smart enough to meet all challenges, since we wanted the same things out of life. I believed we possessed the minimum requirements for a good life: intelligence, ambition, and a desire to have many beautiful children. For me, this marriage was the perfect answer to my problems. Pleasing mother by being safely married and I would have someone to love me. The best of all circumstances, I could get on with my ambitions for my life.

Still in the throes of rebellion when we were wed, I built a marriage and lifestyle that I thought would be the exact opposite to what I saw my mother lead. Part of my rebellion was to not follow her advice concerning birth control, so one month after we married, our first child was on its way.

What we really had in common was domineering, insufferable parents. His overly religious background left him with little sense of direction except to stay out of church. The ambition to have a great job he claimed he wanted did not exist. His drive had been to possess and play with toys like his train set and his truck. That was what he had spent most of his time and effort developing. Otherwise, he wasn't available to me or the children and, of course, not interested in getting financially ahead.

For Thad, although he had escaped to the service, had never been alone or on his own, and some part of him still expected sheltering and to be taken care of by a strong person not unlike the grandmother he hated. Neither of us ever imagined the built-in disaster, nor recognized that we were undertaking a commitment that would thwart us and later make the future of the children we loved more than ourselves be as unsatisfying as our own lives. Our actions toward each other with discord, arguments, and separations have crippled them for their future relationships.

Disillusionment marked our relationship with each other, and basic disagreements how often to have sex, how to manage our money, and how we would conduct our social life. Even our values of life were not the same. I had strong beliefs about God and Thad confessed he didn't have any faith. We struggled with the realities of our relationship and confided to our friends that we were unfulfilled. Nonetheless, we carried on, two very needy individuals, not wanting the life we had, and neither of us having enough self-worth to be on our own.

Three pregnancies and two surviving children marked the first five years; love or dependency cemented the relationship through stormy and painful times. Even family strife brought upon us by his relatives did not pull us apart. They drew us closer together. Ten years later and several affairs sent Thad away from my mothering and self-sacrificing. I was living up fully to the person I was sure my mother never was. He was married to someone who was reliable yet identifying my obsequiousness as maneuvers once used by his grandmother to control him when brute force didn't work. Through my self-sacrifice, I sought to show him how great a person I was. Somehow, through this great love I showed, he would find the real man I imagined was lost somewhere inside of him. Better still, he would grow into this perfect husband and father I was setting the example for by my behavior.

I continued to deny my part in the failure of this fantasy we were in. My expectation was that loving was the key to changing him, thus making our marriage work. How naïve I have been.

We continued to struggle in our relationship until Thad became ill with the autoimmune disease, sarcoidosis, that was quite serious. He spent weeks in the hospital. When the doctors released him, coming home was not healthy for him because our discord hindered his recovery. We decided he should go to New York to be with his uncle, Bill Langoire, to help him recover. While there, he got involved with a young woman. When he returned to California, he moved in with his stepmother, Rowena. His father had passed some years earlier. A week later the young lady arrived, and she stayed with him at Rowena's house. This relationship lasted for a few months until the differences between Thad, the woman and Rowena came to a head. Thad packed her up and sent her back to New York. Later Thad and Rowena found their differences were making it hard for him to continue living with her, so he came home to his family. Yes, I took him back.

The same neediness and fear brought us back together, disguised as doing what was best for the children. Denial still in control as I remained numb and shielded myself from the pain I felt so that I could carry on despite the unresolved conflicts between us. The children grew over the years amidst arguments and constant separations, sometimes physically and many times emotionally.

There were good times too, I must admit. We shared a love of music, playing some form each day. We traveled around the country and even saw a little of Europe while I worked for an airline company. I worked on many business ventures with him, sometimes two jobs to satisfy my drive to be successful. Thad avoided most responsibilities except for his steady job working as a technical representative for a national company and the refinishing business. He left the care of the children with me. I had no time to continue the pursuit of the law degree I had dreamed of. Resentment for this failure always remained just below the surface, frequently showing itself through nightmares and bouts of depression. Gradually depression manifested itself into chronic stress ailments.

A debilitating illness with no clear diagnosis occupied me for three years. It started with a sexually transmitted disease. I had no contact with anyone but my husband. The doctor prescribed a very strong antibiotic, which caused my immune system to shut down. Thad vigorously denied any sexual contact with another person. He wanted to confront the doctor about a misdiagnosis. I was able to prevent that confrontation. Meanwhile, I became so ill that Thad took me to Las Vegas to be with my sister. He was unable to care for me. My condition worsened, and my doctor had me flown back to Los Angeles and into critical care, concerned that I would not survive. I was in denial about my illness. I did not associate it with the state of my life.

It had taken many years to get past the shock, denial, anger and depression, and into the stage of constructive anger. Constructive in that it motivated me to do something about the anger and disappointment at myself as well as at Thad for the disillusionment of my marriage. This legal separation had afforded me the space to think about what my future should look like. As time had gone by, the children were much older now: one was in college, the other working for an airline. Doing what was best for them was no longer an excuse. I hoped to be out of this marriage; however, I couldn't afford a physical separation. Tests and medications were expensive, and the physical demands of my illness made it impossible for me to work.

I received permission from my doctor to enroll in a college to work on the degree I had coveted. We were sure that I could muster enough strength to attend class. Once working toward my goal, my illness was no longer my focus, my body began to heal. I was plagued though with nightmares about my life with Thad. One of my many nightmares was being on campus looking for my classroom and unable to find it. Finding my way off campus became a problem too as I roamed from building to building until I no longer recognized where I was, discovering I was no longer on campus. Wandering around trying to get on track, but I kept ending up somewhere I didn't recognize. I woke up frustrated. I've had this dream often. My other nightmare was being on a rollercoaster with Thad by my side. We were together on the incline to the top. Once there, Thad disappeared. Not only did he disappear, but I was looking down into space no longer in the rollercoaster car alone caught in midair. I woke up rather than fall into space.

We live in a small town in southern California where Thad is the manager of the office for the tech company. I have a home business inviting housewives in for cosmetic sales. Edward is a young black man who came to connect my new phone system. He was happy to meet us because there were very few Black people in this community. It became a habit for him to drop by when he was in the neighborhood for a cup of coffee. I spent my days writing assignments for class. Edward was married with two children, and after a while on these coffee breaks, he would talk about his family, in particular about some problems they were having. I was the older, wiser woman giving him advice. My nonfiction writing class was an opportunity for me to write a story about his family situation. The piece was called "The Rescue Attempt." Thad knew I was writing this piece, having read excerpts of it. It became a very interesting piece even though Edward was not much of a hero in his saga. It revealed that he was at fault for many of the problems he spoke of in the marriage. So much for the rescue of this relationship. My writing piece was my final exam for the class, and the story had no conclusion. It ended, leaving the story unfinished as it was for Edward's problems. I turned it in and was delighted to receive an A+ for my efforts in writing the piece, nothing for helping Edward to solve his problems.

As manager, Thad traveled throughout his territory, which spread to San Luis Obispo County. He stayed away for many days of the week, coming home only on weekends to wash his clothes and prepare for the week ahead. There were weekends he did not come home at all. I didn't question his absences because we were separated. Attending classes and working on recovering from my many ailments had my full attention. What I didn't know was that he was living with a woman when he was out of town. I'm not sure I would have cared about this situation because I was done with the marriage.

I had just returned from my class that day and drove into our semicircular driveway. It was about five o'clock in the evening, and the sun was setting. As I got out of my car, Thad drove in the opposite end of the driveway, blocking my ability to exit without backing up. He slammed the car door shut with a force that echoed through the quiet street. His face was twisted in a scowl, jaw clenched, and eyes dark with fury. I hesitated, then walked toward him, confused and concerned. What had happened? Why was he so angry?

He didn't speak. Just opened the front door, waited for me to step inside, then slammed it behind me with the same violent energy. I turned to face him, ready to ask what was wrong—but before the words could leave my mouth, his fist collided with my cheek.

Pain exploded across my face. I stumbled backward, but he grabbed my arm, gripping it tightly, preventing me from escaping. Blow after blow followed, and I cried out, pleading, asking him why—what was happening—what had I done. I was terrified; was he really determined to hurt me?

While he was hitting me blow after blow to my face, my chest, my body, he was referring to me as his grandmother. He was beating his grandmother. I couldn't believe it. "I'm not Julia!" I shout. He was not listening to me. I tried to pull away and bowed my head to deflect the blows and to protect my face, but he jerked me forward and I lost my balance. He held me tight and I didn't fall.

Trophies gleamed under the overhead light, lining the kitchen wall behind him. Some stood nearly five feet tall, their bases heavy with wood and granite. I tried to twist free, desperate to put distance between us, but he reached for one of the towering trophies.

I realized he was going to kill me. I have to save myself.

He lifted it high above his head, his eyes wild, his breath ragged. I raised my arms instinctively, shielded myself as best I could, my voice trembled as I begged him to stop.

I shout, "Please stop! Tell me why you're doing this to me. If you are going to kill me, I should know why!"

He seemed to be in a daze, referred to me as Julia again. He was killing his grandmother. I have become her image to him. I try to pull away.

Crying, "I am Laurie, not Julia." He seemed to hear what I have said and paused his arm in the air. The trophy remained high above his head.

Then with great thrust, he slammed the trophy to the floor. It broke with pieces of it scattered about the room. His face was red and sweat poured from his temples, snot dripped from his nose. Spittle came from his mouth as he tried to explain his anger. He wiped his mouth with one hand, and the other hand was still clenching me. Words spilled out of his mouth, making no sense. As he tried to speak, his anger seemed to subside. He pushed me roughly into a chair. He continued to hold my arm, preventing me from moving in any direction away from him. No longer referred to me as Julia, I was relieved that the raging attack appeared to be over for now. His eyes were red with anger as tears formed in the corners. I asked again why he was doing this to me. What had I done to deserve this? Did he know I wasn't Julia? I was shaking; my body was in shock. My face was burning from the blows. I could feel it beginning to swell.

When he finally spoke, he said he was in his office today and overheard the secretary talking about Edward. She said he was a womanizer, having affairs with women all over town. She said Thad should be aware he may be screwing his wife. Talk is that they are friends.

"I will kill that son of a bitch if he comes around here ever again."

"You think I am having sex with Edward? How dare you!"

"He's around here all of the time. He's a sneaky bastard. I know his kind."

"I am not having sex with him. I have tried to help him figure out how to solve the problems in his marriage. You read his story."

"That's what you say. That was just a cover up."

"I am years older than him."

"So what, that doesn't make a difference."

"It does to me!"

I tried to loosen his hold on my arm as he tightened his grip whenever he spoke. The force of his efforts to control his anger and speak caused his spit to fly. I'm not able to wipe the spittle from my face. I can't move from this chair, shocked that this was happening. Thad had never been violent with me throughout all our arguments. He has broken furniture and dishes, never touching me.

"You are gone all the time. We have been married over twenty-five years; I have not been unfaithful to you. I can't say as much about you."

"You can't prove I've been unfaithful; we're talking about you now and Edward."

He tightened the grip on my arm further. The pain was intense.

The sound of the phone ringing broke the mood.

I tried to stand up to answer. He pulled me back into the chair. He released his grip on my arm to answer the phone himself. It's my sister. She and her husband. It was surreal that they were calling at that moment.

"Hello," says Thad.

"Hi, Thad. How are you guys doing?"

"We're fine, what's up?"

"Is Laurie there, put her on the phone," says Jim.

"I'm here," I said in a shaky voice. Thad glared at me, threatening me not to tell what was happening. He took my arm again jerking me forward.

"You sound funny," said Jim. What's going on? We haven't heard from you guys for a few days."

"Are you all right Laurie?" asked Pat.

"Not really," I said.

"She's upset; we are having quite a disagreement here."

"Oh! I see," said Pat. "We were thinking of coming up to see you guys. We can come this evening."

"No, that's not necessary."

There was uncomfortable silence while no one spoke.

"Well, I think you guys may need a break. How about you, Laurie, wanna come here for a brief visit?" said Jim.

"No, we are just fine. She doesn't need to go anywhere; she's just upset she'll be alright," said Thad.

"Say man, you know how women are, just let her spend some time here with her sister. Give you some space."

There is a long silence. I cried silently. Thad looked at me and seemed to relax a little.

"How long?"

"Just a few days, we can come to get her."

"No, I'll bring her."

"I would rather fly." I say it out loud. "There are flights every hour or so from Los Angeles airport. You can drive me there tomorrow morning."

"Good idea. That's a deal. How about it, Thad? Laurie, tell us what time you will arrive," said Jim.

Thad hung up the phone, and we didn't talk about my leaving, but I was determined to go. We couldn't leave the next day. Thad kept me in the house, never leaving my side. He made calls to get time off from work. He held me hostage for three days. I couldn't go from one room to another, or even to the bathroom, without him being at my side. I realized later that he wanted the swelling on my face to calm down before my family or anyone could see my scars. Each day I asked him when I could leave. On the fourth day, I reminded him again of my desire to go.

"You don't need to go to Vegas. You need to stay here so we can talk."

"You promised I could go."

"You going to tell them I hurt you?"

"No, no, I will go for the weekend and when I come back, we will talk. We just need a break."

"Just the weekend, okay?"

"We have not seen Antoinette for a while. She can meet us at the airport, and we can go for lunch."

"Yeah, yeah I guess so."

I call and Antoinette answers after one ring.

"Hi, mom."

"Hi, sweetie. I'm flying to Las Vegas to see my sister, why don't you meet us at the airport and we can have lunch?"

"Well, I'm not sure."

"Please darling, we have not seen you for a while."

"I have a paper to write but okay. What airline?"

We drove sixty-five miles to the airport, and Antoinette met us at the gate. I was wearing sunglasses to hide my black eye. This would not be normal for me not to remove the glasses, but Antionette didn't ask questions or act as if it was unusual. I was nervous because Thad had threatened more than once to change his mind about my leaving. She and I hugged, and while she hugged her father, I had an idea to distract him.

"There's a display downstairs a history of the aircraft industry. Why don't you and your father go see it. My flight is over an hour away. I'll wait here."

"Great idea, Dad. Let's go."

She took her father by the arm, and they started down the aisle toward the escalator.

I breathed a sigh of relief. I couldn't sit; I was so nervous. My flight was more than an hour away. I paced back and forth constantly, looking toward the escalator anxious that they might return before I could get away. Standing near me was a lady who looked familiar. I couldn't place where I had seen her. She smiled at me and said, "How are you doing?"

Before I could speak, I realized she was the actress, Sheryl Lee Ralph. Seeing her filled me with joy. She reached out to shake my hand. It was like she knew me. This was the first familiar face I had seen in four days and when she asked how I was, I blurted out.

"I am trying to get away from my husband. My daughter has taken him away to distract him from changing his mind and not letting me go."

She put her hand on my shoulder. "It's going to be okay. Don't worry. I had a feeling something was going on with you. Are you hurt? We can get you some help."

"I don't want help; I just want to get away. My flight is more than an hour away and he could come back and change his mind."

"Okay, okay. The flights leave every forty-five minutes to Las Vegas. Is that where you're going?"

"Yes, my sister and her husband will be there to meet me."

"They are boarding a flight right now. Why not try to take this one?"

I turned to hear the call for final boarding. I thanked her; she hugged me, and I ran to the podium. I was able to board that flight and was gone before Thad and our daughter returned.

When I arrived in Las Vegas, my sister and her husband met me at the gate.

As soon as my sister saw me, she ran toward me to hug me. "He hurt you?" my sister observed.

"Yes, he tried to kill me."

"I'm so sorry. I knew it. I had a feeling something was terribly wrong. We should have him arrested. Did you call the police?" said Pat.

"No, he never left my side. Besides I can't do that. What will the children think? I know his temper; he would never let them take him away. The police in our town would just as soon shoot him. I can't be responsible for that."

"Is this the first time this has happened? Why didn't you tell us?"

"Yes, it was the first time, of course. We have had terrible arguments before, but never violent. I don't know what has come over him. He acts like he's crazy. He even called me his grandmother."

"What! His grandmother? What's that about?"

"I don't know, spooky, huh!"

"Yeah, he's losing his mind."

"Maybe. I'm so thankful you called when you did. It was like you knew I was in trouble. It was a miracle for me."

"We just assumed something was wrong; I could feel it. What took you so long to get here? Jim said. "If you hadn't come today, I was going to pick you up."

"He held me hostage for three days. I thought I would never get away."

“Jim and I were just talking about you and how you two are living together separated as you say, that is under dangerous circumstances. He said it was not a good idea. We decided we should talk to you about it. We were planning to visit so Jim could talk to Thad.”

“He’s gone most of the time. I thought I had no reason to be concerned. But when he came home this time, he was so enraged. Unlike I have never seen before.”

“What do you think has him all riled up? Jim frowns looking at me.”

“It’s outrageous, he thinks I have been having an affair with a neighbor.”

“Well, have you?

“Absolutely not. Not like him who has had several affairs over the years.”

“Where did he get the idea?”

“Somebody at his job said because the guy gets around to many women, he must be involved with me. Unfortunately, he and I are friends. I mean he has been a friend of ours.”

“A friend of both you and Thad?”

“Well, yes, he has been around when Thad was home. They have talked, they aren’t friends, so to speak, but friendly.”

“So, it looked suspicious, didn’t it?”

“No, nothing suspicious. Our relationship is platonic. He is married with small children. Thad is losing his mind. I told you while he was beating me, he called me his grandmother. He was beating his grandmother, maybe killing her. He has been angry at her for so long a time. Me too, but I didn’t feel violent towards her, at least not most of the time.”

“That’s not funny. You say he called you by her name?” asked Jim.

“Yes, he called me her name. He said ‘I hate you, grandmother’. This was more of a shock than the idea he was trying to kill me. It was her he wanted to kill.”

"Now I realize he is crazy. You can't ever go back to him," said Pat.

"I never intend to; you don't have to worry about that. I'm finished with this marriage."

When I arrived at their home my body relaxed for the first time. My shoulders were tight and my muscles tensed. Close to someone who made me secure, my body let go of its stress. Suddenly, exhaustion overcame me as the adrenaline subsided, ending my efforts to maintain control. Observing someone who adored me respond to my situation, caused the truth of the event to sink in deeply. I was ashamed of allowing myself to be in this situation. I had done nothing wrong. I was angry with Thad, at the situation, and at myself for letting this happen. I never thought he would attack me.

Pat put her arms around me to steady my gait as we walked toward the house.

My body ached as I fell into her. My face was sore. It was still swollen. After removing my sunglasses, she could see the blood spot in my right eye and the blue and green marks underneath it. Pat pulled back to get a better look at me, shocked at my appearance. She gave me an ice pack to help the swelling. I was deeply shaken as I realized what I had gone through.

"We need to get you a lawyer and get him out of the house," said Pat.

"We can deal with that later. You can't stay here in Vegas with us. I talked to your brother; he's sending a ticket for your flight," said Jim.

"Flight, where?"

"You're going to Connecticut. It's not safe for you to be here where Thad can get to you."

I flew out the next day. I stayed in Connecticut for two months, taking time to heal. I had to relate the entire experience to my brother and his wife. They were shocked because they had never heard about bad experiences with Thad from me. He got along very well with my brother. Some of our best experiences were while we visited together. It was comfortable to be with family and know I was safe. My thoughts turned to reclaiming my house. The place I personally provided the down payment for from my earnings in real estate. I could not let Thad stay there and end up losing it. I filed divorce papers and made plans to get Thad out of the house It was all I had from this farce of a marriage.

After I returned to California, I stayed with a friend since Thad was still occupying the house. While he was out of town working, I picked up my car which was still parked in the driveway. The court scheduled the hearing date for the divorce at the Los Angeles Superior Court.

I hired a female lawyer to represent me. She had a reputation for being tough. Unfortunately for me, newspapers were running a story about a woman who faked being beaten by her spouse. She wore convincing makeup to court to sway the outcome to her benefit. The judges found out about the ruse and decided not to hear any cases presenting evidence of beatings in domestic relations. Although I had the scars to prove my case, the judge would not hear it. To add to my problem, Thad wrote a threatening letter to my lawyer. Her fear of him kept her from mentioning the letter, so much so that the majority of my complaints were sidelined to expedite the hearing. When we stood in court, the judge asked me if I was sure I wanted a divorce.

"Yes, your honor, I want a divorce."

"Mr. Langoire are you ready to proceed with the dissolution of this marriage?"

"Ah, well, ah I didn't ask for a divorce, she, your honor said she wants the divorce. I have not agreed to it."

"You are not in agreement with the divorce at this time, am I correct in hearing this?"

"Yes, your honor, you are correct."

"There will be no divorce granted at this time. You may benefit from counselling since only one party agrees to dissolve this marriage. Counselling is so ordered."

I was furious. The judge disregarded my wish: if my husband did not want a divorce, I couldn't get it. Information concerning his running us into debt while using the money to entertain other women and holding me hostage after beating me was not presented in court. The judges disregarded a woman's plea, even if her life was in danger. Just because of one case made by a woman who probably was desperate to get away. Her life could have been endangered too.

Thad had his own therapist, and I had mine. We were supposed to have joint therapy, but scheduling it proved impossible. Thad would not cooperate. It took a year to finalize our divorce.

My original college course was conveniently located in town. I was ready to attend classes on campus fifty miles away. While driving the freeway, Thad would pass me. He drove very close to me threateningly to frighten me. I just looked ahead and pretended not to see him. He called a few times to threaten me, and I threatened him right back. I had no weapon and I assumed he didn't have one either.

The day Thad received his final divorce papers, he received a call from the hospital; his mother, Hannah, was having her leg amputated because of diabetes. There was no one to care for her. Julia, as well as her other siblings, had already made their transitions. Thad was the only relative left to care for her.

Thad and his girlfriend cared for his mother. Hannah couldn't get around having lost her leg. She suffered a great deal for years, eventually developing dementia, and then she was bedridden. Word was she lingered for a long while and then she died unexpectedly one day. Thad was free.

Michael kept close contact with his father. He reported some goings on of his father to me. He said Thad's relationship with Linda was fraught with chaos. Their fighting was such that she often threatened to call the police on him. She was hesitant for fear of his being put in jail and fear of the attitude of white policemen and their overreactions on Black men. She was white and that may have something to with how it was handled.

I continued my classes enjoying college and the experience of learning, graduating Summa Cud Laude. I received an award for first place on a short story published in the university's W. E. B. Dubois Writing and Photographic Awards of that year. I was the second oldest graduate, the other a woman was ninety years old and I was fifty-three. During our studies we became friends and created study groups and included much younger students. Studying and discussing information with others in the group cemented it in our brains, leading to high exam scores. Professors sometimes challenged us. I remember we failed to take a history class which was required as freshman. We were classified as seniors and could not graduate unless we completed the U. S. history course. We had to finish the four-month semester class in four weeks and pass the final. The book was over four inches in diameter. I remember the smug expression on the professor's face as he handed the big thick book to us believing we could not possibly cover all of that material and get a grade high enough not to spoil our grade point average. We divided the book in half and met to instruct the other on our portion of the book's contents. When we arrived at the class to take the exam, the instructor put us in different rooms saying we might share information. To his astonishment we aced the final exam making A's. It says a lot about the opportunity to get an education late in life. It could be the best experience you'd have to reach a long-held goal.

Life after divorce was so much better than I imagined at this stage of my life. I was free to come and go as I pleased. Sometimes it was hard between employment opportunities, somehow, I managed until the opportunity arose to teach at a college. Those were good years teaching adults who needed to reach their delayed goal of an education.

Retirement didn't come until I was seventy-six, such was the joy of teaching adults. My sister and I lived together until she passed. Her husband ten years earlier died suddenly. The idea of marrying again was not the experience I wanted to repeat. To compromise and be subject to another man's will was far from my agenda. I moved to another state and lost all contact with Thad. He didn't keep up much with his children, busy I assume with his many car shows.

While in therapy I learned that Thad's life had so many layers of trauma. The possibility of him having a successful relationship and marriage was doubtful. As hard as we tried, our inherited trauma influenced our lives. I guess we never had a chance. He was abandoned by his mother and father, given a violent origin story, and then he was raised by someone who both loved him and harmed him. His grandmother, his only caregiver, used religion to justify abuse of him, which distorted his moral compass. He rejected religion altogether, and it was never a part of his life. He had conflicts of loyalty and resentment. Love mixed with fear, guilt, and anger, he could not express.

There are no heroes in Thad's life except for his Aunt Mary, the only relative he spoke kindly about during our marriage. I lived with him for over thirty years, and I thought I knew him. He often spoke of violence and committing violence on a large scale against a group of people. I never took him seriously, assuming he was just letting off some steam. I perceived him as a coward because of his typical retreat when confrontation with another person. For this reason, I feared for his safety should law enforcement get involved in our arguments. I still didn't think he would commit violence toward me.

My background though much better still created feelings of unworthiness in me. Married to a man whose background was full of chaos, I did so despite seeing all of the red flags. I made it happen to please my mother. Then while being abused, I wasn't able to leave the relationship that hurt me so much. Using any and all excuses to remain in what kept me ill and depressed.

I can't say I am angry with Thad. I don't hate him either. However, forgiveness is not what I can do. My predominant emotion regarding him is indifference. Our arguments may have been the only way he knew to bond with me. Why he decided to kill me has never been explained. When I hear or see violence toward partners, I reflect on what happened to me and feel thankful I survived.

Epilogue

We find Laurie sitting on the veranda of a café in an upscale retirement community. She is dressed elegantly in all white. Her sister-in-law, who is also dressed beautifully, is sitting next to her pouring tea from a delicate porcelain pitcher obviously antique. The occasion is the yearly charity event. As she looks out over the horizon the sun is slowly fading in glorious colors of red, orange and grey. The hills are lush with grass in various shades of green. Surrounding her are couples also wearing white, some toasting each other and others engaged in conversation, some intimate and others full of laughter. For a moment she has a tug of envy, but she quickly waves it away because she admits she is happy without a companion.

The memory of her marriage reminds her that having a companion was not enough if there were anxieties and disappointments to contend with the coupling. The unhappiness she experienced living with Thad long behind her. She sees him when she visits their daughter, Antionette. He's spending his final years working on his show truck and calling friends he has made across the country.

Laurie's social calendar is full; she exercises daily and visits with her children and friends often. She occasionally travels with friends. Yearly, she visits Michael's daughter, Amber, who lives in Paris.

The healing for Laurie has taken years as she devotes time to getting in touch with her happy, confident self. Now with the wounds of trauma behind her, she reflects with sadness on the life of Julia who never seemed to get a break. Her dream of having a career, and a good marriage was not to be. Julia had so many odds against her, the loss of her mother, the times, her race and her gender. Laurie wrote the story of Julia's life and struggles to help her children understand and heal from the family trauma they inherited. It is interesting to see how her life and struggles paralleled Julia's. Laurie's dream was delayed and later partly realized. History seems to repeat itself. It is hoped in reading this story the reader can recognize patterns of abuse that may be present in their past and may be relived in the future. It is also hoped that anyone who reads this story and can relate to the generational trauma, find a way to recognize the symptoms and seek help to heal.

Rowena reached the age of 100 years and died five months later. Thad died a year later at the age of 91 years four weeks before his ninety second birthday.

Family Tree

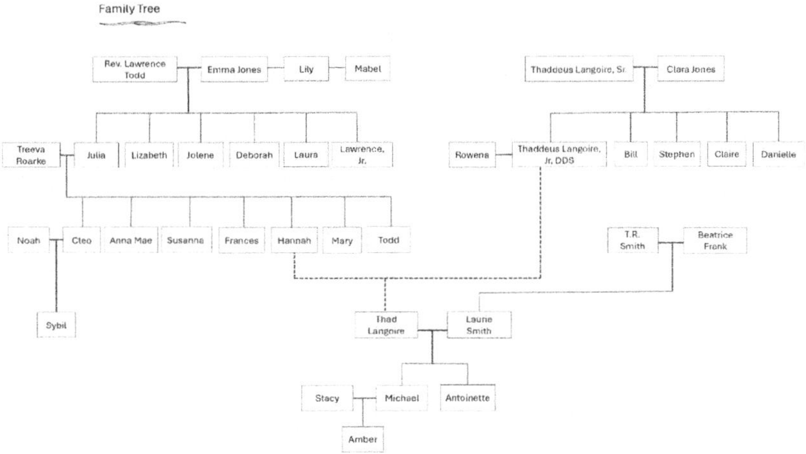

Family Tree
Rev. Lawrence Todd
Emma Jones
Lily
Mabel
Thaddeus Langoire, Sr.
Clara Jones
Treeva Roarke
Julia
Lizabeth
Jolene
Deborah
Laura
Lawrence, Jr.
Rowena
Thaddeus Langoire, Jr, DDS
Bill
Stephen
Claire
Danielle
Noah
Cleo
Anna Mae
Susanna
Frances
Hannah
Mary
Todd
T.R. Smith
Beatrice Frank
Sybil
Thad Langoire
Laurie Smith
Stacy
Michael
Antoinette
Amber

Acknowledgements

I express my deepest gratitude to everyone who helped bring this book into the world. This work is meant to name and heal the patterns of trauma passed through generations. It is for my readers to recognize patterns of abuse and trauma inherited and to get help to heal them.

To Julia whose dreams were shattered time and time again, yet she forged on. My thanks to her for telling the story of her life which has helped me in understanding her struggles and the anger she carried through her lifetime.

I am especially grateful to Isa Segismundo, who has been like a second daughter to me. For years she helped me organize my thoughts and shape the manuscript; I am not sure this book would have been written without her steady support.

Thank you to my friend and neighbor DeeDee Cleveland, who read the original draft and offered encouragement then came up with the title '*The Promise*' and designed the family tree. She supplied practical and editorial help with word processing and formatting. Her patience and direction kept me moving forward every day.

I owe a special thanks to Teresa Holliday, who wrote the Prologue and mentored me in finding the clearest way to express my ideas. To Frazine Jasper, my best friend, and to Charlotte Bentley and Frances Peterson, who read chapters aloud and checked for clarity—your careful listening made this story stronger.

To the friends who gave me their time and patience when I could not be available, and who met deadlines so this project could move forward; your generosity sustained me.

My heartfelt thanks to my son, who designed the cover and cheered me on through the long hours of writing. He has been a light, companion, and comfort when I needed one. To my brilliant daughter, whose love and care have been a constant source of strength, this book is a tribute to your kindness as you cared for our aging father. To my granddaughter who rescued my manuscript when I thought it lost. She is our bright light of the future.

Finally, I thank my brother Clayton and my sister-in-law Johnene Adams for being a steady rock through my every challenge.

With gratitude to all who held me, read with me, and believed this story could be told.

Made in the USA
Las Vegas, NV
11 July 2026

50754424R00115